EVERYBODY
loves
SOMEBODY

ALSO BY **JOANNA SCOTT**

Liberation

Tourmaline

Make Believe

The Manikin

Various Antidotes

Arrogance

The Closest Possible Union

Fading, My Parmacheene Belle

EVERYBODY
loves
SOMEBODY

STORIES

Joanna Scott

BACK BAY BOOKS

Little, Brown and Company

NEW YORK   BOSTON   LONDON

Back Bay Books / Little, Brown and Company
Hachette Book Group USA
1271 Avenue of the Americas, New York, NY 10020
Visit our Web site at www.HachetteBookGroupUSA.com

FIRST EDITION: December 2006

The characters and events in this book are fictitious. Any similarity to real persons, living or dead, is coincidental and not intended by the author.

The author gratefully acknowledges the editors of the following magazines in which versions of these stories were published: *Black Clock, The Cincinnati Review, Common Knowledge, Conjunctions, Daedalus, Salmagundi, The Southern Review, StoryQuarterly, Subtropics, The Yale Review,* and *Zoetrope.*

Library of Congress Cataloging-in-Publication Data
Scott, Joanna.
    Everybody loves somebody: stories / Joanna Scott. — 1st ed.
        p. cm.
    ISBN-10: 0-316-01345-5
    ISBN-13: 978-0-316-01345-1
    1. Love stories, American.   I. Title.
PS3569.C636E94 2006
813'. 54 — dc22   2006012310

10 9 8 7 6 5 4 3 2 1

Book design by Fearn Cutler deVicq

Q-FF

Printed in the United States of America

For Jim, Kathryn, and Alice

CONTENTS

EVERYBODY
loves
SOMEBODY

HEAVEN AND HELL

On a July day in 1919, beneath the blue dome of the summer sky, the guests watched from the base of a hillock as a young woman was joined in marriage to the man she thought she'd lost forever in the war.

Do you—

She does.

Do you—

He does.

Lazy waves lapped and sucked at the rocks below. Seagulls floated on tilted wings over the gazebo, where a five-piece band was waiting to play. A dog down at the far end of the beach plunged into the water to retrieve a stick thrown by a boy who had grown bored with the ceremony and wandered away. A soft breeze rustled through the dry leaves of hawthorn bushes.

After the exchange of vows, the bride and groom stood unmoving in front of the pastor for such a length of time that some of the guests began to wonder if the young couple knew what to do next. Then the bride reached for the groom's hands, together they lifted the lace veil, and as they turned their lips met perfectly, pressing together in a kiss that two years earlier no one thought would be possible. That this kiss almost didn't happen was enough to draw the assembled guests together in shared relief. At last, Gwendolyn Martin and Clive Crawford were husband and wife.

Unfortunately, Tom Martin, father of the bride, was missing the great event, his absence a result of bad luck so typical that he almost relished his despair, since it reinforced his sense that he couldn't help what he did. The fact that he wasn't where he wanted to be at that moment would eventually become an addition to his long list of mishaps, his entire life being a sequence of contests with fate that he kept losing, but not without a struggle. To prove that he didn't give up easily he slammed the weight of his whole body against the bathroom door. But the door was made of sturdy oak, and with the newfangled bolt irreparably jammed, Tom was stuck inside the bathroom rubbing the darkening bruise on his shoulder while his only daughter married her true love.

Seated on wooden chairs arranged in rows along the relatively flat part of Madison Point, the guests were happy to watch for as long as the kiss would last, which, with the bride and groom clamped greedily together, was turning out to last longer than the usual kiss to mark a union, longer than any wedding kiss anyone had ever witnessed, longer than it had taken the couple to say their vows, and, at this rate, longer than the entirety of the preceding ceremony.

The pastor, rotund Father Gaffner, kept his head slightly bent, his posture suggesting infinite patience, making it impossible to guess how long it would take until he intervened. Apparently, he saw no reason to intervene. He would let the bride and groom go on kissing for as long as they pleased while the guests watched with growing awe that any kiss could last this long—long enough to turn the remarkable event into something that would become the stuff of legend. Gwen and Clive had begun kissing and would keep kissing. In that other dimension where the miraculous future of their love had been born, they would never stop kissing.

Keep kissing, Gwen's uncle Hugo wanted to urge. Break the record of kissing. Kiss through the day, dear Gwen and Clive. Kiss through the night. Kiss for as long as it takes cause and effect to be reversed and all the damage that has ever been done to be undone. Kiss away Clive's blindness. Kiss away the memories of war. Kiss away death. Keep kissing until the end of the world, or at least until the arrival of Tom, that scoundrel of a younger brother who had made Hugo's life difficult for all of his fifty-one years.

Where was Tom? Not where he was supposed to be, of course. Tom had never been where he was supposed to be. When he was a boy, he could be counted on to drift from whatever game he'd started to play. As a man, he drifted from job to job and woman to woman. And as a father, he had just drifted away.

Hugo couldn't know that his brother had spent the morning locked in the bathroom of a seaside inn, where he was treating himself to a hefty dose of self-pity. If he were a better man, Tom thought, he'd accept that the only thing left for him to do was put the revolver to his chest and pull the trigger. *Click.* If only he had a revolver. He had a toothbrush and Arm & Hammer paste. He had Pepto-Bismol. He was ready. No, he wasn't ready and wouldn't be ready until he'd been given the chance to improve his predicament. Even if he were entirely blameless for everything that had gone wrong, he knew himself as well as Hugo knew him and would have readily admitted that he was a selfish man. He was also sunken-eyed, yellow-haired, white-whiskered, and hungry for meat after being locked in the bathroom in room number 4 of the Tuckett Beach Inn for hours—days, it seemed to Tom, or at least long enough to miss his daughter's wedding.

No one except Hugo would have cared enough to wonder at his absence. The bride didn't even suspect that her father had been invited. To Gwen, Tom was the strange man with tufted ears and a ridiculous handlebar mustache who appeared in her life no more than once a decade. She didn't pretend to feel any familial attachment to him. It was fair to assume that while Gwen stood there kissing Clive, there was no one further from her thoughts than Tom.

The kiss went on and on. The guests stared, their amazement making them simultaneously tense with expectation and confident that such a kiss could only be a deserved reward. The scene was marvelous, unending, and unrepeatable. Just to witness the kiss gave each guest an expansive feeling of worthiness.

And yet it appeared that Tom Martin had decided he had someplace better to be than at Madison Point on this fine summer day. Unless Tom had simply forgotten how to get there. He had last visited the estate when Gwen was eleven, the event preserved by Hugo with his Kodak Brownie in a photograph of Gwen perched on the seat of a bicycle and Tom standing by the front wheel looking as if he'd just realized he'd taken the wrong road and was hopelessly lost.

Damn that Tom. Hugo had even wired money for his brother's train fare from St. Louis. But Tom had probably used the money to travel in the opposite direction. Instead of coming to his daughter's wedding—to begin at noon, *promptly*, Hugo had added on the invitation to his brother—Tom was probably hundreds of miles away, heading nowhere in particular and inadvertently attaching himself to some new, doomed scheme.

Down on the beach, the dog, a Newfoundland, emerged dripping from the water, the stick clamped between her jaws. The dog's quick shudder was familiar to the boy, who leaped backward to avoid being soaked as the dog shook herself dry. The boy's laughing shriek, though muted by the shushing wind, startled the guests, who weren't ready to be reminded that life was continuing beyond the circle of their assembly. Though none of the guests made any visible move, a rippling unease traveled forward through the rows, passing from one person to another until it finally reached the bride and groom, provoking them to pull slightly away from each other, their minuscule separation dramatic enough to suggest that they were preparing to bring their kiss to an end. The guests continued to stare, savoring this culminating vision of love. The bride and groom had kissed a wonderful kiss and were about to be done, or so the guests thought— mistakenly, as it turned out, for in the next moment the couple fell back toward each other, mouths latched eagerly, for after all they had been through they deserved to kiss and would go on kissing no matter what.

Uncle Hugo admired their defiance. But he had enough foresight to know that eventually the world would intrude. If only he could predict what form the intrusion would take, he'd try to prevent it. Gwen and Clive deserved to kiss for as long as they wanted to kiss. And if they kept on kissing, sooner or later Tom Martin would have to show up.

But Tom couldn't show up unless someone opened the door and let him out. Here he would stay, alone with his thoughts in this tomb of a windowless bathroom, a tub for a coffin, water dripping with torturous irregularity from the faucet. What could he do to improve the situation? His boss at the furniture store in St. Louis would have advised him to make a mental list of ten positive outcomes and ten things that bring him joy. Also, he would have warned him to avoid chocolate, white sugar, mushrooms, and foods that had been pre-served, reheated, or fermented. And he definitely should avoid thinking about the wedding he was destined to miss.

It was a wedding as lovely as the guests had predicted it would be. But no one had expected it to be as transfixing as a dream, as deliciously unpredictable. Time itself seemed to have broken from its normal pace and had taken to swooping in reverse then swirling forward like the cottonwood seedlings that blew about in the breeze. In the grip of their fascination, the guests wouldn't have exclaimed if nymphs and satyrs had cavorted across the lawn.

A baby, set down by her mother to crawl between the rows of chairs, chortled happily. Bees flitted in the honeysuckle vines woven through the gazebo's trellis. Down at the beach, the boy wrestled the stick from the jaws of the Newfoundland. Women enjoyed the sunshine warming their shoulders through silk shawls. Men enjoyed the way the breeze rippled the linen of their wide trousers. Even the lemony, thick scent from the mudflats to the south was something to savor, especially when mixed with the perfume of honeysuckle and driftwood and salt. The only melancholy element was the vague sympathy that some guests felt for those who hadn't been invited.

Tom Martin had been invited. It could be, Hugo considered, that Tom had planned to attend but was running late. Though ordinarily Tom couldn't be roused to run. He preferred to walk. Hugo's brother Tom was never in a hurry and considered any commitment an inconvenience.

It seemed that Tom Martin didn't care enough to tolerate the inconvenience of his daughter's wedding. But Hugo cared. He hoped that simply by his being present at this important event, Tom would set in motion what was sure to be a long and difficult process of reconciliation, made more difficult because the two people involved were content with their estrangement. Wasn't it always easier to forget rather than forgive? When Tom had left Carol, Gwen's mother, for another woman, he hadn't even known that she was pregnant. After Gwen was born, it had taken Hugo three months to locate his brother, who was hiding out in Cleveland, and tell him that he had a daughter, an effort that Hugo would allow himself to regret from time to time, though only in secret, along with the agonizing love he secretly felt for Carol, dear Carol, who was never more than grateful to Hugo for offering her and Gwen a haven.

Beyond the point, whitecaps wrinkled the dark surface of the sound. Seagulls continued to wheel silently overhead. On the beach, the boy waded into the shallow water after the dog. The baby, sitting up in the grass, found an empty nymphal shell of a cicada and fingered it gently. Still standing humbly in front of the kissing couple, Father Gaffner tightened his jaw in a subtle grimace, as though he were suppressing a burp or a chuckle. And buzzing in jerky exploration among the buds of the honeysuckle, the bees kept at their single-minded work.

Tom, in contrast to the bees, was an expert at doing nothing. He could sit on the edge of a filthy blue tub staring at a blue toilet bowl, the air in the bathroom like an August afternoon in St. Louis. He could play the part of the vagabond his brother thought him to be, a man with his slouch hat rolled up in his suitcase, who was never in a hurry. Or rarely in a hurry. Well, sometimes he was in a hurry. Sometimes he got hungry for his breakfast. He was hungry now. Someone, let Tom Martin go! Free him from the prison of his soul, redeem him, make him innocent again, lift him up, open the door to this stinking bathroom, give him beef jerky, ten cents for a pack of cigarettes, and a ride to Madison Point. Believe it or not, he wanted to attend the wedding of his daughter, even if she didn't want him there and greeted him with those icy blue eyes, blaming him for being who he was. But really, as he sat in the sapping warmth of the bathroom, it had begun to seem possible that he was not necessarily equal to his actions. Even if he couldn't undo what he'd done he might be able to avoid repeating his mistakes, his worst mistake being leaving that crackerjack Carol, the first of the many lovers he'd left behind and the one who died before she learned to stop loving him. Carol, Gwen's mother, never enjoyed the luxury of indifference. For the pain he'd caused her, Tom was sorry—sorrier now than ever. With no one but himself for company, he couldn't be distracted from wondering how things would have been different if he'd taken Carol with him when he'd left twenty-three years ago.

Hugo could have told his errant brother what would have been different. If Tom had taken Carol with him, Hugo wouldn't have had the chance to raise Gwen and escort her down the aisle on her wedding day. After all they'd been through together, from Gwen's scarlet fever, her childish tantrums and joys, her engagement to Clive, the war, Clive's disappearance in France, his blindness and slow recovery in a military hospital in Nyons, their reunion, their marriage, Hugo could only be glad that Carol had stayed when Tom left, and that he'd kept his love for her a secret until the end, and beyond. He never had to ask her what she felt for him—he understood that he was like a brother to her. If she'd known he wanted to be more than that, she would have left Madison Point. He would have lost not just her but Gwen and everything that followed, and his life wouldn't be culminating now, despite his brother's absence, or perhaps because of it, in this record-breaking kiss on a perfect July day in 1919, with the guests mesmerized, the seagulls floating like angels overhead, a boy splashing in the water down at the beach, a baby lifting the shell of a cicada to her mouth, and one lone honeybee diving into the roses of the bride's bouquet.

The scene being exactly what Tom was trying not to imagine in the bathroom of the Tuckett Beach Inn. He didn't have to be a genius to guess that his daughter's wedding would include equal parts of beauty and guilelessness, acceptance, risk, ferocity, and resistance. All in the name of love. The daughter of crackerjack Carol wouldn't marry a man she didn't love. Right, Carol? Carol? It was only out of boredom that Tom called Carol—first in a whisper, then with a murmur, then with a shout. But don't think that Tom Martin believed in ghosts. He didn't need metaphysics to be certain that death is the end of life, period. Still, Carol, you could do Tom a little favor and unlock this door, or, short of that, talk to him. He could use the company. Carol, are you there? Carol!

Hugo could have told Tom that it was useless to call Carol, since even if she did exist as a singular entity in the spirit realm—a possibility that Hugo, like his brother, didn't entertain for a moment—surely she wouldn't have left her daughter's wedding just to open the door for a man who had abandoned her twenty-three years ago. Tom was stuck, and Carol was the last person on earth—or elsewhere—who would help him come unstuck.

Yet Hugo knew that it would be just like Tom to lay the fault of his absence with Carol. Go ahead, blame a dead woman for the fact that Tom was missing this kiss of all kisses, love making the burden of expiation as light as a feather, with the guests restored to their primeval nobility by the advantage of their presence here at Madison Point. What? Simply put, Hugo was thinking that this must be similar to Paradise—layers and layers of pure happiness, like pages in a book.

Given the transfixing quality of the scene, it wasn't surprising that no one noticed when the baby, balanced on her pudgy rump between the forest of legs, put the shell of the cicada in her mouth. No one noticed that the seagulls abruptly flew away, one after the other, in the direction of a fishing boat on the horizon. And no one noticed when the boy, who had waded up to his thighs after the Newfoundland, slipped off the edge of a sandy shelf and disappeared into the deep water.

What the guests did notice was the bee. While Gwen and Clive kissed, the bee that had been exploring the bouquet rose from the flowers slowly, like a spider on a thread, hovering for a moment near the bride's shoulders, and then rising toward the buttery sheen of her cheek. Its thorax vibrating hungrily, the bee seemed to search Gwen's skin for a good place to pierce it. Gwen and Clive continued kissing, oblivious, but the guests, along with Uncle Hugo, watched with concern.

Someone had to stop the bee from stinging the bride, Hugo thought, leaning forward, privately trying to reason his way free of his reluctance to intrude. Wasn't there anyone who could help, someone who could intervene without being noticed?

Neither Tom nor Hugo would ever know that they were similar in one essential way: when they needed help, they thought of Carol. Watching the bee buzzing near Gwen, Hugo thought of Carol. Stuck in the bathroom of the Tuckett Beach Inn, Tom thought of Carol.

"Who's Carol?" asked the maid after opening the bathroom door with her skeleton key. She addressed Tom with the frankness of a child half her age. He noticed that her brown eyes slipped off center as she stared. Her unkempt hair was more orange than red. There was a canker scab on her chin, and her cotton dress fell loosely over her hips.

She was too pretty to look so awful, Tom thought. And she was too forward with a strange man standing before her wrapped only in a white bath towel.

"You were calling for Carol," she persisted. She squatted to take a better look at the lock.

"She was my wife," Tom lied.

"Was?"

He answered with an impatient snort.

"Bless you," she said, as though he'd sneezed. She turned the lever of the bolt back and forth until it jammed again. "Not a day goes by when something doesn't go wrong," she announced, without exasperation. "I need a screwdriver." When she stood, her odd gaze alighted on one side of Tom's face. Without thinking, he moved his hand through the air as if to bat away a mosquito. She started visibly, teetered as if she'd been struck in the face. For a moment Tom thought he had hit her inadvertently, and he was seized by terrible, feverish guilt. He wanted to fall down on his knees and apologize. But she smiled at him as if to indicate that an apology really wasn't necessary, especially from a man dressed in a bath towel. Go on, she seemed to tell him, lifting her chin and looking toward the room where he'd left his suitcase. You're free.

While he gathered his clothes, the girl warned him not to shut the bathroom door, and she set off to find a screwdriver. Tom scrambled into his suit, combed his mustache, snapped the buckle of his suitcase, and left in such a hurry that he forgot to pay his bill.

Out on the road in front of the inn, he waved down a dairy cart being pulled by a round-bellied mule. When the dairyman heard that Tom wanted to go to Hugo Martin's estate at Madison Point, he said he'd take him there himself. Coincidentally, he had a wheel of cheddar in back to deliver to the wedding reception.

"Does that ol' mule go any faster?" Tom asked.

The dairyman looked at him askance, not unlike the way the maid had looked at him.

"You want my Rascal to go faster?"

"Yes, please."

"Real fast?"

"Sure."

The dairyman tipped back his cap, revealing the youthfulness of his face. He couldn't have been older than seventeen, Tom thought. Leaning toward the mule as though he meant to grab its tail between his teeth, the dairyman gave a short laugh, warned Tom to hold on, and cracked his whip in the air. The mule flattened its ears against its head and took off, trotting faster than Tom had ever known a mule to trot.

Tom Martin was somewhere between Tuckett Beach and Hugo's estate when the wedding guests first noticed the bee rising from the bride's bouquet. Their attention couldn't have been any more intense at this point; what changed with the bee was the unity of their responses. One man coughed into his hand in warning. A woman whispered audibly enough for her husband to hear, "Oh no." And the mother who had set her baby on the grass glanced down and noticed the shiny tip of an insect shell sticking out from between the baby's grinning lips.

A mere few yards offshore from the narrow stretch of beach, the boy, submerged in the murky salt water, was holding his breath. Though he didn't know how to swim, he'd taught himself to hold his breath during bath time. Once he'd even held his breath for as long as it had taken him to count in his head from one to twenty-five.

He began counting silently. As he counted, he wondered if it was possible to learn to breathe underwater. He tried to propel himself by pulling at the water in the same way that he'd pull himself up to the next branch when he was climbing a tree. Five, one thousand, six. When he relaxed his arms and legs, he felt himself turning a somersault, and when he stretched out again he couldn't tell which direction was up. Nine, one thousand, ten. It was strange that he couldn't see the sky. He was glad, though, to have the chance to feel brave. Feeling brave was the best feeling in the world, better even than the sleepy feeling when his mother kissed him good night on the tip of his nose. She would think him very brave when he told her what had happened, though she'd be angry that he'd gotten his clothes wet. Twelve, one thousand. Or had he reached thirteen? It was frustrating to forget how far he'd counted. He'd been hoping to make it past twenty-seven. If he'd been counting straight, he might have already reached twenty.

He felt his shirt suddenly tighten around his chest. In the next moment a tugging force caused him to turn on his back, and his face broke through the surface of the dark water. It was good to see the sky just where he'd left it. And it felt good to loosen his collar with two fingers and take a deep breath. He felt a little disappointed that he hadn't been given the chance to count to thirty underwater, but he was glad to be floating on his back, with that big black friendly dog dragging him toward shore by his shirt as though he were one of the sticks thrown into the water for the dog to fetch.

In their chairs around the hillock, the guests couldn't have said reliably how much time had passed since Father Gaffner had declared Gwen and Clive husband and wife. Some believed, in hindsight, that the kiss hadn't lasted longer than a minute. Others were sure that at least half an hour had passed. But to Hugo Martin it was as long as he could have wished, for just as the bee dove through the narrow opening below the chins of the bride and groom, a mule pulling a dairy cart came trotting along the sandy track leading to the gazebo. Even before the cart stopped, Tom Martin jumped off.

"Was that fast enough?" the young dairyman asked.

"That was plenty fast," Tom assured him as his gaze turned toward the mound where the bride and groom were standing and kissing. Despite his nearsightedness, Tom could see the couple clearly enough to tell that there was something willfully permanent about them as they kissed, as if they were trying to turn themselves into statues.

It took Father Gaffner to finally break the spell. Father Gaffner, who had once nearly died in an anaphylactic response to a sting, noticed the bee for the first time when it passed to his side of the bride and groom.

In the seventh row of guests, the mother pulled what was left of the cicada shell from her baby's mouth. Down at the beach, the boy climbed up on the Newfoundland's back and rode the dog through the few remaining yards of shallow water. At the base of the gazebo, Tom suddenly remembered that the name of his daughter's husband was Clive. And since Hugo had swiveled around to watch Tom, he didn't see Father Gaffner frantically shake a hand to wave away the bee, his gesture causing the bride and groom to separate with a sucking sound that one man would later describe as like water going down a drain—evidence that tongues were involved, he would insist in a conversation similar to others that would go on through the banquet. What actually happened? How long had the kiss really lasted? The guests weren't sure, and their uncertainty would only increase, every new exchange adding details that confused them more until there was nothing left to do but drink too much champagne and dance.

STUMBLE

Frank's sister Ruth wasn't exactly beautiful, nor was she ever deliberately coy. She wasn't stupid or desperate or even naturally sweet. She was simply the one girl in town mysteriously identified as easy. And if she gave up trying to keep her willingness from bluntly announcing itself, it was only because curiosity got the better of her. She wanted to understand why the value of her affection was considered necessary and why necessity was always only temporary. Week by week, with every new invitation, she understood a little more.

It was only a matter of time before she understood enough to know that she'd gone too far. Her mother had been right to warn her that a reputation couldn't be washed away with soap and water. By the age of sixteen she'd become the kind of girl *nice* girls avoided, and though she felt that her ruin was a mean trick played on her while she'd been having fun, she decided she had no option left but to make a clean break.

It was late summer in 1927 when, with her parents' blessing, she moved to Brooklyn to claim space on the floor of her brother's cold-water flat. This was her first mistake—not asking dear Frank to take her in but timing her arrival to coincide with his departure. She managed to show up at his door just as he was leaving for the weekend. Frank was sorry, but he had to go to his friend's wedding in New Haven—which left Ruth alone with Frank's roommate, Boylston Simms.

Ruth should have known he'd be a problem. After plying her all day long with highballs, he kissed her. She let him kiss her. And then she remembered who she was trying not to be and pulled away, smoothed her skirt, tucked her hair behind her ears, and looked around for diversion. She asked about the birds in the cage across the room—a pair of finches, Boylston said, and explained that they belonged to his grandmother, who was in the hospital. Ruth asked if she could pet their pretty feathers. He shrugged. She sashayed in her usual inadvertently lusty fashion across the room, unlatched the cage door, and poked a finger at one of the birds, trying to scratch its soft throat as she liked to do with her cat at home. The bird hopped away from her and then fluttered forward onto her finger. Unprepared for the shock of rough talons against her skin, Ruth jerked back her hand, carrying the bird with her. The second bird darted out and veered as though ricocheting across the room. The bird on Ruth's finger flew in pursuit of its mate. One after the other, the finches escaped through the open window and disappeared into the dusky Brooklyn sky.

Although Boylston Simms didn't come right out and ask her to leave, Ruth figured she'd better find somewhere else to stay. She made her way to the station and boarded the train for Manhattan. It was dark by the time she arrived on the Upper West Side, where a friend of her cousin's was supposed to be residing. But the friend had long since moved from the address. With nine dollars and sixty cents in her purse and her suitcase in hand, Ruth walked around the neighborhood until she found a vacancy in a boardinghouse on 103rd Street. She slept that night for a solid fourteen hours. She dreamed she ordered a pancake breakfast in a fancy hotel dining room and was served a platter of fried birds. She dreamed she had a newborn baby girl with a marvelous crop of silver hair.

THE NEXT DAY, she walked along the mall in Central Park. A man who introduced himself as Fitz Greene Halleck sat down beside her on a bench by the esplanade and offered to row her around in a party boat. She refused. He bought her an ice cream, which she accepted. After a long conversation he told her that he worked as a stage manager, and he asked her to audition for a musical. He wrote down the Lower East Side address where the auditions would be held the following Monday and then politely bade good-bye. She wondered if a man as easy to be rid of as Fitz Greene Halleck was really as untrustworthy as he seemed. She decided not to audition for Fitz Greene Halleck's play but instead to investigate other theaters.

On Monday she went through the *Variety* ads. On Tuesday she auditioned at the Princess Theater for a small show called *Nobody's Perfect*. In this show, announced the director to the group of auditioners, imperfection would be a virtue. Ruth danced with a strong partner who led her easily through unfamiliar steps. Still, she must have distinguished herself as adequately imperfect, for she was given a chorus part in the show and was on salary by the following week.

She lasted all the way to the first dress rehearsal, two months later. In the final weeks she became friendly with Sam Amwit, a song plugger from Harms Music who was helping the actors learn the tunes. He played his own tunes on the piano during a take-five, and everyone in the chorus thought his music was better than the music in the show. When the cast returned to continue rehearsing, Sam Amwit's last song was still playing in Ruth's mind, and when the chorus moved to the right, she moved to the left and tripped over another actress's foot.

Apparently, her stumble was only the most noticeable of many awkward moves—Ruth's imperfection was of a different nature from the imperfections of the other cast members. The director let her continue with the rehearsal, but afterward he told her not to return. In a note she hastily scribbled, Ruth asked Sam to come see her soon and gave him her address. A few days later she received an apologetic letter from Sam explaining that he was engaged to a woman from Virginia.

Nobody's Perfect flopped, Ruth was pleased to hear. She went to other auditions and eventually landed a part in a girl-and-music show at Margot's, a cabaret on East Fifty-second Street. She danced in a chorus line for an entire month there. Certain male customers returned night after night to see certain dancers; claims were implicit, though relationships were usually limited to postperformance lap-sitting and a few shared drinks. Ruth sat on the lap of an older man named Wallace. She drank gin spritzes and taught him the songs Sam Amwit had taught her.

Her brother Frank came to see one of her shows and waited around afterward to talk to her. Luckily, Wallace wasn't in the audience that day. But Frank didn't approve of either the show or the establishment. He told her to quit, insisting that if their parents found out what she was doing they'd drag her back to New Jersey. She refused to quit without another job lined up, and Frank promised to find something for her.

She asked about Boylston Simms. Frank said that he had fallen in love with an upstate girl and was working for a newspaper in Albany. What about the finches? Boylston Simms had bought two new finches for his grandmother, who believed them to be the same birds she'd left in his care.

Frank returned to the cabaret three days later to inform his sister that he'd found her a place at the Biltmore as a receptionist, a classy job with an unclassy salary. She worked there straight through Christmas and New Year's, worked ten, sometimes twelve hours a day in order to earn enough money to buy silk stockings and silk blouses to wear to work. On her breaks she smoked Chesterfield cigarettes and chewed Wrigley's Spearmint, often at the same time. She had the use of a stove in the boardinghouse and liked to prepare simple dinners of sandwiches and canned soup with some of the other girls. Once every two months she went home to New Jersey for the weekend.

SHE MET PLENTY OF MEN in her job—fancy young men who would lay it on thick and windy old men who would yammer at her while she was trying to add up a bill. One middle-aged Greek man invited her to lunch in the Biltmore's restaurant. She ate roast beef and mashed potatoes and then with a giggle declined his offer to see his penthouse room. A retired jeweler who lived in the hotel gave her a tip of five dollars one day, and she went out and got herself a puffy Nestle wave. At work the next day the reception manager told her to brush her hair properly or else to leave and not come back. So she left. That was that. It was a cold, drizzly March morning and she was out on the street.

She spent the next couple of hours at the nearest el station, standing close to the potbellied stove and trying to figure out where to go next. She decided to go to her brother's apartment. That same day he helped her find a job at the Roxy theater, a movie palace where Frank was an usher and wore a uniform with polished buttons. Ruth worked as a ticket taker for three months and saw *The Crowd* seventeen times.

She left the Roxy for better pay at the Rivoli, the Rivoli for the Rialto. She grew older and more confident. She wrote to Vitagraph for autographed pictures of Mae Marsh and Norma Talmadge. She dated a man who looked just like Buddy Rogers and after she'd spent the night with him a couple of times she asked him to marry her, but he confessed that he was already engaged.

Why were all the men she'd ever known always already engaged? A month passed, and then another month. One day Ruth thought anything was possible, and the next day she realized her fate had been sealed when she wasn't looking. All the men in the world were always and already engaged.

She slept with any man who would have her. A medical student, a policeman, and her boss at the Rialto, who had no patience for contemporary picture shows and quoted Mary Pickford as evidence: "Adding sound to movies would be like putting lipstick on the Venus de Milo." She wondered when she'd fall in love. She told her boss she loved him, just to try out the sentence, and he told her he was—

"Not already engaged!" she interrupted.

"No. Already married."

She quit her job at the Rialto. She worked as a secretary for a stockbroker. She worked as a waitress. One by one her friends in the rooming house on 103rd Street moved away, so Ruth decided to move too. She rented a studio apartment for herself on Jane Street. She quit her waitressing job and found a ten-dollar-a-week position at Woolworth's, which is where she met Mr. Freddie Harvey the Third.

SITTING ON THE SODA-FOUNTAIN COUNTER one day after work, she was arguing with another Woolworth girl, Mary Beth, about the virtue of tattoos, though really she was arguing with herself, trying to persuade her more practical side that she might benefit from a tattoo and with it attract the kind of man who, for every *why not?* that can't be answered, goes ahead and takes a risk. She settled upon her right buttock as a prime location and was idly considering the possibility of a pink rose when she heard Mr. Freddie's voice.

"Pour me a cup of coffee," he ordered, adding, "pumpkin," not out of affection but because after a full month he still didn't know Ruth's name, though they'd had plenty of brief exchanges, mostly concerning the topic of the cash register and Ruth's tendency to come out a few pennies short at the end of the day.

So that was the first time Mr. Freddie showed up where he wasn't supposed to be. Ruth waited for him to fire her for sitting on the counter. But he simply eased himself onto a stool and spun to the left while he waited for his coffee. Coffee? Mr. Freddie had asked for coffee—and how about a piece of pie? Mary Beth crept off to finish restocking shelves, and Ruth cut a piece of pie for her boss, stale cherry pie stiff with tapioca, the crust streaked with hard-baked lard. She stepped back from the counter and watched him eat.

What a remarkable transformation Mr. Freddie accomplished in those few minutes. Up until then he'd cut a ridiculous figure; all the girls thought so—he fancied himself a bantam cock in the henhouse when in fact he was too scrawny to be of interest and too much of the dandy to be trusted. Everything about him was made up, and the girls enjoyed mocking this amateur trouper behind his back.

Ruth, however, didn't laugh at Mr. Freddie that day. She couldn't believe he hadn't fired her, and she stared at him from beneath the smoky blue of her eyelids. Unexpectedly, she found herself growing interested in him. Maybe it was because she suspected that there was more to him than she'd thought. Or maybe she was just ready to believe that she'd finally met a man who would treat her fairly. Whatever the cause, Ruth was no longer simply one of the girls in Mr. Freddie's eyes by the time he finished his pie.

"Call it favoritism, sweetheart, but I'm going to do something special for you," he said with a wink, brushing crumbs from his mustache with his knuckles. "I can tell you're deserving."

How did Mr. Freddie know she was deserving? Ruth must have had neediness written all over her—a whole set of tattoos that only the manager could see. Clever man. The draw by the end of their conversation was his implied knowledge of her. As she watched him walk away from the counter she became aware of a new curiosity, the kind that once in a while would take her by surprise—when she was deep inside a tedious novel, say, and the plot abruptly thickened. She didn't trust Mr. Freddie and because of this she wanted to be intimate with him, to circumvent his evasions and find out who he really was.

Life went on after that conversation, routine continued to dominate the days, and Ruth worked the register for an extra five cents an hour. But within the routine the challenge of Mr. Freddie grew. He learned her name. He'd wander out from the back office to chat with her about the weather. He'd join her at the counter during her lunch break. He'd tell his war stories, which all seemed contradictory versions of a single story about a U-boat sunk off the coast of Ireland. Ruth would hardly listen, having long since concluded that all his testimonials were lies, or at least exaggerations. What she liked better than his puffery were those promises, those delicious representations of the future, about how she would get her promotion, and Mr. Freddie's mysterious investment in an outfit on Long Island would begin to pay off. The accumulation of profit seemed a much more certain thing than the adventures of his past, and Ruth liked the man all the more because of his contagious optimism. So she hung with him, as the other girls noticed, and in doing so became the store outcast, having contracted, in their opinion, the disease that was the boss.

What began for Ruth as curiosity became, in part, defiance. She was Freddie's girl, though how she made that leap to the possessive she'd never know for certain. It was one of the few hypotheticals in her life that ever came true. One morning she woke up in her room on Jane Street, and her first thought was of Freddie's smooth-as-silk hands caressing her, even though at that point she had never met the manager outside the confines of the store.

Freddie's girl she became—in her eyes and in the eyes of her co-workers. Yet as far as she could tell, Mr. Freddie had no opinion about the matter. Or at least that's what he seemed to want her to believe. Yet as time went on she became convinced that the enigma of Freddie the Third would be irresistible once he let her know who he was.

He kept her believing that they were guaranteed a happy future together right through most of their first night out on the town, when Ruth in her boa and heels and Freddie in his Panama were a head-turning smash. She enjoyed the admiration of strangers. But even more than that, she enjoyed watching Freddie in action, handing out five-dollar tips and ordering oysters and rib eye and champagne. Somehow, after a series of taxis and nightclubs, they ended up in a back street south of Linden Boulevard, in a pleasure palace hideaway, where Ruth was willing to throw caution to the wind. *Throw caution to the wind.* A lovely phrase, she thought with a giggle as she stepped out of her dress, having already been assured by Freddie that there was nothing to fear.

"What's so funny, precious?"

"You are, Freddie!"

Her opinion had been influenced by innumerable glasses of champagne, and right then Freddie the Third was about as amusing as they come, pretending to be Mr. Debonair when in fact he was an awkward dancer who didn't know the next step. What fun Ruth had stripping for him, all the while thinking that she had finally found the true Freddie—a meek little understudy who preferred hiding in the wings.

She'd never known a man to be afraid of her. No sooner was she stark naked, her remaining stocking flung across the cracked lacquered bureau, than Freddie started stuttering about how he hoped she was having a good time. She assured him that the good time was just beginning, and she grabbed him by the collar and pulled him onto the bed.

They did have a good time together that night, though Ruth had to teach Freddie a thing or two. When they were done, she felt pleasantly sleepy, and she closed her eyes to better enjoy the tingling aftereffects inside her. She didn't bother to open her eyes when she felt Freddie rise from the bed, so she didn't see him gather his clothes. She kept her eyes closed all the while he was getting dressed, blinking only when she heard the clink of coins on the bureau.

"What are you doing, Freddie?"

He was peering at his reflection in the mirror above the washbasin, straightening his tie.

"I hope it's more than your usual," he said. He explained that he didn't know the going rate, but if she expected more, she shouldn't hesitate to ask. And she shouldn't worry about getting home, since he'd included cab fare.

She stared at his back in amazement. He turned around and tipped his hat foolishly as he let himself out. And then he was gone, leaving Ruth behind to wish that he'd tried to kill her. If he'd come at her, slapped her and kicked her, then she could have returned the treatment and broken a glass against his head.

It took some time before she could catch her breath. With difficulty, she dressed herself and abandoned the room, leaving the money from Freddie on the bureau—she was halfway down the stairs when she realized that she had forgotten her stockings and that her dress underneath her shawl was on inside-out. But she had no inclination to improve her appearance. She only wanted to get out into the fresh air and collect the frenzied memory into some vaguely ordered whole, which she tried to do as she walked up the empty street between two warehouses.

She began her long journey back to her Jane Street apartment, an expedition that took her through the empty, unmarked lanes of Canarsie to the swamplands reeking of seaweed and mud and frying fat. It was a cool night, with a mist shrouding the half-moon, and in the gloomy light the shacks built on pilings seemed to have hollow eye sockets where there should have been windows and gaping dark mouths instead of doors. Ruth would have thought them all uninhabited if she hadn't seen a kerosene lamp flickering on a back porch, hung there to warn away vagrants. Ruth was no better than a vagrant. Circumstances had turned her into the kind of woman that most of humanity reviles, and she couldn't blame them, couldn't in her dazed state figure out who was to blame, and couldn't figure out how best to get home.

A single room with a bath and an electric burner: this was Ruth's home and she wanted to be there so badly that she began to run. She crossed a gravel driveway, scrambled down and out of a drainage ditch, and began fighting her way through the wet salt hay, swamp tassels bobbing and nodding at her as she passed. She lost one of her high-heeled shoes when she crossed the mucky bed of a tidal creek. She threw the other shoe far into the swamp and kept stumbling over the soft hummocks as fast as she could toward the highway in the distance. She would wave down a driver, beg a ride into Manhattan, and be home in an hour.

An occasional truck rattled along the road, and in the intervals of silence she heard her own panting and the *shush* of the wet hay. There were fewer shacks in this area of the meadows, and the ground was soupier—Ruth fell twice, and by the time she reached the bottom of the highway's steep embankment she was shivering and spattered head to foot with swamp mud. From her neck down she looked more like some monster from a picture show than the fancy gal she'd imagined herself to be earlier that same evening, and she clutched the corners of her shawl together to hide her body from herself.

She was about ten feet below the verge, scooting forward on hands and feet through the grass, when one hand landed on a soft, clammy, contoured something. She popped up, revulsion preceding comprehension. For a few seconds she couldn't look down, wanting to believe that she had nothing to fear. When she did finally look, she saw not a fish but a bulging shape that resembled nothing more than a naked human torso tucked snugly in the grass. The broad, spongy surface, mottled by shadows, had a fleshy pallor to it, in fact was flesh, and belonged, she thought at first, to a person, the back hidden beneath coarse hair—hair that with a better look she recognized to be the fur of an animal, a dead opossum that Ruth could only imagine had been planted there to humiliate her.

She ran from the carcass, scrambled up the last part of the embankment, careened along the verge calling for help, but the wind washed away her voice and the truck approaching didn't stop— fortunately for Ruth, she realized in the next instant, because if she was discovered covered with mud here on the edge of Jamaica Bay, she'd have a hard time convincing the world that she didn't belong locked in the solitary confinement wing of The Tombs.

She tried to collect herself, folded her arms together, trudged forward. She was heading toward Brooklyn, she discovered at the first roadside sign, in the wrong direction, though now at least she knew where she was. Another truck rattled by without slowing. At Rockaway Boulevard she turned her nose toward Manhattan, walking more steadily, even automatically, along the sidewalk. Eventually she came to a bus station, where she splashed her face at the sink in the ladies' room and bought a ticket from a dull-eyed vendor who didn't glance twice at her. She waited nearly an hour for the bus. She rode it as far as the Flatbush Avenue station, then took the IRT into Manhattan. No one noticed or cared that she wore no shoes. Miraculously, she was back in her own bed, asleep, before sunrise.

SHE WOKE LATE the next day, the sound of her laughter echoing from her dreams. When she glanced at the clock and saw the time her first thought was that she'd be late for work. She even began to wash up before the embroidery of dried mud on her legs reminded her that she couldn't go to work.

She bathed in deep, bubble-bath comfort for more than an hour. Later, after a bowl of canned chicken noodle soup, she lay back down on her bed and stared at the ceiling. She listened to the noises of life in the street. She made herself a cheese sandwich, which she couldn't bring herself to eat. She went to bed shortly before eight.

She passed the next day, though she woke earlier, in much the same fashion. Out of this solitary existence she began to fall into a new routine for herself. A week later she left the Jane Street apartment and moved into a women's boardinghouse on West Thirty-eighth Street. Someday soon she would have to find another job.

With so much time on her hands, she took to strolling through Paddy's Market underneath the Ninth Avenue elevated. Initially the chaos of the place unnerved her, but eventually she grew used to it, and even to like it. She enjoyed taking in the scenery and imagining countless plots to explain the mysterious lives of strangers. Really, the market was better than any show she'd ever been in, funnier than vaudeville, with each gesture part of a routine and the overheard conversations verging on song. The funniest thing of all was that when a train passed, clanking overhead, the noise entirely drowned out the voices in the market, yet everyone kept right on talking.

She was at noisy Paddy's Market on the day her brother spent a fortune to put a message in the newspaper: *Ruth. Where are you? I would like to help if I can. Please get in touch with me for anything you need. Brother Frank.* The appeal ran at the bottom of the front page of the *New York Times*. But Ruth didn't bother to read the *New York Times*. Instead, she wandered around the market trying to envision a better life for herself, a life in which everything would fall perfectly into place and she'd put all her troubles so far behind her that she wouldn't even be able to remember them. Even here—surrounded by heaps of luscious oranges and lemons to flavor iced tea; cages packed with terrified turkeys, chickens, pigeons, and ducks; carts full of wilting parsley and Bibb lettuce and Carolina tomatoes; stout, aproned women haggling in thick accents with the merchants; men shouting over dice in a corner—Ruth found it hard to recall that she'd ever felt alone. Sure, this was just the place for a girl to come if she was looking to start over. She'd better be ready, since her perfect new life might begin any time. Or maybe, she considered, it had already begun.

WORRY

Through the first decade of her marriage, Mrs. Helen Weech Owen didn't have a worry in the world, unlike her husband, Dexter, whose responsibilities as vice president of a pharmaceutical company left him little time to spare for his family. And while another sort of wife might have wondered what her husband did, exactly, on those frequent business trips to Boston, Mrs. Owen wasn't that sort. She knew her husband too well to fret about him acquiring a mistress. If he didn't always adore his wife, he depended upon their attachment, clung to the idea of their alliance much as the creeping ivy attached itself to the stone wall bordering their backyard. Simply by agreeing to be his wife, Mrs. Owen had insured herself against betrayal. Dexter had risked love once—and won. He would never take such a risk again.

Redfield Doyle Pharmaceutical managed to flourish right from its inception, and the Owen family seemed to all a paragon of good fortune at a time when so many fortunes were being consigned to memory. Helen grew increasingly satisfied with "the lot of it," as she liked to say. She grew in other ways as well: she didn't resist when her already square figure began to expand, puffing at the wrists and ankles, pouching a bit on either side of her jaw. She was too confident a woman to worry about pounds and dimensions. As the years passed and her friends found themselves losing control of their lives, they turned to steady Helen Owen for consolation, finding in her a faithful listener who had no turmoil of her own to relate.

The women tended to confide in Helen over coffee during the blank hours of midmorning. While the babies napped, Helen's friends told her of unpaid bills and second mortgages. They told her of heirloom jewelry that they'd been forced to pawn at a shop over in Great Neck. They told her of husbands who insulted them in public, slapped them in private, ignored them, berated them, even threatened to abandon them. Helen led the women through their monologues with a frown that conveyed her concern more fully than any words could have done. But it wasn't enough for them to tell—and to be heard. Helen could do nothing to help them. She found herself privately predicting the mistakes they would make and wasn't at all surprised when, once their children started school, her friends began taking lovers.

They were wrong to think that she would disapprove of their behavior, but apparently their shame was strong enough that they stopped visiting her, and Helen had to learn the details of their affairs through gossip at club luncheons. Though she'd expected to hear of such adventures in their lives, she couldn't help but feel deserted. She guessed that nothing short of a serious illness would revive the old intimacies.

To ward off the loneliness of vacant mornings, she threw herself into charity work. She wanted to help those truly in need of help.

With her characteristic determination, she set out to become the kind of community volunteer who would be recognized one day with a full-page obituary in the local paper.

As it turned out, the two people who needed her least were her own children. In their early years, Jackie and Gregory—or Gimp, as Jackie had named him when he was three—had been polite, mild children, perhaps more inclined to sob over little disappointments than others their age, though Helen attributed this to their intelligence and felt sure that their weakness would develop into impressive strength of character. Indeed, by the time Jackie was twelve and Gimp ten, they were admired by other parents for their studiousness and self-control. Dexter, though he didn't spend much time with the children, saw in them his own best traits and never found reason to punish them. His pride verged on happy foolishness, and the infrequent Saturdays he was at home he liked to sit in the garden watching his children play their make-believe games.

Everyone agreed that they were beauties, miraculously so given the plain generations preceding them. Helen liked to think of them as two angels sucked to earth by the vacuum of their mother's love. For she'd loved each of them before they'd been conceived, had seen the children in her dreams dancing across the cotton-ball floor of heaven: a girl first—chestnut hair lit with strands of yellow; round, chocolate eyes—and then her son, blue-eyed, his blond hair streaked with brown. In life, as in heaven, they seemed perfect complements to each other, both of them insistently alive and, in some magical way, invulnerable. Helen had complete, unquestioning faith in their mutual safety. Without quite articulating it to herself, she considered them the necessary manifestations of existence itself, and for many years she wasted no anxious thoughts pondering the many dangers that threaten children. That her offspring would thrive was too solid a conviction to doubt.

Yet doubt did come to her. It came from within, remaining latent for months, perhaps for years. She first became vaguely aware of it at about the time her beautician took to plucking iron gray hairs from her head. She was thirty-nine years old, blessed with such reliable comforts that she considered it disgraceful to fret. She'd always known that a woman's mind has a way of quietly damaging satisfaction, shaking one's confidence in the situation at hand with phantom catastrophes so that experience begins to seem a quagmire of possibilities and change the only certainty. But she continued to believe in her happiness, and her anxiety betrayed itself only in trivialities, a chronic twitch in her right eyelid and a tendency to clear her throat every few minutes, symptoms that Helen shook off as inevitable, like her gray hair.

Then one morning following a particularly restless night, she decided to walk her children to school, her excuse to herself being that she would benefit from the fresh air. At their age, Jackie and Gimp didn't need their mother as an escort, but neither did they seem to mind. They played tag with friends they met along the way while Helen ambled along behind, and at the first sight of the school they raced each other up to the building, finishing their uneventful journey with hoots and laughter. After the doors closed behind them they ran to a foyer window to wave good-bye. As Helen raised her arm to wave back, she hesitated, struck by an immense and unfamiliar fear. Her children were mere apparitions behind the dusty glass, insubstantial, weightless, and as soon as they disappeared, she burst into tears.

Had she been an experienced worrier, at least she would have understood what she was feeling. But she understood nothing more than that she had to reckon with the fear, whatever its source. Reckoning must involve reason. So she reasoned her way home and spent the rest of the tearless morning planning the next meeting of Jackie's Girl Scout troop.

Through that fall and winter, Helen rarely had cause to remember her bout of worry. Heavy snowfalls gave the children plenty to do outside, and holiday fund-raising events kept their mother fairly well occupied. With the approach of spring, however, she began to grow restless. She would have taken long afternoon walks, but that wasn't done by women of her age—not in this town, where the only sidewalks connected the stores along Main Street. Instead, she bought herself a new radio and spent the empty hours learning the words to such popular songs as "The Dipsy Doodle" and "Harbour Lights."

Toward evening one day in May, while the children played outside in the warm, grainy dusk and Helen attended to bills, the newscaster pressed in monotone through the previous day's list of crimes, including one involving a hobo who was doused with gasoline and lit on fire while he'd been sleeping on the edge of a playing field in Huntington. The name of the nearby town startled Helen, as if she'd suddenly heard her own name on the broadcast. She dropped the letter opener and almost turned over her chair when she stood. She hurried outside, where she found her children behind the garden shed pounding nails and securing wire mesh to tall wooden stakes. Helen had no idea what they were building and didn't stop to ask. She just swept them into her arms with rough, impossible strength and squeezed them together as though trying to press one into the other, to make a single child out of two. And for the first time in their lives, as far as she could remember, they struggled to push her away.

THE POINT BEING that squabs beat hens no matter what, and at two dollars and fifteen cents a dozen, the Owen children are sure to turn a fancy profit. Or such is Jackie's notion, though Gimp feels compelled to point out that it's no work for a get-rich-quick kind of person. Which causes Jackie to seize her little brother by his shirt collar and dare him to back out now. But Gimp just wants to be sure, a fair-enough request, so Jackie takes him through her calculations once more: they buy twelve breeding pairs today, they'll have six hundred birds within eight months. Gimp reminds Jackie that they'll need a supply of buckwheat. Jackie reminds Gimp that squabs prefer barley during the molting season. And then there's the cost of two large cages to transport the birds home.

They fall silent when a sudden spasm of darkness turns the morning into night. They hear only the churning of the train's wheels and the murmuring voices of passengers in nearby seats.

"What's happened?"

"We're in a tunnel, Gimp."

Their hands meet, clasp in the dark, the grip of clammy fingers still comforting to them, though they are almost too old for this contact— old enough, after all, to make a real-life investment. Their business venture, the gist of which they've kept to themselves for the simple reason that neither parent has asked them what, precisely, they've been up to, will be common knowledge soon enough, once the twenty-four birds are flashing and tumbling across their flying pen.

The children don't think it at all unusual that neither parent has inquired about the exact purpose of the huge pen they've built in the backyard. To them, life at home is like this ride through the tunnel, their privacy intensified by a surrounding darkness. Not that they mind. They prefer to be left alone. Besides, their parents have never found reason to blame them for anything, and while the children don't exactly think of themselves as perfect, they know they can do no wrong in their parents' eyes. Even this trip to the city will be forgiven, in light of the practical motive: twelve white-fleshed, fertile pairs of Plymouth Rock homers.

They are still holding hands when they follow the other passengers across the gap separating the train from the platform. The crowd is not the early-commuter throng; they are noontime tourists and travelers, and instead of surging toward the gate they trickle, carrying the young Owens along their surface, two fallen leaves with stems entwined.

And then, nearly as quickly as the tunnel had engulfed daylight, the small group disperses, leaving the children alone in the lower concourse of the station, where they have been once before, on a trip to their father's office. That was years ago, and the only memory of the visit they retain is of the company's doorman letting them play with the elevator controls. Now, on their own in the city, having skipped out on their school fair, they are too confused by the many possible directions to be terrified. But terror soon comes to them—delicious, illuminating terror—when they see an old man shuffling along a vaulted corridor, a bent, shrouded figure, and though motion seems difficult for him, he manages to increase his pace as he approaches. He reeks of urine, and the newspapers he has wrapped around his feet crunch softly as he walks. The children stand still, both of them enjoying the strange luxury of fear even as they pray silently that this ghost will pass by and keep walking down the platform and into the endless darkness.

He drags himself to a halt. They can see the perspiration glistening inside his wrinkles. His voice, magically amplified, startles them with its volume and clarity. "What's that? *Ark!* Now take a penny, each of you, *ark!* Give me your hands, come on now, a penny for good luck, two shiny new pennies for two—*ark!*—naughty pussies." After grabbing their reluctant hands and pressing a penny in each, the mad old man shuffles on, his head bobbing so close to Jackie that with a quick, wicked thrust he could give the girl a smack of a kiss on her lips. But the man has already forgotten his recent dispensation and

engaged one of his many selves in some incoherent argument punctuated by *ark*s and scornful laughter.

The children close their fists around the filthy pennies and wander up the same sloping corridor the man had come down. They
know now that they are in a treacherous place, if not actually threatened, and this sense of risk makes them feel important, momentarily
raises the purpose of their lives to extraordinary heights, which, after
all, has always been their main ambition, ever since they were left to
wander where they pleased. They have spent their first decade increasing the simple risks of life in whatever way they could: climbing pine
trees up to the wavering top, scooting across busy roads, swimming
in forbidden Saverin Lake. Not that they consider themselves more
courageous than other children—they are simply addicted to thrill
and enjoy nothing better than the suspense of a perilous situation.

The astonishing thing is that they have nurtured their addiction
without giving away the secret of their recklessness. At school, they
are model students, praised and then ignored by teachers preoccu-
pied with the more rambunctious children. They risk accident and
death only when they are away from school and out of sight of their
mother and father. Once in a while they invite friends to join them,
but mostly they save their rash adventures for themselves, storing up
ideas in their daydreams like little scientists planning a series of ex-
periments that might, just might, have terrible consequences, though
so far they have survived without a single broken bone.

Lately, under Jackie's maturing influence, they have started to
design new adventures for themselves, ones that are borrowed from
the adult world, that mysterious, alluring Hades, where so many things
can go wrong. Unlike their father, whose main impulse in business is
caution, and their mother, who likes to claim that most everything
"works out," the children have decided that after the many exciting

close calls of their early years, they are ready to invest the small fortune they've accumulated from their weekly allowances in their own squab farm. They are either future tycoons or doomed gamblers, or perhaps both. But they won't know what they can be if they don't try.

And here they are on a school day in this tremendous Roman bath called Pennsylvania Station, making their innocent way along an arcade lined with snack bars and shops and up a marble stairway to the street, where the momentum of so many individuals—some heading into the station, others dispersing to waiting taxis or across nearby intersections, just as their own father must do on days when he's not in Boston—makes Jackie and Gimp feel like idlers, and even worse, like children. They don't want to be just children. They want to be remarkable in some way. But the only reason they stand out from this crowd, if they stand out at all, is that they are children. Children with a mission—on the way to the Washington Market, where they hope to find their pigeons at a bargain price.

They have their neighbor to thank for this, their first business venture. Jackie discovered the book on squabs in Mrs. Parsons's trash bin, where she'd been digging in search of other treasures, the costume jewelry that Mrs. Parsons accumulated and then discarded or the girlie magazines that came for her boarder, Carl. Why either Mrs. Parsons or her boarder had bought and then thrown away a book on raising squabs for profit, Jackie couldn't say and didn't care. But within twenty-four hours of finding the book, financial gain had become her new obsession—and Gimp's too, since by habit he dedicates himself to his sister's schemes. That he is uncertain has only intensified the danger involved. Uncertainty, the children know, means the effort is worthy.

But not worthy enough, not yet. Here on a sultry spring day in Manhattan there are too many people, too many open doors and alert policemen for the children to feel themselves in any real danger. Their mission will be accomplished easily at this rate. Without quite realizing what they're doing they set off walking up Seventh Avenue, away from the direction of the Washington Market and their Plymouth Rock homers. They eat a chocolate bar as they go. They turn east on Forty-second Street, nudging each other as they pass the signs advertising dime-a-dance girls. From a shop on Broadway they buy a malted milk with ice cream, which they share amiably, and after they have finished it Jackie tucks her snap purse into the pocket of her jumper, takes her brother's hand, and leads him across Times Square and through the entrance of the Rialto. A new impulse usually means a new adventure. The children have grown impatient, so they tempt fate by walking through the lobby, where gusts of dusty noontime heat are churned by huge ceiling fans, and past the ticket booth into the theater. No one stops them or calls after them, which both disappoints and relieves the children. Now that they are here they feel compelled to stay for at least a few minutes. Jackie chews her thumbnail, and Gimp shuffles from foot to foot. On the screen, women cheer marching soldiers while a narrator exclaims: *". . . Any action or policy the Reich elects to adopt!"* Whatever he means, it matters little to the children, and they remain standing in the rear of the theater until the newsreel ends. The next newsreel features Chicago policemen who are either grinning or wincing as they club factory workers. The children ease themselves into two seats on the right-hand side of the theater and watch attentively, content to be spectators to something they don't understand.

After the second newsreel, they rise and hurry into adjacent washrooms, emerging at the same time and without a word heading out of the theater. Back on the street, the heat hits them with the force of a slap, and Jackie orders a lemonade from a vendor. She has already tipped the cup to her mouth when the vendor snatches it away and shrieks at her in Italian, patting his shirt pocket to indicate the payment due, which, according to the sign, is just a nickel, almost nothing when you're walking around with more than eight dollars in your purse.

But it's something—more than something—when you reach into your dress pocket, a pocket so ample and deep that you can put your schoolbooks in it, and your snap purse isn't there!

"My purse, Gimp!"

"What?"

"It's gone."

"What?"

"My purse—it's gone."

"Your purse?"

"In the theater, maybe . . ."

"You dropped it?"

"I lost it."

"Or it was filched. What if it was filched?"

"Oh, Gimp, will you shut up!"

"But, Jack—"

"Don't talk to me, do you hear!"

Jackie is screaming now, a typical response for her in a moment of crisis and all too appropriate, given their predicament. The vendor is shouting too, *"Vai, vai!"* splashing the lemonade as he gestures for them to leave, and poor Gimp is hopping nervously, almost running in place, as though trying to escape his sister's wrath. You'd have to look closely to see the mirth behind her fury. For both children, their reactions are those of actors who nearly, though not entirely, forget their real selves on stage. How convincing they are in their panic. How utterly engaging their performance—to themselves, if to none of the indifferent passersby. This is a worthy predicament, one they will remember for years to come. Alone in the middle of the Great White Way, beggared either by bad luck or a pickpocket, reduced to a penny apiece. Never before have they felt so perfectly vulnerable.

HELEN OWEN had a special talent when it came to charity: where other volunteers were met with brittle smiles and refusals, Helen managed to turn virtually every solicitation into a profitable transaction. She'd gone door to door to raise money for the town library. She'd visited her wealthiest friends to raise capital for the expansion of a small local hospital. Helen was known in town for her magical touch, and during the day her face shone with the kind of contentment that belongs only to women who manage to combine prosperity with social purpose. Had she been even wealthier, she would have found her niche as a famous philanthropist. But the Owens were wedged snugly in place just below the pinnacle of the aristocracy. They were what their more desperate friends referred to as *well off*—not exactly the "economic royalists" maligned by Roosevelt but still miraculously unaffected by the difficult times.

On a typical day, the children would arrive home from school, devour the snack prepared for them by Mrs. Minello, the cook, and then run out to play until suppertime. Helen would come home at about four thirty or five to find Mrs. Minello up to her elbows in raw meatloaf. For the next hour, Helen would listen to the radio and attend to correspondence at the rolltop desk in the den. At six she would call her children in for supper, and they'd come scampering across the yard, grass stains on their clothes, twigs tangled in their hair. They would wash their hands at the kitchen sink and sit down to eat whether or not Dexter was expected home that night. During dinner, Helen would drill the children about their successes at school. When they were through, they'd rush outside to continue work on their fort, or such was Helen's notion of their project. Eventually they'd return to the house of their own accord, emerging from the dusk like pieces of pale quartz, though until then Helen would sit near the single window in the den listening for any sound—a crackle of leaves, a cough, a brittle laugh—that might belong to some drifter lurking out in the woods. Not that she blamed those men unfortunate enough to have lost their jobs and homes. But as their ranks increased, so did the violence. While she watched her children playing in the distance, she'd imagine all the harm that might come to them. Only after she had them safely inside for the night would she admit the burden of their absence.

Yet she remained determined not to overprotect them, and she kept her worry a secret, privately condemning herself for indulging the faithless emotion and always greeting the children with remarkable composure, interrogating them about the next day's schedule as though they were her adult employees. They in turn were wonderfully respectful of their mother, unlike some other children she knew, and they'd try their best to impress her. Gregory, she hoped, would grow up to be a doctor. Jacqueline would carry on her mother's good work. But there was plenty of time for them to choose their vocations. For now, Helen tried to allow them ample opportunity to do as they pleased, since she believed that children benefit from privacy—an independent character grows out of an independent childhood, as Helen herself could testify from her own upbringing.

Memorial Day was not unusual in any way. Rumblings of thunder in the late afternoon were not followed by rain, so the children returned outside after their snack. At supper, Jackie described in detail an experiment with helium her teacher had performed for her class the previous week. Gimp announced, for the fifth time in two days, that he'd gotten an A on a spelling quiz. Helen tested them both for a few minutes with words like *appetite, conscience,* and *unanimity,* coaching them gently through the more difficult syllables. Then she excused them from the table, and they rushed off for their final hour of play.

With Dexter away taking care of some sort of business that *could not wait,* Helen spent the rest of the evening in restless solitude. Once the children were in bed, she paged through magazines and eventually fell asleep in her clothes. She woke with a start shortly after 2:00 a.m. Sleep was a useless effort at that point, so she went downstairs to read on the sofa. But though her mind was alert, her eyes were too tired to decipher the print. She tried to doze. She tried rehearsing verb conjugations in French. Finally she decided to go outside for a breath of fresh night air.

She felt the thumping work of her heart as she closed the door behind her—a common-enough symptom of her rising anxiety. A dog barked in the distance. Nearby, branches rustled under the paws of some nocturnal animal. Helen set out on a walk through the neighborhood, and though nothing seemed amiss, she felt the need to stay acutely alert. She imagined she was a guard for her family and neighbors. As long as she was awake, nothing terrible could happen. The night would pass without disruption. No child would be stolen, no band of ruffians would come to prey on roaming bums.

By the third turn around the circle, Helen's anxiety had begun to subside, replaced by a pleasant fatigue. She was already looking forward to her Scotch and the sleep that would finally release her from her vigilance. She paused in a pocket of air rich with the scent of honeysuckle and turned her face up to contemplate the strands of clouds that floated across the moon. She felt as proud of her vigilance as she was sure that the last hours of the night would pass uneventfully. Her neighbors would never know what she had done for them. The phantom warrior of Wakeman Road. The obvious irony of the street's name struck her for the first time, and she slowed her pace to better appreciate her neighborhood. Behind the bayberry hedge was the Raymond house, number 35, a large brick Tudor with a slate roof. The Raymonds, it was rumored, had suffered dearly from the Crash, and since then they'd been kept afloat by Willie Raymond's parents. Mrs. Parsons, who lived in the Cape at number 33, had been renting out rooms ever since her husband's death two years ago. The Owens owned the shingled Colonial, number 31. Separating each house were spacious yards, the grass still fragrant with rotting dogwood blossoms.

How unreal Helen suddenly felt—so strangely voluptuous. *Imagine lying on a sheet of freshly fallen blossoms, your body still slender with youth, a boy leaning over you, your mouths latched. Imagine a touch made more electrifying by the fact that it is forbidden. Imagine lying naked beneath him, feeling him inside you.* The night seemed to insist upon romance, and for a moment she found herself remembering something she had never experienced. She'd known only routine courtship, everything correct, from the rings exchanged to the devotion that bound her to her husband for life, and her memory sternly reminded her of this: there had been no backyard romance in her life, no secret passion that, had it been discovered, would have ruined her, no inappropriate desire impossible to contain. Mrs. Helen Weech Owen had lived a contained life. Of course, all that could change in an instant. She could stand here in the middle of the road and howl at the moon, rousing the whole neighborhood with the sound, an awful temptation that swept over and past her, leaving her drenched in sweat but sedate.

She walked on, recovering her dignity with every step, so by the time she was crossing her own yard she could scold herself for getting so worked up over nothing.

She slept fitfully and at dawn fell into a deeper sleep that lasted until noon. The sound of automobile tires on the brick drive woke her. Her husband was home from his business trip. She felt an immediate rush of joy, which subsided as she watched him slip out of the car. He would be disappointed to find her still in her nightgown, and the thought of trying to make up excuses irritated her. By the time she had arrived downstairs to greet him she felt angry at his intrusion, though he asked no questions about her apparel, and as soon as she had him settled in with his coffee, she returned to her room, where she dressed with the slow, self-conscious movements of an invalid who has forced herself to rise from bed after many months.

The children would already be finished with classes for the day, since the school was holding its annual spring fair in the afternoon. Helen decided to catch up with them there, and since Dexter opted for rest, she walked alone to the school yard, where the small carnival, complete with booths and hayrides and a hot-air balloon, seemed dwarfed by the expansive playing fields. She spent most of the day wandering through the crowd in search of her daughter and son, unable to believe that no one had seen them or knew where they were. By 4:30 p.m., panic made it impossible for Helen to speak coherently, so it was Dexter who finally called the police.

Devious children. Mustering all their guilelessness, they convince the Rialto's red-coated ticket taker to let them in without paying so they can search—unsuccessfully—for the lost purse, then they scurry back across Times Square, west on Forty-second, and down to Pennsylvania Station. Jackie blames the theft on the mad old crow man, but Gimp reminds her that they'd used money from the purse to buy the malted milk. Which reminds Jackie that she is thirsty, though for now there is nothing they can do about it, not with two measly cents between them.

In the station they are drawn by the clash of a tambourine to a crowd that has gathered around a performer, a clown of sorts, only half in costume, with a fool's cap on his head and a frothy pink collar pinned to his T-shirt. He is balancing three eggs on a spoon while he hits a tambourine against his thigh. Except for a few laughing children tucked against their parents' legs, the crowd watches silently as an egg drops and explodes on the floor. Jackie and Gimp push to the front, and she clutches his hand so she won't lose him like she lost the purse. People press against her on all sides. She becomes aware of something—a book, perhaps a package—rubbing uncomfortably up and down, up and down against the small of her back. She shifts forward, but the pressure increases until she begins wondering whether a spiteful stranger is twisting a fist against her back. She jerks her elbows to gain herself more room. In a moment the pressure ceases, and she turns to catch sight of a short, bloated man with balloons for cheeks and a blunt goatee slipping backward through the crowd. As their glances meet, his flushed face and strangely friendly smile give away his intentions, igniting in Jackie a peculiar humiliation she has never felt before. She pulls her brother forward into the space left open for the clown and then through the sparser crowd behind. They run across the main hall and out through an end pavilion. Gimp lets his sister tug him across Seventh Avenue. They keep running until Jackie stops right in front of the side entrance of Macy's department store to catch her breath.

"Let's go home," she says between gasps.

"We don't have any money."

No money, no tickets, no passage home. Across the street shirt-less workers are edging squares of cement for a new sidewalk. Gimp watches them for a while then turns to eye the revolving doors of Macy's. His sister just stands there hugging herself, panting, looking vacantly ahead, so he gives her a playful push, causing her to stumble a few steps, and he runs into the store, knowing that Jackie will have to follow.

She loses sight of him almost instantly, for the interior dazzles with its glittering ribbons wrapped around Corinthian columns, its many mirrors positioned at various angles, its jewels displayed on beds of blue velvet. Even the hundreds of hats propped on racks pul-sate with light. And such heady perfumes, the scents spun into swirls by fans. And the scarves and purses, so many purses, leather, straw, alligator, cotton, all of them stuffed with paper to look plump. It is a magical place, as remote as a painting, populated by slender ladies so comfortable in their elegance that Jackie wonders whether they are actresses hired by the store to complete the displays.

"Oh, sister!" Gimp's voice rises above the crowd—there he is, halfway up the stairs, taunting his sister with his grin, beckoning her to follow. He turns, bumps into a woman carrying two large shop-ping bags. She boxes him on the ear—serves him right—as he dashes by. Jackie tries to pursue him, bounces like a pinball through the aisles and finally reaches the stairs, only to see her brother disappear around the corner of the second floor. Women's wear, perfect for hide-and-seek. Jackie ascends two stairs at a time, dives through racks of shin-length dresses that smell of moldering hay, pushes through the clothes straight into her brother, who lunges toward her, tackles her and knocks her down, then scampers off.

Stupid coot! She'll show him! Still on her hands and knees, she crawls beneath the dresses into the next aisle, catches Gimp's ankle as he runs by, leaves him sprawled on the dusty wooden floor. Ha! Score one!

What a fine adventure this is turning out to be after all. Gimp chases Jackie, Jackie chases Gimp, until a salesgirl catches them both by an arm and starts to drag them toward the rear stairway. But they yank free and each hurtles off in the opposite direction, one upstairs to the third floor, one downstairs to the first.

Safely alone, Jackie decides to let Gimp come after her rather than pursuing him. She wanders through lingerie and shoes and finds another stairway leading to the basement, where she discovers a vast market made to look even more expansive with floor-to-ceiling mirrors on all sides. There are chocolate bars, pints of fresh raspberries, peaches, cheese, fresh breads and rolls, packets of cookies and lemon drops. Jackie imagines herself a poor orphan set loose in Paradise. She manages to stuff her pockets without anyone noticing and even brazenly stops to ask a deli clerk for directions to the water fountain. She is feeling utterly pleased with herself as she bends over the curling stream of water. But when a pair of arms wraps around her from behind she shrieks, choking on the last sip of water, causing nearly everyone in the area to stop what they're doing and stare.

"Gotcha!"

She wipes her lips with the back of her hand, smiles uneasily at all the strangers, and grabs a fistful of her brother's hair. "Never, never do that again!" she whispers, releasing him with a shove. There's still plenty of fun to be had, though Gimp is smart enough to wait until they're outside the store, the two of them sauntering through the exit and up Broadway like flush crooks, feeling ever so proud of themselves, which is only suitable in a city where retailers and restaurants all hang signs advertising themselves as THE WORLD'S BEST. The Owen children fit right in to this cosmopolitan machine—already they've learned how to take advantage of those who'd like to take advantage of them.

They are inexperienced in the delicate art of shoplifting because the opportunity has never before presented itself. During these hard times, stores in their town tend to keep anything of value on shelves behind the counter. Macy's and its ten acres of treasures offered itself up to them, and they'd taken what they could use—two peaches, candy and cookies, and, voilà, a matronly brassiere, size 36C, which Gimp whips out with a shout from beneath his shirt, looping it into a noose around his sister's neck.

So here's one more lively jest, one more farce to break up the monotony, Jackie galloping along a city street, a brassiere strung around her neck, her little brother with the buckled reins in his hands. *Giddyup!* But there's a change in Jackie's frenzy, so subtle that even Gimp doesn't notice until it's too late. *Whoa, wild girl!* This bucking, runaway mare won't be stopped, and now Gimp can hardly keep up with her, so without thinking he pulls with all his strength on the elastic strap, forcing his sister to spring backward while her legs lunge forward. She topples like a tower of blocks, the back of her head landing with a dull crack—sickening sound—on the sidewalk.

The world stands absolutely still, a hush falls over the city, and piles of clouds slide across the sky to shield the sun from this awful sight. Gimp can't make himself move to help his sister, and she's not moving at all. If she is dead, and her appearance would have it so, then he has killed her. He watches strangers come to his sister's aid just as he watched the newsreels, mouth open, eyes wide. History rolls on, and there is nothing Gregory Dexter Owen can do about it.

A man loses his hat as he goes down—genuflects is what it seems from Gimp's point of view, his beloved sister the object of worship, a martyr laid out on a warm stone bed, soon to be beatified. Gimp snatches the hat before a woman crushes it beneath her foot, and from behind he restores the hat to the man's head, the least he can do for this Samaritan, who in turn restores life to his sister. She moans while the man cradles the back of her head with his open hand. "That's quite a lump, sweetheart!" he murmurs. Two women standing nearby begin to titter, as though the man had said something obscene. Gimp reaches for the brassiere and unwinds it from Jackie's neck, not to relieve his sister of any discomfort or indignity but because he's scared someone will identify the garment as a stolen article. Anyway, isn't it time to get going, Jackie? Gimp wishes his sister would scramble to her feet and tell all the gawkers to mind their own business. But she's still moaning, unaware of the attention she has drawn to herself, so it's up to Gimp, now that he's fairly composed, to send the spectators away.

"That's all right, we're fine," he says, trying to drag Jackie up by her elbows.

"You wait a minute, half-pint," a voice advises from the rear of the crowd, which parts to let the policeman through, brass buttons, billy club, and all, a terrifying sight to a young boy who has just stolen a brassiere from Macy's department store and nearly offed his sister on Broadway. It takes all the control he can muster to keep himself from darting away, but he does more than that, he summons his youthful nerve and manages to stare at the policeman with teary, hound-dog eyes while he helps his sister to her feet.

"I'm fine," she lies, finally coming to her senses though her head pounds.

"See, she's fine," echoes Gimp, and they start walking away from the law's scrutiny and the curiosity of strangers. Within seconds the small crowd disperses, leaving the man with the hat standing beside the policeman, who calls after the children, "No more funny business, you got me?"

"Yessir," replies Gimp, stuffing the brassiere into his trouser pocket.

So the children are on their own again. They keep wandering, but Jackie's aching head makes it impossible for them to have more fun. They eat the two peaches and pause to contemplate the displays in bakery windows. Toward four o'clock the sky darkens to the color of asphalt and a few plump raindrops fall. The children don't hold hands as they walk—they will probably never hold hands again, since they no longer care enough about each other to offer comfort. For no precise reason, they have lost a crucial bit of interest in each other and prefer their inward selves. And somehow they both suspect that they will lose more interest over the weeks and months to come, until they are strangers to each other, their sympathies as different as their personalities.

They feel bored rather than sad. At Jackie's suggestion they return to the train station and explain to one of the conductors waiting near their gate that all their money has been stolen—which isn't quite true, since they still have two pennies. The conductor motions them onto the train, and later, after the train has left the station and the conductor is collecting tickets, he winks at the children and walks past them, clicking the money changer on his belt as he goes.

They ride in silence. When the train emerges from the tunnel, they expect daylight but are greeted with a low cloud bed darkened by dusk. Gimp falls asleep, his head bobbing forward on his chest. Jackie rests her face against the window and wonders with unfamiliar melancholy about all the people she will never meet.

•　　•　　•

Could be—no—then what about—about what? Never mind all that, the possibilities, just the possibilities, will kill her, but wouldn't that be a relief, heaven the antidote to worry, how she hates to worry when there are so many possibilities, none of them comforting, though she'd much rather find out that the children have run off instead— instead of what? Never mind about that. This: the possibility of their disgust? Oh, they have every right to be disgusted with their mother, it's her fault they're missing, and she should hack away at herself with a cleaver until her blood fills the streets of this quiet American town. Then she'll never have to know what she doesn't want to know, coward that she is, a failure, and her children will suffer for—but no, don't say that! Having been born, they must live, all children must live, except they won't, not all, and her children may be among the few . . . now there's no use thinking the worst, Helen Weech, no use thinking at all, and if she could she'd lock the door against the possibilities, though the worst has a way of waiting around to avail itself of the right opportunity, so she mustn't let that happen, mustn't give any of those awful stories a chance to be told, as if she were in control of what might have already happened and could go back to that moment when she held them both in her arms, the last time she held them, the day that unlucky drifter over in Huntington burst into flames, her children in her arms squirming to free themselves. If only she had taken a knitting needle and stitched them to her, skin to skin, then they wouldn't be missing—ridiculous, Helen Weech! You should listen to your husband, who has pointed out that most children get themselves lost, and most of those children are eventually found. Leaving the few possibilities allowed by God . . . and then there are the causes to consider, all of them unthinkable until they are revealed, while for the time being there's the worry, thunder in the sky portending nothing more than possibilities, darkness closing in on her from all sides, her voice like the chirp of a lone cricket when she calls out into the night for her children, such a weak, useless noise, though Dexter doesn't want to hear it and is asking her to please stop, stop, stop it, Helen! holding his hands over his ears while Mrs. Parsons and Mrs. Raymond are busying themselves putting away dishes left to dry in the dish rack, pretending that such an effort will help. Here, this will help! Crash of china on the tile floor—but you see, Helen, it doesn't help, the sound disappears into the silence of their false pity, poor dear, why don't you sit down, but sitting only makes it worse, at least when you're up and on your feet you can kick out if need be, or you can bolt, escape from the premier possibility, the one that squelches its fellows and becomes real, like a toy in the nursery brought to life by the power of a child's affection, tender fingers caressing, little lips curled around first words, everything ordered to carry on the process of life, a slow, ordinary turning, no accidents, no interruptions, flesh displacing the air, life miraculously sustaining itself—until something stops or falters or something else intrudes, obstructs, strikes, turning meaning into nonsense, hickory dickory, and the children are suddenly missing, the space around you squeezed by darkness, danger crushing you until you can't bear the pain of it, so you swallow the syrup offered by the doctor—where did he come from?—without feeling yourself swallow, your throat numb beneath the weight of the night, and don't you know about the possibilities contained within the night? You, Helen, are an expert, a nocturnal archangel who can find what others can't in the dark. Minute by minute.

As they settle her on the sofa, she is the first to see her children, unharmed and unconcerned, scuffing up the drive, slumped and disheveled like bums, bums who come to rifle through your trash bins and camp in your own backyard, *godless bums!* If she didn't see them with her own eyes she wouldn't believe it. But already she's too tired to announce their arrival, too tired to call out to them, and certainly too tired to beat them, which she's never done before but would do now if she had the strength, for she is furious, or would be were it not for this artificial tranquillity that distracts her from the rage she wants to feel, forcing her into a dreamless sleep and leaving her to wake the next morning to a household restored to order, everything in place, and she, devoted wife and mother, more dependent than ever upon a serenity that she is certain will fail her.

FREEZE-OUT

I n a sunlit room overlooking Riverside Drive, Sir Maxwell Smedley-Bark, retired major general of the British army, is reading about himself. In Sir Maxwell's decided opinion, reported correctly on the front page of the newspaper and continued on page twenty-six, "Propaganda is a mighty weapon, especially in the hands of the Spanish insurgents, who have hoodwinked the international community and cast Señor Franco as the villain, when in fact he is very quiet, unassuming, and congenial." That's what he had said to the reporter during the interview yesterday, and here it is printed word for word. The public trusts him to know what he's talking about. After all, he spent two months in Spain, covering 3,200 miles, from Málaga to the Bidasoa. "I look upon General Franco as the champion of Christianity against communism in Western Europe," the quote continues. And for those who might wonder about his sympathies, there's this: Sir Maxwell secured a promise from Franco himself that "no Protestant in Spain will ever be molested for his religion." How about that for a diplomatic plum!

As the direct descendant and namesake of Sir Maxwell Bark, the renowned Scottish poet, his inherited gift with language has served him well in the public realm, and he is spending the golden years of his life traveling around the world in pursuit of peace, a rare treasure indeed! In Spain he spoke with civil authorities, prisoners and soldiers, priests and military personnel on up to Franco himself, who proved a remarkably agreeable fellow as well as a tobacco connoisseur, which made for a delightful after-supper smoke.

Here in New York on business relating to the Bank of England, Sir Maxwell was laid up in the hospital for nearly a week with an intestinal infection. As soon as he had sufficiently recuperated, he'd moved into this bank-owned flat and agreed to an interview. As it turned out, a parade in honor of veterans had thumped and trumpeted along Riverside Drive all morning long, sending up fanfare through the open window while Sir Maxwell held forth.

"The churches are full. There is absolute law and order and peace behind Franco's lines." At some point, perhaps before this last declaration, perhaps afterward, he'd wandered over to the window to peruse a military band passing below, and with his back turned to his visitor he'd recited one of his great-grandfather's verses:

> *Come, Mother, lift your wee treasure high,*
> *Innocent aloft glanced by the flashing eye*
> *Of he who urges our good men to war . . .*

But poetry apparently meant nothing to the journalist, who had omitted the lines from his transcription. Like most journalists, he'd wanted controversy and slogans. Sir Maxwell had given him both. "The world is fooled! Propaganda is so frightfully clever. Franco is no dictator, nor is he a fascist. You can see the light of understanding in his eyes." The light of understanding! Sir Maxwell has a way with words, and if he can't devote himself entirely to poetry, he can, at the tip of a hat, use poetry to enhance his opinions.

He imagines General Franco's pleasure when he hears about the interview. He imagines his own name spoken with admiration around the world.

IN THE KITCHEN of the Brown family house on Rogers Avenue in Marwood, New Jersey, two old women drink their thin coffee laced with Schenley's Supreme and chatter about yesterday's adventures: they had gone into the city to watch the parade and then to meet the French liner *Normandie* in hopes of catching a glimpse of Gloria Swanson, who was said to be returning from Europe. Well, they hadn't seen the grande dame herself, but they'd had plenty of fun matching three longshoremen dime for dime in craps. Then they'd gone to the matinee at the Booth, two hours plus spent in such scientifically cooled comfort that both sisters had promptly fallen asleep at intermission and slept through to the end.

"Aunties," their niece, Clara, says the next morning, addressing them as usual in the plural, "have a bite before you go." She slides a plate of buttered toast into the center of the table and sits down to join them. "Let's just pray the weather holds out."

"My bones are telling me—" says the younger of the two old sisters, but the elder interrupts—"Your rattling bones"—leaving the younger to insist, "My bones are always right—"

"Unless they're wrong."

"And today will be fair."

"That's the order."

"Fair skies and warm."

"Too warm."

"Warm enough."

They reach for the plate of toast at the same time, their fingers brush, and the elder slips a piece from the middle of the stack, leaving the top pieces for her sister. They munch in silence, crumbs collecting in the cracks of their lips while their niece, mother of six grown children, stares through the screen door into the backyard, her expression wistful, as though she were halfheartedly searching the yard for evidence that the past had really happened.

"Don't let Tony forget the watermelon."

The aunts plan to spend today at Belmont Park, where Clara's brother Tony will treat them to lunch and share tips when they go to place their bets. It will be a good day because every day they remain alive is a good day. And as it's the birthday of their niece, it will be a special day.

"You'll bring Gabriella back with you this evening," Clara reminds her aunts. Gabriella, Clara's youngest child, is turning twenty today, and the entire family is gathering to celebrate. Twenty happy years. By suppertime there will be little children darting about the house, tangling themselves in their uncle Trip's legs and causing him to fall headfirst into the rack covered with strips of fresh noodles while Clara's husband and Tony and the aunts play cards and Clara's own boys—fathers themselves now—lob a football back and forth in the yard. Amid the mayhem, Gabriella will drift quietly, her silence giving her beauty an ethereal lightness, as though her true self existed in heaven and the form she took in this world were just a reflection.

Beautiful, serene Gabriella, with nothing to say. The aunts like to compare her to a feather hidden underneath corn kernels in a popping machine—lovely and soft and silent. With thick black hair and black lashes shading penny-colored eyes, all she has to do is blink at a man and he'll melt. The trick, the aunts agree, will be to help her find the suitor with the deepest pockets and the best disposition. But there is time for all that, plenty of time. Gabriella is still a precious girl, as marvelous as a fairy child with gauzy wings hidden inside her dress.

"And remember, don't let on," Clara says to the aunts, for the party tonight is supposed to be a surprise.

"Don't spill the beans, sister," says the elder aunt.

"Don't let the cat out of the bath," remarks the other.

"The bag!" the first corrects, and the two old women snort merrily.

READING ABOUT ONESELF is comparable to dining on frogs' legs and calves' brains, Sir Maxwell thinks as he rolls his newspaper into a tube. The idea of such exposure might be distasteful in theory, but in fact it makes him feel that the effort of life has been worth the trouble. He is deservedly proud. But pride, when it goes unfed, is a poor defense against impatience. A hungry man cannot remain a proud man for long. How long has he been waiting for service in this New York chophouse? Too long. Yet the restaurant is half empty. With the aplomb so typical of the serving class in this country, the waitress assigned to his table gazes right past him every time he raises his hand.

He is just about to complain to the maître d' when the girl arrives with a pitcher of fresh water laced with lemon slices. All right, then—he will complain directly to her, and he is about to do just that, in his severest baritone, but he stops short. She is looking at him in a puzzled way, apparently anticipating a reprimand that will only baffle her. He is looking at her in awe.

He knows what he's feeling, what is happening, for it has happened before, but each new time the feeling strikes him as starkly unfamiliar. He wants to look down to assure himself that the floor is still beneath his feet, but he can't tear his eyes from the face of this chophouse waitress, who is, without a doubt, the prettiest girl he has ever seen, at least since the last prettiest girl he'd ever seen, who was . . . he can't even remember who the last one was, in the face of this present beauty.

Immortal lady born to live in blazing glory . . .

He becomes aware that his jaw is hanging stupidly. As he snaps his mouth closed, he snaps his desire into focus. In the brown pools of the girl's eyes he sees two foolish graybeards, himself doubled into a knight doomed to be spurned and yet loving her all the more for her poisonous indifference, a man who in that instant experiences the most profound humility he's ever felt—or so it seems, bound as he is by the intensity of the moment, this emotion supplanting any sense of repeated history so he understands as if for the first time his terrible insignificance, sixty-seven years adding up to nothing.

He is known as a man with a romantic disposition. But he keeps forgetting the meaning of love and feels it now as a confusing external pressure, a force that will flatten him at the moment when he allows himself to give up hope. He doesn't have the wherewithal to think about his potential for self-deception. He can only believe that he has never before truly loved another human being. Truthfully, his

wife had been no more than an ornament. Even Magdalena, his Sevil-
lan joy, had meant little to him in the end—the pain he felt upon
leaving her had been sweet, the memory of his pleasure a kind of
souvenir he could revive from time to time. But there will be no sou-
venirs from this brutal experience, only terror as suspicion hardens
into the certainty that the waitress will remain separate from him,
unmoved by his suffering, though it wouldn't matter even if she did
come to love him, for she could never love him enough.

Paladin cursed by eerie love doth seek
His blessed cushat dove in stormy bleak
Tossed by the wind. Hear the doleful sound
Of solace sought and never found.

His only hope is to confess, without delay, his love for her. It
would do no good courting her with an account of his honors, mere
hindrances to him now, like an elaborate costume on a drowning man.
Perhaps, though, the girl will take pity on him when he describes this
newborn terror and the transformation that has occurred in him.
Love at first sight. It's one of the sublime experiences available in life,
awful and inspiring and, from a distance, ridiculous. He can't help it
if he's worthy of ridicule, nor does he care what his friends might
think of him if they were here. The only one he cares about is the girl
before him. Why, Sir Maxwell mustn't keep her waiting any longer,
he must tell her exactly what he wants without startling her, the
lovely creature, without wasting another precious minute—

"I'll have the lamb chops, miss. Pink. And bring me a whiskey
sour. Don't dawdle now. I haven't all day!"

Stupidity's deadly weapon—spontaneity. How could he have spoken to her like that, as though she were just an ordinary waitress and

he weren't devastated by love? What an idiot, courting her with tyranny and a sneer and thus destroying any shred of interest that might have been stirred by kinder words. Come back! But she is already heading into the kitchen, lost to a first impression that can never be undone, her indifference calcifying into contempt even as she walks away to fetch him what he wants.

His only solace is his imagination. He pictures her in the kitchen spitting angrily into his drink, giving him a chance to taste her sweet soul. He'd rather taste the salty surface of her skin, her breasts, her lips, the nectar of her sex—he tries to imagine stepping out of time into the dream world where she would make herself available to him, tries to picture her in place of his mistress Magdalena lying naked on the bed. But the real place he's in oppresses with its dim electric chandeliers, so he closes his eyes against the scene, opens them again a lifetime later, and finds before him his drink. He eats the speared cherry first, then sips the whiskey, taking in only enough to wet his tongue, for he wants to make this drink last, along with the others that will follow, each full glass an excuse to keep him sitting in this restaurant. He'll sit here all afternoon, all evening, all night, and into the morrow. He'll sit here until he turns to dust.

CLASS C, one-thousand-dollar purse on the Widener course, and with Stout on top of Deep End there's no telling what will happen. Jolly Jack breaks too quickly and drops, while Suntime holds on gamely, but it's Deep End the aunts have put their money on—against the advice of their nephew Tony—for Deep End is a handsome, high-stepping horse, a plucky sprinter who last week ran third and usually does even worse but today has that look of ambition in his eye. Indeed, he seizes the lead at the quarter post and holds it, increases his advantage at the last sixteenth, coming under the wire a half-length ahead of Suntime. And that's at twenty-to-one odds at the last call-over!

Lucky as gypsies, these two sisters, with their fistfuls of cash. They count their money dollar by dollar and then send it back, putting it all on Dundrillon in the second heat, though the four-year-old gelding unfairly carries 151 pounds. Dundrillon runs sixth, the aunts are penniless again, and there's not even time to watch the next race, for they've promised Clara that they'd pick up Gabriella and bring her along to the birthday party.

"So long, aunties!" Tony calls, after giving them each a dollar for train fare. Although he's a professional picker, he, like his aunts, usually comes out no better than even at the end of the day. Right now he's down fifty bucks. His mustache, sticky with sweat, looks like it's been dipped in molasses.

"Don't be late," the younger aunt says.

"And don't forget the watermelon," the older one reminds him. But Tony has turned his back and is too busy studying the call-board and jotting down numbers in the margins of his paper to reply, so the aunts blow him a kiss and hurry off to the train, bumping each other with their broad hips as they turn and letting out such peals of laughter that a husband and wife nearby shake their heads grimly at the sight of these two old spinster sinners who are obviously long past saving.

SIR MAXWELL CUTS INTO THE LAMB, finds it brown in the center but does not complain. In fact, he's glad that the chops had been plucked late from the griddle, for this gives him a chance to make up for his harsh order with penitential silence. He is a gentleman; he will accept whatever hand life deals him, whether it be an unreachable girl or overcooked lamb.

He leaves a fair amount of meat on the bones in hopes that the waitress will notice the cook's error. But the girl is nowhere to be seen. Instead, the busboy, a freckled lad of sixteen or so, clears the table, brushing bread crumbs off the linen cloth with a series of quick strokes that suggest a powerful disdain. Has the waitress already warned the busboy about the peevish old man at the corner table? Perhaps all the workers in this restaurant have heard from her that the gentleman who ordered the chops is a scoundrel, and so all of them have agreed to treat him with cruel civility.

"Dessert, sir?"

"Eh, what's that?"

"Dessert?"

"No. Yes. Where's my waitress?"

"Should I send her over?"

"Oh, for God's sake, yes! No! Tell me, what's her name?"

"Marshall Johnson, sir."

"Marshall? What kind of name is that for a girl?"

To Sir Maxwell's astonishment, the busboy makes an about-face and stalks off, treating the major general to a double dose of contempt. Can it be so? Is the entire establishment of this restaurant conspiring to make a fool of him? On any other day Sir Maxwell would ensure that rudeness was adequately punished, but today he wishes to avoid creating a scene and is quite dismayed when he sees the maître d' approaching.

"I say," he bursts out, just as the man is about to speak, "an apology isn't necessary."

"But it is," replies the maître d', a thin, reptilian fellow who smells faintly, Sir Maxwell thinks, of bus exhaust.

"I'd rather forget the matter."

"In all deference, sir, my boy Johnson deserves an apology," the maître d' persists. "In this country, you should understand . . . ," and he goes on to explain certain expectations Americans have, whatever their station—most important, that boys expect to be addressed as boys and girls as girls. But Sir Maxwell can't quite follow the gist, for he's still pondering the maître d's reference to "my boy Johnson," and in the private struggle of misunderstanding he wonders whether the waitress, so quaintly named Marshall Johnson, is actually a *he*.

"Yes, yes, of course," he says, motioning with his hand as if to wave away a gnat, for he can't think clearly with the man rambling on.

"Otherwise, sir, I'll have to ask you to leave," the man says, standing tall, obviously emboldened by the threat.

"You what!" Sir Maxwell rises from his chair, unable to resist the challenge, hearing in his head his own voice chant, *Not mine a race of craven blood,* for when pushed to the wall he's a proud old dog. "Do you know who I am?" He picks up the newspaper and smacks it back down on the table. "Can you even guess?"

By now the scene Sir Maxwell had wanted to avoid is drawing wondering and disapproving glances from around the room; the waitresses have stopped serving, the customers have stopped talking, and Sir Maxwell stands at the center of attention, pathetic in his rage.

"Good God," he says, blotting sweat away with a napkin, "I'm mistaken," for in a flash he has understood. "The boy, you see, your boy Johnson, he must have misheard my question. I was asking about . . . about . . ." He searches the room and points: "Her! The little beauty!"

All eyes follow the line of his forefinger a few yards to Gabriella Brown, who alone among his audience is smiling knowingly, her satisfaction prompting Sir Maxwell to see her for a passing instant as the perpetrator of a successful dupe.

With somewhat forced laughter, he and the maître d' put the pieces back into proper order while Gabriella watches from a distance. Sir Maxwell learns her name and repeats it quietly to himself while the maître d' whispers, "She's a dandy server, but what an oddball!" touching his forehead to indicate the source of her strangeness. "The owner took a fancy to her when she came in to apply for the job," the maître d' explains. "He didn't much care that she kept her thoughts to herself. Hired her anyway." As in most such cases of doomed love, her mysteriousness only makes her more intriguing to her infatuated customer, and over a refreshed drink, compliments of the house, Sir Maxwell lets himself begin to hope that when he finally leaves the restaurant, he'll leave with her.

By THE TIME THE TWO AUNTS ARRIVE at the restaurant, Gabriella, finished with her shift for the day, is on her third martini and looking more beatific than ever, a captive audience, apparently, to Sir Maxwell, who is boasting about the bottle of port he brought to General Franco—put down in 1853. Sir Maxwell has been sipping whiskey sours since lunch, and now the tip of his nose is the same blush red as the candied cherry in his drink. "Ho, ho," he laughs, oblivious to the similarity between himself and that old charmer Saint Nick. The aunts watch quietly for a few minutes. When they see that he's casting his spell with Bombay gin and that the twinkle in his eye has an avaricious gleam, they decide to interrupt.

"Precious Gabriella," they sing, taking turns squeezing her chin in their plump hands and kissing her cheeks. "Are you well?" the elder asks, and the younger chirps, "Are you done for the day?" and then they tell her about their luck at the track, clearly expecting no reply from the girl, happy just to have her listening intently, that look of calm interest on her face enough to make the most tedious subject seem marvelous. And without pausing in their account, they each take an arm and lift Gabriella right out of her chair, for they intend to catch the 6:05 from Pennsylvania Station.

"Hello there, not so quickly!" Sir Maxwell cries, placing his bulky self in front of the women.

"Pardon me, Santa," says the elder sister.

"We have to go," says the younger.

"But we've been having a jolly time," he persists. "Don't take her away."

"We have to catch a train."

"So if you'll excuse us."

"Why don't we let the lovely girl decide?" Sir Maxwell suggests.

"Ah, that will be one day!" retorts the elder.

"*The* day," corrects the younger, attempting to nudge Father Christmas out of the way with her elbow. But he won't be budged; neither will Gabriella, who is useless when it becomes necessary to direct a situation toward an appropriate conclusion. The aunts will have to reckon with this opponent themselves—they'd better make quick work of him or they'll miss their train.

Gabriella slips back into her seat while the old women contemplate Sir Maxwell. "Shall we . . ." begins the elder.

"Play?" fills in the younger.

The elder huffs; the younger shrugs. Then they grin the grin of familial conspiracy, and their faces suddenly seem flooded with light, as though a window shade has been raised nearby.

"I suppose there's time," says the younger.

"There is always time," replies the elder.

"For cards," explains the younger.

"We do like cards."

"A freeze-out game of five-card stud—"

Sir Maxwell looks perplexed.

"A matchstick game," the elder declares and then rattles off the rules: two players, bets no higher than twenty, outside dealer, and the winner wins the right to accompany Gabriella for the evening.

Sir Maxwell is muddled by the proposal. "You are . . . are you serious?"

"Of course we are," says the elder sister with a snort while the younger announces, "Certainly."

Sir Maxwell needs to think. With the stakes so high, he can't refuse. Unless this is a joke, at his expense. The whole country seems privy to the joke. Sir Maxwell, the foreigner, is trapped. But if he plays and wins . . . ? All right, then—he accepts the challenge, though he insists on using a deck supplied by the restaurant and appointing the dealer himself: who else but Gabriella! She tucks her face against her shoulder for a moment as if to hide her smile.

"Are you able?" Sir Maxwell asks her. She nods.

The aunts see nothing wrong with these terms, so they pull chairs up to the table. The busboy appears with a deck of cards. Once the glasses have been cleared, the game begins, with the younger aunt opposite Sir Maxwell and the elder aunt sitting to her sister's right. Gabriella treats the cards with a tenderness an ordinary girl would save for an arrangement of flowers. Sir Maxwell lifts the card she lays facedown in front of him, sniffs it with dreamy pleasure, and puts it back on the table. The younger aunt examines her card while the elder looks on, then she returns it to its place, and together they let out an enigmatic sigh when their first upturned card is the king of diamonds.

"You did say *two* players, ladies," Sir Maxwell reminds them, and the elder aunt leans back and folds her arms beneath the precipice of her bosom. The younger counts out six matchsticks; Sir Maxwell sees her and, upon being dealt the ace of hearts for his third card, raises her ten. She sees him and, to Sir Maxwell's obvious delight, folds when she's dealt the five of clubs.

He collects the pot and blows a kiss to the dealer. She lays out the round of hole cards and gives Sir Maxwell the advantage, the ten of hearts, on the next round. He bets twelve matchsticks. The elder aunt fans herself with a menu; the younger ponders her new card, the eight of spades, as though it were a chess piece. "I'll see you and raise you five," she says. Sir Maxwell counts out five matchsticks and pushes them toward the center. The elder aunt lights a cigarette and passes it to the younger, who inhales deeply as Gabriella deals her a second eight, the eight of clubs. The younger aunt counts out fifteen sticks. Sir Maxwell raises her five. Her fourth card up is a jack, and she raises him ten, then calls. He turns over a pair of aces, but the aunt wins with a pair of eights and a pair of jacks.

By now the busboy, the maître d', the bartender, an assortment of waitresses, and even a few customers have gathered to watch the game. Gabriella lightly taps the cut deck of cards against the table and deals the hole card to each player. Sir Maxwell's second card is the king of hearts, giving him the advantage again, but this time he checks the bet and passes to the aunt, who bets a cautious five match-sticks on her seven of clubs. Gabriella deals Sir Maxwell another king, and he counts out twenty matches. The aunt receives the ten of clubs and sees him. Sir Maxwell's fourth card is the five of diamonds, the aunt's the jack of clubs. Sir Maxwell bets another bold twenty matchsticks to make up for his losses. The aunt receives a fourth club and raises him five. Sir Maxwell raises her with the rest of his matchsticks and calls. At the very least, she has a four-card flush, which will beat a pair of any rank, if that's all the gentleman has. But the gentleman has three grand kings, God save them! And the lady? She turns over a mere deuce—but a deuce of clubs!—and with a definitive *humph* gathers the matchsticks into a tidy pyramid in the ashtray, strikes one against the flint of her empty matchbox, and lights the pile. The flame flares, sizzles, and collapses into a compact ball of fire.

"A fair-and-square freeze-out," she declares. "You understand, yes? In this game when you lose, you lose, Mr. . . . Mr. . . ."

"Smedley-Bark." His despondency works like a noxious smell upon the crowd, dispersing it.

"Well, Mr. Bark, hats on to you." And out go the two merry ladies clutching their beautiful grand-niece between them and loving her more than ever.

AND HE, battered old heath cock, has given up all hope of happiness. He could come back here tomorrow; he could order the lamb chops and a whiskey sour and invite the girl named Gabriella to join him at his table when she's through with her shift. But the effort would be useless. It doesn't take a philosopher to understand the girl's deception.

> *When he thinks upon her smile,*
> *O Misery, his heart is liquid fire.*
> *When he thinks upon her soul,*
> *O Treachery, he knows her for a liar.*

He can't be sure that she cheated at the game and dealt the old woman a winning hand, but he does know that if she'd wanted him to win, if she'd *wanted* him, she could have made it happen. He would have won if she'd desired it. Desired him. That smile. Instead, she let him lose. He'd empty his mind of a lifetime's worth of memories in order to forget her. He tries, stares at the mural scene on the restaurant's wall of cowboys mauling Indians, thinks of nothing: the nothing in place of the girl. Not holding her. Not ever making love to her. His resolve slackens, and he lets himself imagine her wherever she might be: walking, no, half-skipping like a child along the sidewalk toward the steps leading down to the subway. She descends two steps at a time. Hop, her legs disappear from his view beneath the lip of the entrance; hop, her hips are out of sight; hop, she's gone altogether, lost in that black hole where Sir Maxwell Smedley-Bark, dependent upon servants and chauffeurs, diplomats and chairmans, presidents and dictators, has never ventured.

So he can't follow her, not even in his imagination, onto the train, through the tunnel, across the Meadows, and into New Jersey. He can't picture her arriving at home, where she is greeted at the door by her mother, Clara, who feigns confusion: "Gabriella, we weren't expecting you. Well, you're here, so come on in"—her performance so convincing that the younger aunt forgets herself and says, "But Clara, you told us to bring her along," while Gabriella walks ahead into the darkened living room, as content as ever and just a touch unsteady from the martinis.

Surprise!

Back in the restaurant, Sir Maxwell is contemplating a life that will never include the girl named Gabriella, who at that same moment is being celebrated in the house on Rogers Avenue in Marwood. The family emerges in a pack from the dining room, the children rush forward to grab Gabriella's legs, her brothers and their wives dance across the rug, Uncle Trip trips with his intentional clumsiness over a footstool and lands on the sofa, Uncle Tony wears his cap at a tilt until Clara grabs it from his head, Gabriella's father holds the cake lit with twenty candles, and the aunts stand with their arms around Gabriella's waist while she shakes with soft laughter, clearly grateful for the party and yet amused, as though she thought love a comic thing, the grandest jest a person could play on the world. And while no one in the family really knows what she is thinking, they don't care, for together they have created this serenity, nurtured it, and will go on protecting it, keeping their treasure to themselves.

ACROSS FROM
THE SHANNONSO

While my aged father slept soundly in his bedroom at the back of our apartment and my husband danced to Johnny Messner's band at the McAlpin with his mistress, her featherweight polka-dot dimity flaring smartly as she twirled, and while the Simms sisters in 3D argued in their kitchen about the volume of the radio and Therese Poulee snored her delicate French Canadian snore in 3B and the Latvian bachelor in 2A wrote a poem about foxgloves and the captain's wife pleasured the captain in 2D and in the basement Mr. Gonzales dreamed of the sea and on the first floor the Webbers and the Peets and Glenn McDuff all settled deeper into sleep, a man and a boy stole across the lot that separates our building from the Shannonso Hotel.

I have to do some presuming in order to piece together the circumstances of that night, but I know this much without a doubt because I saw it from my window while I was brushing my hair: in the lot between our building and the Shannonso, a man dressed in a light blue Palm Beach suit led a boy by the hand. Moonlight and neon brightened the sky, but the brick bulk of the sixteen-story hotel drenched the lot in shadow. From my window I could see the two figures moving quickly, furtively, between the cars. At one point the boy stumbled and almost fell, and the man wrapped his fingers around the boy's wrist to steady him.

Neither of them said a word as they approached our building. Their silence was as inevitable as the vaporous mist that rolls off the Hudson on warm spring nights, as our country's declaration of war, as the pounding of my heart. A glance from a fourth-floor window would have told you this much and more: the boy down below had taken if not this exact journey then similar ones many times before. And maybe at the same time you'd have sensed, as I did, the presence of a second man; maybe you too would have caught the whiff of cigar smoke drifting from the sky and realized with a start that someone else was waiting on our rooftop.

I lost sight of the pair beneath the fire escape, but I could antic-ipate to the second the time it would take them to reach the plat-form outside my window. I pressed myself against my bedroom wall as the man climbed past. He drew in a wet suck of air and piv-oted to climb the last flight. When I renewed my watch, the boy was directly in front of the window, which I'd left open a few inches to let in the cool night air, and he snapped his head around to look at me. As our eyes met, he shook his head slightly, as though to indicate that I should look away. But I would see what I could, and more.

He sprang to life then, struggled to find his footing on the metal steps, and was lifted by the man in a single motion. He rose to the top of the fire escape as though secured to a huge elastic band, disap-pearing over the lip of the roof.

Ordinarily, I mind my own business. I shake my head and cluck my tongue and go back to sleep. That's easy enough to do when it's my husband dancing at a downtown hotel with his mistress or the Simms sisters fighting over the radio. But when the problem appeared right outside my bedroom, I figured it was time for me to get involved. So that's what I did. That's why my tea shop, Scarooms, is no longer. That's why you're not sitting by the window looking out on traffic and sipping peppermint tea as you read this.

I slid each foot into a pink slipper and grabbed my father's raincoat from the rack in the hall, draping it over my shoulders. When I stepped out of my apartment, I stupidly let the door swing shut and lock with a click behind me. That click was my first warning, a sign that I should have left destiny alone. But I just headed for the stairs, telling myself that if I couldn't wake Daddy by pounding on the door, then I could climb down the fire escape from the roof and enter our apartment through my bedroom window.

The second sign I chose to ignore was the stairwell lightbulb, which burst with a pop when I pressed the switch. I persisted, climbed stair by stair through the pitch-black to the rooftop door.

The third sign was almost enough to dissuade me: the metal door was locked, as usual, but in the darkness I couldn't find the key ring hanging on the wall. I poked around blindly, searching with my hands, and felt the nail where the ring usually hung but didn't find the key ring there. I slumped onto the top stair and wondered what I'd been hoping to accomplish. Velma Dorsey in her pink cotton nightgown to the rescue?

The sound of my breathing was absorbed by the thick air. A distant, inexplicable *ping,* the sound of glass against metal, rose from the floors below. I thought about my husband dancing with his mistress. I thought about the previous afternoon, when my crazy old dad had threatened my husband with a shoehorn. I thought about the look in the boy's eyes as he stood outside my bedroom window, and I realized right then that I was sitting on the key, which must have fallen free from the ring.

After a fair amount of struggle, I managed to fit in the key and turn the lock. I eased open the door and stepped outside onto the roof.

I GREW UP in a village at the bottom of Chariot Mountain in the Alleghenies. My father worked as a handyman; my mother was best known for her tendency to daydream. Her friends resented the fact that she didn't bother to go to church or to stanch the rumors that her husband was an atheist. My father, who insisted that people should believe whatever they want to believe, argued that anyone with any sense must recognize the world to be pitiless, disappointing, raw, without intention, and life no more than a series of mistakes and inadequate reparations. In his opinion, it was a mistake for me to marry Ted Dorsey, whom I met at a party while visiting a cousin in Philadelphia, and it was an even bigger mistake to move with Ted to New York City. But Daddy didn't try to stop me. He just wrote me weekly letters cataloging the dangers of the big city and advising me to be careful crossing the street.

I found work as a hostess at a Broadway coffee shop, but I kept my eye on the failing delicatessen located in our apartment building, and when the deli finally went out of business I leased the space. Three months later, I opened Scarooms. In the years since then, I did just enough business to turn a small profit. My tea shop didn't attract the guests from the Shannonso as I'd hoped it would, but between the occasional customer wandering in off the street and residents of the building stopping in, Scarooms was seldom empty, though just as seldom bustling.

After my mother passed away, my father came to live with us—against his wishes. I put him in charge of Scarooms' maintenance. He was an expert at taking things apart. Not putting things back together, though. A single cabinet hinge could keep him busy for weeks. I'd station him at the table by the register and there he'd go at his task with his assortment of tools, chattering to whoever would listen.

Toward evening, back in our apartment, Daddy would grow irritable. I knew better than to try and reason with him then, so I'd continue washing the dishes, making the beds, dusting, or plumping the cushions on the sofa while he grumbled. Eventually Ted would appear and yell at my father to shut him up, which of course incited Daddy further. Their shouting would rattle the glass in the windowpanes, and within minutes Ted would storm from the apartment. As soon as the door slammed Daddy would fall abruptly silent, take a deep drag on his pipe, and grin.

The boy was named Jack, I decided. Yes, he looked to me just like the boy named Jack in a novel I'd read part of and misplaced before I could finish it. Jack Vizzone, who'd been sold by his mother to a childless woman, a woman named Catherine, if I recall correctly, who took him to live in Canada with her aunt. And then because it's the way things often happen in novels, the woman named Catherine died suddenly, and the aunt died a few months later, and a man who identified himself as Jack's uncle appeared and took Jack away to live with an elderly couple on a sheep farm, where he stayed for about a year. When the uncle came to pick him up a year later, he found Jack riding around on the back of a sheep as though it were a shaggy pony.

From then until the point where I'd stopped reading, Jack lived in many different homes. No one mistreated him. No one raised a hand against him. The women called him their little popover and fed him roast beef and chocolate pudding. The men chewed tobacco and watched while he drew pictures, studying the boy as though trying to figure out what to do next with him.

In real life he had a heart-shaped face, his eyes separated by the bridge of a nose that dipped in a concave curl and then turned up so sharply at the end that you could see the dark interiors of his nostrils when you faced him straight on. But from my position on the roof I could only see, at best, his profile, the line of his nose pinked by the neon of the hotel's rooftop sign, his upper lip bunched in a pucker as he sucked the tip of his thumb. The men were talking in such low voices that I couldn't make out a word of their conversation. They were at ease with each other, I could tell that much, and the wariness of the man who'd led the boy up to the roof had given way to casual interest. He perceived no danger; he'd done his part of the job, now it was the second man's turn. Together they could take the time to consider the cityscape around them, the scarlet blaze from the Shannonso, the depths of space, the joy of a fine cigar, the vulnerability of mankind.

Huddled behind the chimney, I absently fingered the matchbook my father had left in a pocket of his raincoat. I edged my thumbnail along the tinder and thought of the hours I'd spent as a child rubbing sticks together, generating heat but never a spark. I felt the urge to sprout wings and fly away from there, and then a leaden feeling of hopelessness. I wondered if this was what a soldier felt in the midst of battle. And out of this confusion emerged a single, sharp urge to scream.

And then what, Velma Dorsey?

Then I didn't know. I drew my hands up through the pockets, bunching the raincoat near my chin. The men abruptly stopped talking, and I could hear the squish of their shoes on the tar paper. Somehow I managed to keep quiet. I pressed myself against the bricks and waited. One of the men lumbered right past me to the stairway door and tried the knob, which turned easily in his grasp. He opened the door, holding it as though he meant to let the darkness escape from the building's interior—and so it did, a faint *whoosh* of shadow that stretched across the surface of the roof to the tips of my slippers.

My only chance was to reach the door before the man grabbed me, but just as I prepared to lunge past him, he let the door swing shut, flicked a stub of ash from his cigar, and wandered back to his friend on the other side of the chimney. I heard him catch his foot on a metal object. With a clatter and flurry of curses he freed his shoe and sent the whole contraption sailing in the air across the roof.

Though I couldn't see the thing, which landed close to the roof's western perimeter, I immediately knew what it was: the Latvian bachelor's kerosene stove. On hot nights he came up here to cook his supper, and later he'd be joined by the Webber and Peet children, and sometimes by the captain, all of them preferring the bright expansive dark to their airless rooms. They would stake out areas as their own, and they'd spend the night there, the children tucked away on the opposite side of a trellis erected by Mr. Webber two summers earlier and laced with grapevines, the captain and the Latvian bachelor lying close enough so they could share a bottle of vodka but not so close that they could have much of a conversation. With my window open

I'd hear them belching and snoring, and in the distance I'd hear the muted giggles of the children.

So now, thanks to the misstep of a stranger and to an unusually warm week that had brought my neighbors to the roof the previous night, the Latvian's stove was somewhere on the other side of the roof, upended, spilling fuel.

On the afternoon of my last day as the proprietress of Sca-rooms, I had watched Therese Poulee wagging her spoon around in her cup. ". . . out in Great Neck," she was saying. "A reception hall, a marble staircase, steel cabinets in ze kitchen, and also, how do you say eet, a garbage disposer!"

Her friend had snapped shut her makeup case and asked Therese how she came to know such men, gentlemen with money and style. Therese said that working at her company's reception desk had its rewards.

Judy Simms leaned over from her table and apologized for inter-rupting, but she wanted to know where Therese worked and if the company had any openings. Nancy Simms suggested to her sister that she mind her own business. "How else will I ever find work again?" Judy Simms barked.

"There's a war on. There are plenty of jobs to be had!" said her sister, pulling the classified ads, curled in a tube, from her red leather purse and slapping the table with it, accidentally knocking Judy's teacup, spilling the milky tea onto the table.

I remember noticing Therese Poulee glance coldly at the sisters. I remember Glenn McDuff limping across the room, rocking off his stronger right leg onto the braced left, dragging the left leg forward and pushing off with some effort onto the right leg again. He shook out a dry rag and blotted the surface of the table around Judy's saucer.

"Oh, Mr. McDuff, you don't need . . ." It was Nancy Simms who said this. Nancy Simms, the one who at least made an effort to be polite.

"Did you see what my sister did?" Judy burst out. "Attacked me with the classifieds! Just because I lost my job last week."

"McDuff!" called the captain. "We want our bill!"

"Come and pay me, sir," I directed, moving to the cash register. "Sandwiches, was it?"

"Cucumber," said the captain's wife. "Cucumber and a pot of tea." Glenn McDuff dragged himself back behind the counter and squeezed the rag into the basin.

I remember that day the Peacock Bread and Muffin man came in with his delivery two hours later than usual. I paid him with cash from the register. My father looked up from his newspaper and said, "You should cut back your orders, Velma."

"Better to have too much than not enough," I said.

"That's the way it is in this city, everyone always wanting more more more. What do you think, Mr. McDuff?"

"I think we should trust the missus."

"You hear that, Daddy?" I said, arranging corn muffins on a tray in rows.

"The missus, the missus," Daddy muttered as he tried to flatten the crease of his paper. "Looky here, will you?" he said after a minute. " 'The motorized machine has made man not a soul but a hand.' Tell me what you think about it, Mr. McDuff. The Reverend Dr. William Ward Ayer said yesterday morning in his Calvary Baptist Church, West Fifty-seventh Street . . . here, let me read it to you word for

word. 'I cannot picture Jesus, the carpenter, in an automobile factory on an assembly line. People were happier in our grandfathers'
day.' What do you think, Mr. McDuff? I'll tell you what I think. I
think those are the wisest words ever spoken by a zealot, Mr. Mc-
Duff. Our great motorized machines. It's the machines that make
this terrible war possible. The breakneck speed of life in our machine age, the flywheels spinning, the shafts turning, no time to sit
back and consider what we're doing. Why, Mr. McDuff, we're a
species suffering from grand delusions, pretending we share a like-
ness with some mysterious divinity when in fact we're just what we
are and no more!"

IN A MOMENT the two men and the boy would be gone, spiraling
down the fire escape. I could think of nothing better to do than follow through with my impulse to scream. So this is just what I did, or
tried to do, but the scream got stuck halfway up my throat so the
sound that did escape was no more than a grunt.

"What the hell!" exclaimed one of the men.

I leaped backward to escape the men, though they were so startled by my strange behavior that they didn't try to grab me. I made
no sense to them and had no obvious intention. I was just there, all of
a sudden *there*, hopping about in my pink slippers and raincoat, a
crazy lady—ah, now this made sense, yes, a crazy beggar lady camp-
ing out on the roof because I had no home of my own. I was just one
of the city's castoffs, that's what they were thinking. I was someone
who deserved to be ignored.

One of the men tossed away his cigar stub. The other stifled a laugh. They were about to leave me to my madness when the rooftop was suddenly split in two by a glare of red. A trail of sparks hissed in a zigzag at our feet, spurting away from one of the cigar stubs and across the roof, and instantly broke into roaring turbulent cone-shaped flames, which, by spinning wildly, forced themselves deep into the cracked surface in search of combustible material.

We all grew still and watched in wonder, transfixed by this spectacle that had replaced the lesser spectacle I'd been, forgetting the danger as we considered the beauty. Miracle of fire. From a glowing cigar stub and spilled kerosene to this: animate, ravenous fire. Through the flames I saw the men shielding their faces with their hands, their blue suits given a metallic sheen in the glare. The boy stood farther away from the fire, and as the blaze spread toward the wall he leaped back, landing on my side of the flames.

I pulled him toward the stairway. If he'd resisted I probably would have given up and fled without him. But he was strangely compliant. Down I ran, pushing him ahead of me, down the top flight to the fourth floor, down farther to the third, down to the second, where I finally halted on the landing and listened for the sound of the men pursuing us. I heard nothing and so nudged the boy forward again and we continued down to the ground floor and into the hallway, where I flung the door open right into my husband, who had finally decided to leave behind the fun at the McAlpin and come home.

"Christ's sake," he moaned, rubbing his sore forehead. "What do you think you're doing, Velma, at this time of night . . ."

"You idiot," I murmured, pushing past him with the boy. But I stopped in the middle of the small lobby, for in front of the building, through the wrought-iron cage over the front door, I saw one of the men rush up the stoop, the same man who had led the boy to the roof, and tug at the handle of the locked door. When our eyes met, he released the handle and ran off.

Ted tried to grab my arm but I pulled free. "Vel, sheesh, just tell me——"

"You win the prize for stupidity, Ted, you really do, now go, just go!" I pushed the boy against him and then herded them both toward the rear hall, crying out, "Fire! Fire!" pounding on the Peets' door as we passed. "Fire!"

"What fire?" Ted gasped. "Fire? Where? Do you mean fire?"

"Fire, you thickhead! Fire! Ted, get out of here. Keep the kid with you and get help."

"What kid, what are you——"

"You've been taking those imbecility pills again, Ted, you've got to stop that. All you Webbers, get up! Everyone, get up!"

The Peet door opened and the oldest Peet boy stood there, blinking sleepily. Then the families started to emerge, comprehension set in, voices shouted into back rooms, children cried, doors slammed, and my husband finally understood what he had to do and disappeared out the back door. With the occupants on the first floor warned I ran up the stairs to the second floor and out into the hall, where I pounded and shouted until the captain rushed out wearing nothing but bright yellow-and-red-striped boxers that flared open as he moved forward and revealed his stiff and ruddy member ready for action.

"Sir!"

"Fire, you say?" He was sober, dignified, quietly pleased to have an adventure to experience.

"On the roof. Evacuate the premises, sir," I said, suppressing a sudden urge to laugh.

He saluted. I saluted in return and started to run up to the third floor but stopped, swung around, and cried, "The girls, wake the girls!" meaning Judy and Nancy Simms and Therese Poulee.

"I'll attend to them," said the captain, waving me away. "Go on, do what you must do, Mrs. Dorsey."

"And the Latvian!"

"Go on, Mrs. Dorsey."

As I ran up to the fourth floor I smelled smoke and could see a faint veil hanging in the air. I pulled the raincoat around me and pressed forward into the hallway, expecting a blast of heat, a rush of acrid smoke, flames breaking through the walls. But the air was clear, the hallway quiet. I wondered whether I'd been wrong about the power of the flames—perhaps the fire had already burned itself out, the danger was past, and I'd been a fool for stirring up a panic.

I went to open the door to my apartment, remembering only as I struggled with the knob that I'd let the door lock behind me.

"Daddy!" I called, pounding on the door. "Daddy!" I looked around for something to use to force my way in. I grabbed an empty bucket left by Mr. Gonzales. "Daddy, wake up!" I beat the door, cracked the bucket, bruised my knuckles, but could not rouse my father. He was an old man, partially deaf, and he slept in a windowless room at the back of our apartment. "Daddy!" When I stopped to listen I heard only the rushing sound of my own inhalation. The pressure of silence made my skin tingle. I thought I smelled smoke now—or was it the stale smell from my father's pipe? I stood there panting, trying to inhale through my nose and identify the scent. Tobacco? Wood? Kerosene? A roach emerged from a crevice in a wall and scooted down the wall and across the floor. Another roach scuttled from beneath the door. I became conscious of a new sound, a sound I recognized immediately—the crackle of a light rain falling against a canopy of new leaves. Rain? I looked up to see the white paint of the ceiling bulge in a plump blister.

Wake up, Daddy! Wake up!

He was awake. He was always awake. He never did more than drift toward sleep and turn around and drift away from it. Well, he wasn't drifting now. He was wide awake, thanks to that racket in the hall, a lively party to which, as usual, he was not invited. He couldn't have cared less. He'd rather lie in bed and smoke his pipe. Where was his pipe? He coughed gently, then inhaled, tasted the bitter smoke on his tongue and wondered who had sold him such foul tobacco. Judging from the sensation in his bones, dawn was still hours away, though he couldn't tell much from the quality of light in his windowless room; he'd left the door ajar, but the hall light had been turned off. He didn't mind. Night should be dark—moonlight outside, pitch-black inside. Pitch-black night, and the revelers were going at it. Or maybe the noise was coming from the old one-tube Crosley 50 in the living room. No one cared a smidgen about his comfort. His daughter ran a tea shop on Amsterdam Avenue, his son-in-law was a rascal, his wife was dead, and his country was at war. These were facts. Facts bled like cheap dye until people who should have known better weren't sure what was true.

He coughed again, more emphatically this time, in an effort to call attention to himself. Hello there, Velma. Where was his pipe? Could someone find his pipe for him? Was it morning yet? Was it winter? Look at him, silky white beard curled beneath his chin by the force of the wind as he skimmed along the dirt road from the summit of Chariot Mountain, picking up speed with every rotation of the wheels. Old daredevil, surging on his sturdy Schwinn, the one he'd sold to a neighbor and then bought back when the neighbor moved away.

Daddy!

I was waiting at the bottom along with the rest of them—his wife, his brothers, his cousins, his own ma. We were all waiting at the bottom of the mountain for the reckless old charioteer to descend from Olympus, his beard wound around his neck, his white hair surrounding his skull like the white cloud of breath blooming in front of his wife's face on a cold autumn day or like the smoke surrounding him in the black box of his room, smoke from his pipe, he'd forgotten to tamp his pipe and now—

Vel, where are you, Vel?

Look at him go, speeding downhill as though on the crest of a flood, his beard tightening in a noose around his neck, his eyes tearing, his lungs burning, his wife out in the kitchen mindlessly dipping tripe in batter while I sewed a new wool patch on his winter coat, willfully ignoring him as I so often did, though he was an old man and I a hardy young woman who could have lifted him on my shoulders and carried him to safety.

I'D ALWAYS KNOWN FIRE to burn steadily. Before that night I'd never seen fire pretend to lie dormant and then without warning explode through the walls and ceilings and then shrink back into the crumbling plaster and then explode again so I couldn't tell where it would appear next and my mind was seized with such panic that I could think of nothing but escape.

I have no recollection of deciding to leave the fourth-floor hall-way. All I remember is a flare of intense heat, and the next thing I knew I was running down the stairs, descending so fast that at one point I lost my footing and fell to the landing. I picked myself up and kept going, and within moments I found myself out on the street standing in a crowd, and Therese Poulee was asking me what had happened to my eyebrows, and I was screaming at her, demanding this delicate young French Canadian woman, who represented no less to me than my last desperate hope, to help my father, *help him, damn you!*

From the opposite sidewalk the crowd watched smoke seep from crevices and broken windows. Here and there a flame appeared to wave wickedly and then hid before the firemen could steer the hose. Little Rosie Peet stood clutching her doll and hopping back and forth from one bare foot to the other, splashing her toes in the spill-off that collected against the curb, squealing with delight. The older children watched solemnly, even proudly, for they were taking part in a mag-nificent event and would have something to tell their friends in school the next day.

A fireman named Floyd Coolidge climbed the fire escape to our apartment. He found my father lying in a stupor in the hallway out-side his bedroom. Floyd picked him up like he would have picked up a suitcase and then dragged him by one arm through the smoky apartment and out to the fire escape. With the help of another fire-man he carried my father down to the street, where he was roused to sputtering rage by the ammonia a medic held under his nose. The two firemen returned to join their crew, who kept the hoses blasting even after the fire was out, as if filling a huge container.

My father spent two days in the hospital. I went to fetch him on Monday morning. While I buttoned his shirt to his Arrow collar, he stared sullenly at me. I knew by then that he'd heard the story about the cause of the fire, and I guessed what he was thinking: his own daughter had been willing to sacrifice her father, her own dear father, for the sake of a hoodlum boy. Sure, he'd be better off dead, he'd be the first to admit it, but as long as he was still alive he would never forgive me.

Since the fire, we've been staying in the Shannonso, in a two-room suite on the seventh floor. From the window in the sitting room I can look out upon our building. The bricks are streaked from the rooftop to the third floor with soot, the windowpanes are shattered, and the plate glass of Scarooms has been boarded over, though the sign still hangs lopsided on its metal bracket. The building will be demolished eventually, though it will probably have to wait until the war is over.

I don't know much about the boy I risked so many lives to save. On the way to the precinct he told my husband that his name was Wally and that he'd climbed with his dad to the rooftop simply to see the view. According to the story in the newspaper, the boy's name is Wallace Michaud and he lives with his family in New Jersey. His father, so the reporter claimed, led the boy to the roof of our building to have a smoke and meet a friend, a real estate shark keen on buying up property in our neighborhood. The police say the matter is under investigation.

My husband still has his job cooking at a Midtown steak house. Most of my former neighbors have found temporary accommodations with friends or relatives, though Therese Poulee and Glenn McDuff are both living on different floors here at the Shannonso.

I don't do much more than take care of my father, who sits propped on the threadbare sofa, scowling with indignant satisfaction, having concluded that his own daughter is responsible for everything that's wrong in the world. I bring him his tea and cinnamon toast and settle across from him in a chair. My mind drifts, and I keep thinking about the strange beauty of the fire spreading on the rooftop. To escape my father's eyes I open a book; any old paperback is fine, for I'm only pretending to read.

THE QUEEN OF SHEBA IS AFRAID OF SNOW

The girl didn't want anything to change. She especially liked it when her mama came home late from her job at the lunchroom wearing her juniper perfume and tussled with her across the mattress they shared, tickling her in the armpits, giving her butterfly kisses with her wiry eyelashes, laughing the same way she wept, the fullness of the sound threatening to shatter her bones, which would never happen, the girl knew, since Mama was as strong as the young tree planted in front of the Lafayette, a second Tree of Hope to replace the first, which had finally grown so old it would have toppled some windy day if the authorities hadn't chopped it down.

Granny was growing old. Actually, Granny was the child's great-grandmother and liked to remind her of that, her *great* age being her main claim to dignity. The old woman's own daughter, Mama's mama, had died long ago, so Granny had raised Mama "by hand," as she said, the plan being that someday Mama would take care of Granny. But it hadn't turned out that way. Granny had to keep on selling baked sweet potatoes and popcorn from a cart on Lenox because Mama spent her own wages at a gin mill and every few days came home drunk, which was how the child liked her best, when Mama was in a laughing mood. But there were bound to be words exchanged between Granny and Mama, hardly an even exchange, since out of Granny's mouth flew complaints pitched at top volume, while from Mama came the softest whisper, "Leave off, Gran," her gentle voice enough to make Granny reach for the belt.

The last time Granny lit into Mama was in sticky-hot weather, when Mama came home so saturated that she sweated gin. She'd been too tired to play much, though she did draw her daughter onto her lap and rock her until they both fell back giggling on the mattress. Granny, of course, didn't find any of it funny, and she struck at Mama's bare arms with the leather so hard that by the time the whipping was done Mama looked like she'd been picked over by crows. But she didn't cry. She just stood up, tottered over to Granny, said something in too low a voice for the girl to hear, and walked out the door.

A few days into June, when the girl began to understand that her mama wouldn't be home any time soon, she made herself nice and sick with a throat so swollen she could hardly swallow and a fever hotter than the hottest day in Harlem. She knew that her sweat didn't smell as sweet as Mama's, but Granny paid no mind to the stink. When the child couldn't even stand on her own two feet one morning, Granny slung her over her shoulder like one of those burlap sacks full of potatoes she bought at the market and carried her five blocks to the hospital, where she was told to have a seat.

Now Granny wasn't one to do, necessarily, as she was told, but on this occasion she didn't have much of a choice, what with dozens of sickly souls clamoring like the multitude for salvation and many more just politely waiting their turn, silent except for their coughing and heaving and their wailing children. The girl noticed that what she at first took to be a pillow held by the woman next to her was really a baby bundled in its mother's arms. It wasn't asleep—its little eyes were half open, dull as the eyes of an old dog, while the mother's eyes were glittering and so fixed on the wall clock they might have been attached to it by thread. After a while the girl grew bored waiting for the baby to do something interesting, and she shut her own eyes and lay across Granny's lap, the sounds of the hospital melting together, dripping in ice-cold drops onto her skin, making her whole body twitch and tremble. She'd come in red-hot and here she was shivering from the worst cold she'd ever felt. She kept trying to cover herself with whatever was available—her granny's apron, her own dress folded back over her arms, even a corner of the blanket belonging to the sick baby, but when she tried to snatch the blanket her hands were yanked back by Granny, who could do no better than wrap her own thin arms around the girl and try to squeeze away the shivers.

The girl gave up hoping to feel warm and instead let the fever's blizzard bury her in drifts of snow until she could breathe only in quick sucks, as though she were taking in air through a straw. The *clackety* sound her teeth made reminded her of Granny's cart rolling up Lenox Avenue early in the morning, the girl's favorite time of day, when the stores were still closed and the few people walking along the sidewalk all had places to be—women with plastic flowers in their hats, men in fancy bellhop uniforms. The folks the girl liked best were those who stopped to buy the potatoes Granny roasted in a foil tent on her kerosene stove. Sometimes they would chat with Granny while they ate their breakfast, and the girl would bask in their voices, though she paid no attention to the meanings of words, didn't care at all what grown folks had to say to each other, whether it was a conversation held over a roasted sweet potato or over her own sick body, which by the time she became aware of it again had been moved from the wooden folding chair in the waiting room to a gurney in a hallway. A doctor in gold-rimmed glasses poked and probed at the girl while Granny stood to the side, arms folded and that look on her face suggesting she was getting ready to give the spectacled man a good licking. To spare him, the girl managed to rasp, "I don't need nothing," though at first the words stuck in her parched throat, so she said it again, provoking the man to laughter.

"You need plenty!" he said, which made the girl think he knew something about her that Granny didn't. She closed her eyes and returned in her mind to her grandmother's cart and the buttery lips of strangers shining in the morning light.

She woke in a different bed, found herself lying between crisp white sheets, and though her jaw was stiff and her throat ached, her teeth weren't chattering anymore. She was just a little too warm instead of unbearably cold, a preferable sensation, since it made her feel as if she were tucked against Mama's sleeping body in their shared bed. Granny stood in the same stern position, and when she saw that the child was awake she launched into an account of the tribulations caused by the girl's sickness. "You be acting like the Queen of Sheba the way you go on . . ." The girl just stared at the dirty white wall and thought about how much better she felt, listening again only when Granny started telling how that baby in the waiting room had died in its mama's arms without ever having been examined by a doctor, and you can be sure Granny wasn't going to let the same happen to her own kin.

The girl left the hospital the next morning, still too weak to walk, so Granny pushed her in the cart. She perched in front like a figurehead nailed to an old fishing rig, smiling at people who smiled at her as she rolled past. Back home, Granny put her to bed, and the girl spent the rest of the week recuperating, dozing during the day while Granny was away and tossing and turning through the night, unable to sleep soundly without her mama snoring beside her. Finally the girl couldn't stand lying there any longer, and she got up in the darkness and dressed herself. When Granny woke to see the girl waiting in her polka-dot dress with frayed batting and torn hem, she gave her a good scolding because it was Sunday, and on Sunday little girls should beautify themselves for the Lord. So the girl changed into her one fine dress, a frilly pink confection, and they set off together for the Metropolitan Baptist Church.

From then on, everything seemed to fall into place. The only piece missing was Mama, and after a few weeks the child stopped expecting her to come home. At the end of that boiler-room summer the landlord raised the rent five dollars, and Granny decided to move. She packed their suitcases and paid two boys a nickel each to carry the mattresses and load their belongings on her cart. The girl filled a paper bag with her few valuables—a box of seashells she'd scavenged from rubbish on the street, her dresses, and a charm necklace her mother had given her last year. By the afternoon they were settled in their new apartment on 134th Street, just a half block up from the river, so if the girl woke early enough she could watch from the rooftop as the sun turned the strip of water brick red. The apartment was even smaller than the last, but the girl didn't mind, especially since they had a toilet of their own, a toilet that flushed! They lived on the first floor, and if a truck happened to be rumbling by on the street, the girl wouldn't be able to hear what her granny was saying. So Granny would just raise her voice and say something like, "When you going to stop pretending you the Queen of Sheba?"— Granny's favorite admonishment ever since the girl had been brazen

enough to require hospital care. Eventually, after months of supposedly putting on airs, the girl found the title had stuck, and her granny
called her Queen Sheebie if she called her anything at all. In no time
her schoolmates took to using the name, flinging it at her first in fun
and then with indifference, so she stopped fidgeting when she heard
it and started turning into Queen Sheebie until, from her point of
view, the name seemed more than suitable.

Not that the child had any sort of queenly shine to her. Her coffee skin was splotched with freckles, and her eyes usually had a startled gleam to them, as if she couldn't believe what she'd seen. Truth
was, she believed too much. She believed that sinners spend eternity
tied to a roasting spit over a huge bonfire; she believed her mother
was a sinner, just as Granny said; she believed that when she grew up
she'd have her own huckster cart and sell sweet potatoes and popcorn along Lenox Avenue; she also believed that the angels were
waiting for her granny, tapping their silver slippers expectantly,
though Granny never said as much and instead kept on like a me-
chanical soldier march, march, marching across a toy-shop floor. But
the old woman had a way of moaning in her sleep that made her
sound like she was saying good-bye to life. The girl didn't think far
enough ahead to worry about who would take care of her when
Granny died—she wondered only about that strange moment when
Granny would drift from her bed up to heaven, imagined that the angels would hover outside the window blowing trumpets while the
neighbors came running. The girl only hoped she'd reach the rooftop
in time to see her grandmother slip through the gilded door at the
crest of the sky.

But the old woman, with typical stubbornness, wasn't ready to
die. And while the simple effort of rising from her chair and walking
over to the toilet would make her pant, she never complained about

her ailments. She complained about Queen Sheebie plenty, of course, blamed her for the high-and-mighty attitude she must have learned from her mama. The harangues grew worse when the girl took to heading after school to the 135th Street branch library. But even then Granny never beat her and never said, *I don't want you going to that place no more.* So the girl, who hated winter ever since her fever had taught her the truth about cold, bided time in the library reading room while Granny wrapped herself in old shawls and tended her cart, the slush and snow apparently bothering her not a bit.

The girl liked nothing better than to page through books looking at the pictures, and one afternoon she was doing just this when a white-haired man pulled up a chair beside her. She felt him staring and was about to move to another seat when he pointed to the word at the top of the page and said, "Read this."

"What?"

"Tell me what it says."

She could read a few words, and that's what she usually did in the library—searched books for familiar words like *cat* and *the* and *Jesus.* But the word at the top of the page was just a jumble of letters. She couldn't even make sense of the book's title, though she had selected it herself from the shelf. So she clamped her mouth shut, and the man with the dust-mop hair began to read: " 'Introduction . . . The subject and method of this book . . . ' " and then he stopped, skipped forward a few pages, and began again: " 'Chapter one. My African Expedition,' " his voice beginning to please the girl, for on the cover of the book was a roaring lion, and she'd been disappointed to find that the chapters contained no pictures. With the old man reading, she could imagine the wounded animals turning to charge, the rifles raised, the hunter pinned beneath a tiger's paw. But he wasn't going to let her get away with dreaming her way through.

"Assist me," he whispered, nearly poking a hole through the page with his finger.

"The," the girl said.

"The what?"

"The err-uhh."

"Roo," the man corrected.

"Roo," the girl echoed.

"Rule," he said. "Rule."

"Rule. The rule."

And so it began, her first reading lesson by Mr. Dosan, as he finally introduced himself. She'd long since figured out that nothing could be learned at school, not with such a din made by thousands of children packed into a too-small building. The girl, impressed by this man who obviously knew everything there was to be known, accepted Mr. Dosan's unspoken invitation and began a course of study that occupied her right through the unkind winter months and dozens of books.

They met after school, finding each other in the library reading room as if by chance, for they never made arrangements to meet, and they worked for at least a solid hour every weekday afternoon. Thanks to her new mentor, the girl came to understand the power of embarrassment at about the same rate that she was learning to read. Sometimes she found herself wishing he would leave her alone, though she never admitted this aloud, and instead tried her best to be a model student, which meant following his directions exactly, sounding out sentences from whatever dull book he'd chosen from the stacks. He never seemed completely satisfied with her performance, never told her what a good job she'd done, yet neither did he scold her for her mistakes. They just kept pushing on, moving farther from "the shores of ignorance," as he grandly said one day, her dependency upon him increasing as she came to sense the vastness of this sea of words, all the unrelated information and so many different meanings that in some ways she felt more perplexed than ever and began secretly resenting Mr. Dosan for knowing as much as he did. On some afternoons she couldn't even stand his peppermint breath, much less his instruction, and she began looking for any opportunity to lord it over the old man and force him to feel as stupid as he made her feel.

By the middle of March, she'd learned a year's worth of phonics, according to Mr. Dosan, who offered to reward her with a sundae. They ended up in a lunchroom two blocks from the library, the same lunchroom where Mama used to work. They sat in a booth by the front window; the grimy panes were streaked with rain, and cigarette smoke turned in spirals beneath the overhead lights. The girl remembered how she would spin herself around on a stool while Mama blended her an egg cream, and she regretted that she wasn't sitting at the counter now. She didn't recognize the waitress who came over to take their order, but the waitress recognized the girl right away. She began clucking and shaking her head, denying vocally what she already knew: "You ain't Sally's girl, tell me you ain't Sally's girl, that itsy-bitsy thing used to come here to give her mama a hug round the knees."

"Sure is me!" the girl said, surprised and proud to be singled out in front of Mr. Dosan, especially since the implication of the waitress's disbelief was that she had grown with such amazing speed that she was hardly to be known. "I'm my mama's girl!" she announced, smiling boldly back at the waitress while Mr. Dosan looked on. But her pride didn't last long, for Mr. Dosan was quick to root out the truth from the waitress, which was, simply, that the girl had been left behind, abandoned by her mama, who had "gone and turned herself into one of those crazy angels, got a bed and three meals a day over there at the kingdom."

An angel. Meaning that Mama had already passed through the gilded door in the sky, leaving her grandmother and her only child to fend for themselves. Meaning that the unspoken presumption, the glue of her soul, was false: she would never see her mama again, not in this life. No more tickling and laughter, no more romps in front of disapproving Granny. Her mama had gone and turned herself into an angel. Her mama had gone and was never coming back. Her mama had abandoned her. Her mama—

"You say she's abiding at one of those kingdoms?" Mr. Dosan asked the waitress, his voice inexplicably calm in the face of such a terrifying revelation.

"One Hundred Twenty-sixth Street, last I hear. Calls herself Miss Love Dove. Miss Love Dove!" With that Mr. Dosan and the waitress both began to laugh, or at least he chuckled scornfully while the waitress hooted. The girl looked on, dumb as a fish in a bowl staring out at the world, colors and shapes beyond the glass making no sense, no sense at all. Her mama was an angel and these two grown folks thought it all right to laugh. If she had been a different sort she would have slapped Mr. Dosan, plunged a fork into the waitress's thigh, and run out of the lunchroom. Instead, she concentrated on keeping her tears from streaming down her face, succeeded for about ten seconds, and then gave up and let the tears do just as they pleased. Most everyone in the restaurant turned to see what the fuss was about, but Mr. Dosan just leaned over the table and covered her hands with both of his, the first time he'd ever touched her, while the waitress smoothed her hair, the two of them treating the girl like a baby who deserved to be indulged.

Once the waitress had disappeared into the kitchen again, the other customers had turned back to their food, and the girl's noisy sorrow had quieted down, Mr. Dosan twisted his lips as though spitting out a bitter taste and said, "So your own materfamilias has seen the light!"

"She an angel?" the girl whispered, keeping her voice low because she didn't want to know the answer.

"She's a fool."

"She ain't!"

"She believes that crimp is God, Sheebie!" he said, suddenly so formidable that the girl felt afraid of him. She withdrew her hands and sank back against the cloth cushion of the booth, trying to disappear inside it. "He has gathered all the misfits of the world together to worship him," Mr. Dosan said, scorn making him spit out the words.

"Mama ain't no—" the girl began, but the waitress, who'd come back to the table with their coffee and ice cream, interrupted: "Word is, you eat much as you want for fifteen cents at one of those kingdoms, chicken and brussels sprouts and mashed potatoes—"

"I've seen that man myself, driving around in his shiny Cadillac," Mr. Dosan countered.

"All that food for fifteen cents. Ribs and apple pie and pudding . . ."

"Wearing fancy suits . . ."

The waitress slid the sundae in front of the girl, who had never in her life had quite enough to eat. She began scooping up chopped nuts and whipped cream, scraped the warm chocolate syrup out from the sides of the glass bowl. After letting a spoonful of ice cream melt on her tongue she decided she didn't like ice cream anymore because it made her cold inside, and she would rather be anything but cold. She wondered if all those feasts at the kingdom kept her mama warm. She pictured her mama wearing angel wings made out of tissue and wire, her mama plump as Santa Claus, her mama standing in some heavenly choir while the man she thought was God stood behind the pulpit the way Preacher Vernon did every Sunday at the Metropolitan Baptist Church.

The girl said she needed to get home. Mr. Dosan stayed right beside her as she headed up Seventh Avenue. Later she would remember an unusual expression on his face, a puckered look, as though a drawstring had been pulled inside his head. "Where is the refuge for our children?" he demanded. "Nowhere in this world! Abandoned by those who bred you . . ." He fell silent for a long minute, and then, with the suddenness of a radio switched on, he launched into his personal account of the "woes of mankind," including causes, consequences, and remedies, the words spilling from his mouth like water over the sides of a cup.

At first the girl was still so involved in imagining her mother as a false angel that she didn't pay much attention to him, and when she did try to listen, his speech seemed as obscure as an argument held between two people in a foreign language. He left out the usual pauses so the sentences blended together and spittle gathered at the corners of his mouth. He might as well have been talking only to himself. Now the teacher who had introduced the girl to written language was just a hunched, drooling old man dressed in baggy trousers without suspenders, a string tie, and a cheap flannel jacket, spouting wild talk as he walked along, throwing out words like *advancement, disorder, anarchy,* and *fidelity,* obviously expecting the child not only to comprehend but to agree with him.

People stared at both of them—she felt the weight of their eyes, their judgment, and, even worse, their pity. They would assume that this foolish old man was her daddy.

He ain't! she wanted to shout. *I don't have nothing to do with him!*

As they passed a bakery window she noticed a stocky woman standing behind an empty bread shelf, her face partially hidden by the lettering on the glass, though enough of the woman was visible for the girl to know what she was thinking: the girl had herself to blame. But it wasn't her fault that Mr. Dosan had decided to supervise her education. She would have gone on minding her own business and never bothered with book-learning. What use were books if this was their effect? Going on about something he called individuation, circling around his vague ideas of social improvement and the importance of educating the young. Mr. Dosan thought himself a genius equipped with enough knowledge to save the world, except that the liars and drunkards kept getting in his way. Liars and drunkards were the bane of mankind. Liars and drunkards had failed in their duty to society. Liars and drunkards—

"I got to go," the girl announced, and with that she raced up Seventh Avenue without looking back, turned the corner onto 135th Street, leaped over flattened cardboard boxes soggy from the rain, ran as though she were being pursued all the way home.

During the days that followed she joined her granny on the street. She didn't want to see Mr. Dosan again. No, that wasn't it. She didn't want Mr. Dosan to see her, for she sensed that he had expectations and had chosen her to fulfill them. He'd been training her like a dog to perform extraordinary tricks, and she'd been trying to please him. Probably wanted to marry her as soon as she turned thirteen. Well, she wasn't having any more to do with him, she knew that much!

Granny kept asking her, wouldn't she like to spend the afternoon at the library, and the girl kept declining, indicating that she wanted nothing better than to sit on the curb beside the cart and watch people going about their business. She hadn't told her granny about Mr. Dosan, though now she wished she had, since Granny might have been able to explain why some old folks accepted the dispensations of God and some flew into a rage over the littlest something. Why hadn't Mr. Dosan come straight out at the beginning and told her what he hoped to accomplish? And what did he really know about drunks? Her own mama was never kinder, never more fun than when she'd been boozing, the girl could have testified. Take a tired, hungry woman, fill her up with cheap gin, and you'll put her in a laughing mood. Sure, the girl could tell Mr. Dosan a thing or two about juniper perfume. Who did he think he was, stealing his ideas from books? Who was he? It occurred to her that she knew next to nothing about the man. Where did he live? Where did he work? Did he work at all, or did he live on handouts?

Why did it matter anyway? She shrugged off her curiosity and pretended that her afternoons at the library belonged to some hazy dream. She was finished with all that. But the one remnant of the dream she couldn't ignore was the bit of information about her mama, who had turned into an angel and was living at "the kingdom," whatever that was, on 126th Street.

No surprise, then, that on a drizzly Saturday when Granny didn't feel well enough to take the cart out, the girl found herself heading toward her mama's new home. Lenox had the spent, hungover look of a man who'd been carousing all night and didn't care where he lay down to sleep. The sky had been painted gray, and each bus or motorcar that passed ripped a thin layer of skin off the avenue with its wet tires. As she walked, she let her hand bump along the iron bars protecting store windows. One summer night a few years back, all these windows on Lenox had been shattered when Harlem went wild, busting and burning, having a fine old time of it, or such was the girl's notion while she'd lain in her bed listening to the distant sounds of shattering glass and sirens. Her mother hadn't come home at all that night, but the girl never worried, for she knew that if there was fun to be had, Mama would be there. Granny made the mistake of sitting up until morning waiting for the riot to end and Mama to return, wearing herself out so that when Mama did finally saunter in, Granny was too tired to whip her.

That memory of the riot stirred a more recent memory. The girl recalled how her mama had whispered something to Granny just before heading off to become an angel. What had she said? She hadn't seemed angry. Of course, Mama only got dopey, never angry. What had she whispered to the old woman? Good-bye? Why hadn't she said good-bye to her daughter? It wasn't fair, the way grown folks kept their secrets. And it wasn't right of Mama to leave home without telling her daughter what she planned to do with her life.

So many questions the girl had, and the variety of answers didn't begin to console. Neither did the possibility that soon she'd find out what she wanted to know. It might turn out that she would have been better off never seeing the kingdom with its marble ramparts and towers, or so she pictured it, realizing even then that the actual kingdom would turn out to be unlike anything she might imagine, much grander, she assumed, perhaps with jewels embedded in the walls and huge stone lions guarding the doors.

It took her more than an hour to find her sparkling castle. She'd walked up and down 126th Street between St. Nicholas and Third Avenue three times without seeing what turned out to be just a sooty brick building that looked like an old bathhouse and identified itself with a hand-painted sign hanging crookedly on the door: WELCOME TO THE KINGDOM. She'd expected to be surprised, but not disappointed. The Kingdom. Why would her mother give up all that she had—a grandmother, a daughter, a paying job—for this? The girl stood in front of the building pondering the sign, working with some effort toward a new comprehension: it didn't matter what words meant, since you could attach any word to anything and make it stick. You could call a man God and an old bathhouse a kingdom. You could call yourself by any name you pleased. You could walk right out of one life and into another.

The light, silvery drizzle turned to a heavier rain, but the girl kept standing there, hatless, almost enjoying the soaking, imagining that the rain would wash away the words on the sign, leaving it blank, leaving everything blank, nameless, without memory or guilt, making it possible for a person to snap her fingers and change into an angel. The girl snapped her fingers just to see what would happen, but they were too damp, too slippery to make a sound, and she remained what she'd been since her mama had gone away: *Queen Sheebie, the only kin Granny got to live for anymore,* reminding the girl that the old woman would probably be wanting something right about then, a bowl of soup or some tea, and with no one to wait on her she'd be steaming like the kettle should have been but wasn't.

She would have left then if a well-bred white girl hadn't accidentally snagged her sweater with the edge of an umbrella as she strutted by, pretending to be the model of perfection, not even apologizing as she unhooked the metal spoke from the loop of yarn. She scooted up the stairs of the brownstone in her dainty high-heeled shoes and entered the kingdom, closing the door behind her with a smack. The girl might have snuck away then if the congregation hadn't started to arrive, first individually, a few in pairs, then in droves, hundreds even, some flocking down the street and others emerging from adjacent brownstones, the commotion as abrupt and yet as orderly as if the curtain had been raised on a dance-hall stage. Still, the girl would have remained outside the kingdom while the people disappeared inside if an elderly woman hadn't taken her by the hand and said sweetly, "Come in out of the rain, child." Mesmerized by this sudden kindness, she let the woman lead her up the steps and into the building that grew in magnificence as soon as the girl entered, not because the exterior hid an elaborately decorated interior, which it didn't, but because the front hall transformed ordinary people into worshippers, drawing from them exclamations of "Peace, Sister," "And to you, Brother," warm embraces, and outbreaks of song. "He has the world in a jug," a woman caroled. "And the stopper in His hand," the crowd echoed, merging into a line and filing through a narrow doorway to the tables.

How delicious the kingdom smelled—of wet clothes and clean bodies and fresh-baked cake, such a comforting stew of fragrances that the girl wasn't afraid, though the old woman who had invited her inside had disappeared in the crowd and no one else paid any mind to her, not even the man passing the collection hat. He looked straight over her head as she entered the dining hall, where the feast laid out was even more elaborate than the waitress had described. Besides plates of fricasseed chicken and spareribs and brussels sprouts there were string beans, asparagus tips, sausage, fruit salad, and a total of eight chocolate cakes set like top hats on the ends of each table. The girl seated herself right in front of a cake, reached up to swipe a finger through the rich frosting, then saw the girl with the umbrella sitting patiently a few seats down, so she tucked her hands in her lap, folded them around the hunger she was feeling, while she waited for the signal to dig in.

The din faded, and after a long minute of expectant silence, she felt the draft of wafting clothes. She turned in her seat to see the procession of young women—ten of them, no, twenty, more than twenty—floating down the aisle toward the head table. They wore identical white berets and white dresses decorated with ribbons and cloth buttons, and their smiles were so similar their faces looked like cardboard masks, angel masks, the girl thought, remembering why she'd come here just as recognition took hold.

"Mama!" she exclaimed, jumping up from her seat. But though her mama surely heard, she just smiled that angel smile without turning her head to look and drifted right on past, showing no special affection for her own child, shunning her with that sticky-sweet expression, pretending not to know her. The girl hardly felt the man's hand pressing on her shoulder, pulling her back, but she obliged without resistance, sat down again as the angels took their places at the head table. Mama had her back to the girl, who knew that you could bore a hole through someone's heart if you glared long enough. She fixed on that velvety groove beneath Mama's shoulder blades and above her dress line, was pleased to see her reach behind to scratch her back, but that's all she did, scratched just once. The only person Mama cared for was the little bald man coming through another door up front. The girl gave up and turned to this man, the center of attention, the kingdom's king, tucked as neatly as a birthday present inside his blue suit. He was followed by a slight, sharp-featured woman, also dressed in blue, who led the congregation in song while the man, the Father himself, sat and laid a napkin across his lap. The woman sang about justice and truth, and the people joined in the refrain, something about a righteous government, the words as confusing as Mr. Dosan's speech. All these folks calling for a better world when what they really wanted was to help themselves to the food. The girl could hear the hunger in their voices and would have heard the same in her own voice if she'd joined in. But it didn't take much thinking to realize that she preferred her granny's temper to these hallelujahs. She stood up a second time and walked away from the free lunch and her lost mama without offering anyone an explanation, walked straight out of this dingy heaven into the rain and headed home.

In the days that followed, she kept telling herself that she was through with her mama, just like she was through with Mr. Dosan. She tried feeling angry, but anger made her too jittery. She tried forgetting Mama. She tried hoping that Mama would have a change of heart. Now here was a feeling the girl could tolerate, the hope that her mama might give up all that foolishness and come on home, if not tomorrow then next week or next month, no need to hurry since her presence didn't much change the routine, and it felt good to be expecting her again, looking forward to the night—surely she would come home at night, just as she used to—when Mama would creep into the apartment trying as best she could not to wake Granny and failing, of course, so there would be an uproar, maybe a whipping, but the three of them would calm down soon enough, and the next morning the girl would tell Mama how she'd learned to read.

It was this hope, her renewed expectation, that kept the girl cheerful during the long months of Granny's sickness. Granny wasn't so sick that she couldn't huck sweet potatoes and popcorn most days, but at night, after supper, the only meal of the day she ate regularly, she spent hours on the toilet and then was so plagued by stomach cramps she couldn't sleep. On Saturdays she went over to the clinic on Seventh Avenue and the girl tended to the chores—she washed the laundry in the sink, using hand soap to make suds, then draped wet clothes over the furniture since they didn't have a wash line. She swept the floor and wiped down the stove and made the beds, and upon Granny's return at the end of the day she stood to the side of the room, waiting for her hard work to be noticed. But Granny just closed herself in the bathroom without offering a whisper of praise.

One week hardly differed from any other week. Granny was

sick, but she wasn't getting sicker, as far as her granddaughter could tell. The girl had stopped thinking about heaven since her visit to the kingdom, had stopped imagining the old woman's death altogether. Plenty of people suffered from ailments that wouldn't go away and grew no worse. Granny assured her that her bellyaches were no more bothersome than the ache in her fingers—two Bufferin always helped to set things right. And as long as Granny still pushed her cart up and down Lenox, still hauled bags of sweet potatoes from the grocer, and still made enough money to pay the rent, the girl could believe that everything was close to fine.

She didn't see through her granny's masquerade until it was too late. But even if she had suspected, she wouldn't have known what to do. The old woman denied that she was failing by clinging to routine with all her strength, and when she finally gave up, she didn't slip softly to the floor—she fell with a great thud in the middle of the night, waking the girl.

"Mama?" the girl said, sitting up in her bed. "Mama?"

"Your mama ain't here, Sheebie."

"That you, Mama? You come home?"

"It's just you and me, girl. Now get on back to sleep." She growled the command and lay still. The girl stood up and switched on the lamp. She stared at her granny sprawled on the floor, seeing not the living woman but the hollow form of the woman who was almost dead, Granny already different, an unworldly stranger to the girl, the change signaled by the vicious sound of her teeth as she snapped at the air, chomping the space to show that she'd turned dangerous and would bite the girl's hand if she could only reach it.

"You all right, Granny?"

"Spoilation ain't pretty. Now do as I say, get on back to bed!"

"Lemme help, please. . . ."

Snap of teeth again, a vile, liquid fart. Poor Granny roaring from her grave at the bottom of the river, her voice bubbling up through water.

"Please, Granny . . ."

Granny was a puppet coming to life. She was a statue rearing its stone head. The girl took a few steps away from the old woman, who propped herself first on her hands and knees and then managed to grasp the table and pull herself up. She had no strength left to scold, but the girl didn't need words to know that the ordeal was over, at least for the present. Granny would clean herself up and they'd both return to bed, never to speak of this night again, though from then on the child would be privy to the truth that her great-grandmother refused to admit: she was dying, and when she took her last breath the angels wouldn't swoop down for the fanfare. The angels wouldn't even bother to stop by for the occasion, and Granny would collapse in a puddle of her own filth, snapping at any hand that came too close, as mean and helpless as a cat with a broken back.

The next day was Sunday, but the old woman didn't bother to get up and dress herself for church. She slept through most of the morning. Though Granny didn't ask for it, the girl left a cup of water on her bedside table, and from across the room she waited, as though she'd set a trap, for her to drink. When the cup was empty she'd refill it. Granny didn't say a word all day, except when she dozed, and then she recited lists of items to be purchased—"Thirty pounds taters, five pounds popping corn, factree-made dress, pair of Florsheim shoes, nickel loaf, quart of milk, butter brick, bobby pins"—and on, her voice fading as she woke until she was completely silent again, her set lips the ashen color of the November sky beyond the window, her body rigid one moment then straining to expel the pain she wouldn't admit to, until finally the girl felt herself being expelled, driven out of the airless room by some mysterious force so Granny could suffer alone.

Outside, she stuffed her hands into her pockets and kept her head down. Where could the girl hide from the cold? The library was closed, and the service at the Metropolitan Baptist Church would already be half over. For some reason Mr. Dosan came to mind, uselessly, since the girl had vowed never to have anything more to do with him. Besides, she didn't know where he lived. She knew where her mama lived, though. Granny hadn't asked for Mama, not in so many words, but the girl had started to pay attention to her own intuition, which was telling her now that Granny needed Mama, even though she would have denied it. Or maybe what presented itself as intuition was merely the child's own desire in disguise: she wanted to be warm. She wanted to put warm food in her empty belly, and she knew of only one place in the world where she'd be invited inside to share a meal. But whether she was making the journey on her granny's or her own behalf didn't much matter, for by then she'd reached the corner of Lenox and 126th Street and would only reveal herself to be a coward if she turned back.

She kept edging forward, as though along a lightless hallway, until she stood outside the kingdom. She waited for a crowd to assemble and draw her into its midst; she waited for the girl with the umbrella to dash by. But the street remained empty and the building seemed as impenetrable as a huge boulder, so lifeless that the girl wondered whether the Father had lost interest in his mission and dispersed his congregation. She climbed the steps and cracked open the door, half expecting to be met by silence. Instead, as she stood on the threshold she heard the intonations of a voice as powerful as the Pied Piper's secret melody, inviting all who heard it to *believe, believe, believe*.

The girl tiptoed across the front hall and down the corridor. In the dining hall she discovered the worshippers feasting not on food—the tables were empty, though the fragrance of hot grease and baked goods still lingered in the air—but on the words of the Father. He stood alone at the end of an aisle, without either a pulpit or Bible, and as the girl watched he raised his right hand and snatched at nothing, as though pulling his sermon from the air.

" 'Jesus,' said the sinner, 'Jesus, remember me when You come into Your kingdom,' and Jesus said, 'Truly I say to you, you will be with Me in Paradise.' Now I say to you, my people, you will be with me in Paradise."

A woman kneeling in the aisle cried out, "We love you, Father!"

Another woman called, "My heart is beating faster!"

A man sang, "He's our father, and he's walking in the land!"

The Father scanned the room like an overseer surveying a field until his eyes, iron nails hammered into the bald globe of his head, settled right on the girl, locking her in place. "They may prosecute me," he seethed. "They may persecute me. They may strap me to the electric chair."

"No!" screamed the kneeling woman.

"It's a new day, Father!" a man shouted.

"They may hang me by the neck. But I tell you now, they will never keep me away from you!"

To the girl, the man seemed to be speaking only to her. He lifted his hands, palms flat, above his head, and the people rose from their chairs in unison and began chanting, "Father, O Father, give me the victory," the clamor increasing as he spread his arms in a gesture of embrace, still fixing his stare on the girl.

"I know you are God, God, God!" the people sang, and finally the Father lifted his eyes, releasing the girl from his gaze, and beckoned farewell to the worshippers before he slipped out of the room.

In his absence the noise of devotion peaked and quickly sub-sided, and during the few moments of reverent quiet the girl looked around, at first just to regain her bearings, for she felt as though she'd been swept up by an eagle and dropped hundreds of miles away from home, and then to search the crowd for her mama. But today the angels stood in a row up front, facing away from the congregation, and the girl couldn't get a sufficient look as they filed out to tell whether her mama was among them. She tried to follow the angels but couldn't push through the crowd. Men and women clutched and kissed their closest neighbors, and the girl was swept up into the ecstasy and passed along like a loaf of hot bread, finally ending mashed against the ample bosom of a lady whose grin revealed a gap where her two front teeth should have been and whose name, the girl would learn later, was Miss Smile All the While.

Miss Smile All the While loved the children "long as they live a holy, clean life." Miss Smile All the While took it upon herself to bring the "starveticating" girl into the kitchen and fix her a plate of leftover chicken and baked beans. Over the meal she described some of the Father's miraculous cures—her own rheumatism had disap-peared the first time he touched her hands, five years earlier. The girl revealed that she'd come looking for her mama, and Miss Smile All the While said, "In good time," then led her four flights up to a small room furnished with seven cots spaced no more than a foot apart. "You take this one," Miss Smile said, indicating the cot closest to the door, and left her alone, not once asking her whether she needed to rest, though somehow giving the impression that they'd all be in-sulted if she refused.

So the girl sat on the mattress and scuffed her heels along the floor, hoping that her mama would come find her. After a while she grew tired from waiting—she settled back on the bare mattress, tried to keep herself awake by holding her eyelids open with her thumb and forefinger, and finally gave up, drifting off into a sleep so busy with dreams that when she woke a few hours later she was more exhausted than ever.

The room was dark and her cot had been made up with freshly washed sheets and a wool blanket. Voices were murmuring softly in the room, like pigeons chortling, such a comforting sound that the girl was lulled back to sleep. When she woke again she found herself alone, and daylight shone through the single window. As the fog of sleep cleared, it occurred to her that Granny would be wanting her supper. Not until she'd made her way downstairs and smelled breakfast cooking did she realize that she'd slept straight through to morning. In the kitchen, Miss Smile All the While stood by a huge pot of percolating coffee, singing a duet with a woman frying some bacon. When she saw the girl she gave her a wet kiss on the forehead and said, "You be blessed, chicky. We got a sewing job just waiting to be filled."

The girl didn't understand at first. Sure, she needed a pair of stockings darned, a torn dress repaired, but how could Miss Smile know that? It took a once-over look from the other woman to give the girl the necessary clue: they wanted to put her to work. But she was planning to sell sweet potatoes and popcorn out in the open air, not sit in some musty back room pedaling a sewing machine. Besides, she still had a couple of years of schooling to finish—Granny wouldn't let her huck a single potato until she'd made it through the eighth grade.

She didn't feel right disappointing Miss Smile, though, especially since she needed her to help find Mama. So she accepted the cup of black coffee sweetened with a tablespoon of sugar and listened to the ladies trade praise for the man who made room for even the tiniest lamb.

And then the stories began. The woman at the stove—Miss Cheerfulness Good—spoke of an angel named Holy Light, who'd had twelve children and no food to feed them until she met the Father. He put her up in a fabricated house down in Miami for three months, then he brought her to New York, where she gave her children to God. The girl wondered what this meant: "gave her chillun to God." She wondered if her own mama intended to give her to God. She didn't ask any questions, though, just sipped the sweet coffee and listened to another story about an angel named Miss Beautiful, who got sick working in the nightclubs. Luckily for her, it was the Father who found her lying in the gutter one day, and he scooped her up and brought her to his kingdom. Next came the tales of Miss Charmed Life, Miss Sweet Soul, Mr. Disciple, and Mr. Righteous Government, all of them damned to sickness and poverty and all of them saved by the Father. It began to seem to the girl that the kingdom might be a haven, after all. Food was abundant, the rooms had working radiators, the toilets were clean, and the Father provided for anyone who arrived on the doorstep. Even if he wasn't God, he might be one of those spiritual-contacting folks she'd heard about, and maybe he'd make Granny well. The girl resolved to get her granny and present her in person to the great wizard. Then she and Granny and Mama could live together again under one roof.

Miss Smile and Miss Cheerfulness served her a breakfast of scrambled eggs, hash browns, and bacon, and they didn't hesitate to load her up with more food as soon as she'd cleaned her plate. Here at the kingdom a girl didn't have to live on sweet potatoes. A girl could eat as much as she pleased. A girl could drink black coffee as though she were all grown up. When the two women began singing, the girl stood and did a little dance for them, spinning across the room, feeling as carefree as she did in the old days when Mama came home laughing. The girl was intoxicated by food and kindness, and she spun around and around and around, landing right in the strong arms of the man entering the kitchen, who said, "Now if she ain't absotively posilutely the prettiest dancing soul I ever seen, I'll eat my hat," and lifted her up until she could touch the ceiling.

Miss Dancing Soul she became, thanks to the man called Mr. Loving Jeremiah. She spent the whole day at the kingdom helping with the meals and listening to the angels tell their happily-ever-after stories. She hadn't forgotten Granny—she planned to go to her before the day was over, but when darkness fell, the distance between the kingdom and the apartment building seemed so vast, the cold so bitter, that she decided to fetch her great-grandmother the following morning.

She didn't see her mama at all that day and couldn't bring herself to ask about her. She'd find her *in good time,* Miss Smile had promised, and the girl believed what she'd been told. Gratitude filled her with a warmth that saturated her flesh, making her face and fingertips tingle with joy. She felt so excited when she went to bed that night, surrounded by gentle angels, that she couldn't sleep, so she lay awake and imagined her future as Miss Dancing Soul, loved by all who lived at the kingdom, and loving them.

Another day passed before the girl bothered to return home. She intended to stay just long enough to pack up her possessions and convince Granny to come with her. As she let herself into the apartment, she braced herself against the wild scolding sure to greet her.

"Granny?" she called out. There was no answer. "You here?" She checked the bathroom. Only when she returned to the main room did she notice that the bedding had been stripped from her granny's mattress. The smell of sickness hung in the air, and, inexplicably, crumbs of mud were scattered across the floor, as though booted soldiers had stomped through. Granny must have gone out with her cart, the girl figured, not quite believing it herself, for by then the knowledge of something else, something too terrible to name, began to come to her. She resisted the thought, and after stuffing her dresses and seashells in the net bag Granny used for groceries, she set out for Lenox in search of the old woman.

It was midday Tuesday. As she stepped from the building the door to the basement flat opened, and a woman, Mrs. Jenny, leaned out to shake dust from a throw rug. "Why there you is, Sheebie," she said, wiping the back of her hand across her forehead, painting her face with pity, "you poor orphan girl."

It was true, then: the terrible thing had happened while Miss Dancing Soul had been gormandizing at the kingdom. The simple permanence of the situation turned everything familiar—the street, the building she'd called home for nearly a year, the woman in the doorway—into her accusers. Had she stayed with her great-grandmother she would have proven that she was not scared. Now everyone in the world knew that she was scared, so she had no reason to pretend otherwise and could run away without worrying about what others thought, for they already thought the worst of her.

Queen Sheebie ran from the poor orphan girl she was supposed to be. She ran so fast that the city seemed to fold beneath her, and it took just a few giant steps to reach the threshold of the kingdom, her home now. She flung open the door and collapsed in a heap. Soon people were murmuring above her, and a man lifted her gently into the cradle of his arms. She didn't open her eyes when someone said, "Miss Dancing Soul," for she knew that she'd be cared for here—all she had to do was live a holy, clean life and earn her keep as a seam-stress and help wash up after meals.

The man carried her into a small parlor and laid her on a divan. Someone draped a warm washcloth across her forehead. She heard a group of women whispering, thought she heard her mother among them, but still she didn't open her eyes. She craved blindness, tried to will herself sightless as she lay there, for more than anything she wanted to be coddled, helpless, dependent upon these people who were so good to her. She wanted to feel the caress of their fingertips upon her skin, which had an appetite of its own that would be satis-fied only by the loving touch of angels.

But they left her alone. The washcloth grew cold on her forehead so she laid it, folded, on the floor. Eventually, that more pressing ap-petite belonging to her stomach roused her, and she made her way to the dining room, where the congregation had already gathered. For the first time since she'd come to the kingdom, one of the men held his collection hat out for her, but she didn't have a penny and just shrugged at him. His scowl felt like a fist on her teeth. She picked up her knife and fork and idly danced them together, fidgeting to hide her shame. It occurred to her that she'd lost the bag full of her pos-sessions somewhere between the apartment and the kingdom. Now she had nothing except the flesh-and-blood part of her that filled this little bit of space at the table, along with the flower-print dress she'd been wearing for three days.

It was this sense of herself as almost but not quite nothing that made the skin-hunger unbearable. So later that evening, when the angel named Mr. Loving Jeremiah met her on the landing of the back stairs and gave his precious Miss Dancing Soul a hug, she nearly fainted with gratitude. The next day, when he found her alone in the kitchen drying the last dishes from lunch, he surprised her with an embrace from behind, curling his strong arms beneath her own and lifting her right off the floor.

In the next weeks, the girl spent mornings and afternoons sewing buttons on organdy dresses and mealtimes listening to the Father trumpet the rewards of faith. Miss Smile All the While taught her hymns, which they sang together with Miss Cheerfulness Good in the kitchen. She learned from Miss Smile that the angel named Miss Love Dove had gone to the Father's kingdom up north, and Miss Dancing Soul would see her "in good time." The girl stopped thinking of her mama as an object to be retrieved—instead, Miss Love Dove was another member of the huge family to which the girl herself belonged, along with Miss Smile and Miss Cheerfulness and all the others, including Mr. Loving Jeremiah, who was like an older brother to her, protective and conspiratorial. Though he never admitted it, she could see that his fondness for her fell just short of romance, which wasn't allowed in the kingdom, fortunately, so she could feel safely tempted, as long as she kept her daydreams to herself. Here in Paradise, the girl knew she had nothing to fear from her Prince Charming, no matter that his face was as inviting as a sun-drenched lake and that he took to sneaking upstairs to her dormitory and leaving candy on her pillow. He wouldn't try to take advantage of her, she felt certain.

But his affections weren't restrained enough, as it turned out. Somehow the Father himself got word of the chocolate heart Mr. Loving Jeremiah gave to Miss Dancing Soul on Valentine's Day, and he ordered meetings with each of them separately. Mr. Loving Jeremiah went first, and when he came out half a minute later he didn't even glance at the girl, just skulked on past looking every bit like a thief caught red-handed. But just then the angel named Miss Pleasing Joy stepped up and took the girl's hand, clenching hard, as though trying to squeeze fortitude into her and prepare her for her first face-to-face meeting with the Father.

Everyone, including the girl, knew that the Father considered children nothing but annoyances. She had been lucky to have the protection of Miss Smile All the While, one of the kingdom's most important angels, and she'd been treated as a grown-up, given coffee to drink and work to occupy her during the day. Now, as Miss Pleasing Joy released her hand and nudged open the door, she was reminded that she was just eleven and hadn't even completed the fifth grade.

The office was long but hardly wider than the sofa at the far end, where the Father sat prying open a pistachio shell with his thumbnails. The girl gave only a passing glance to the angel working as the great man's secretary who was sitting in a chair beside him, her face turned down while she scribbled in a notepad. The room was furnished simply, though with lush accents: red velvet drapes covered the window behind the sofa; red flowers, like the paw prints of small dogs, filled the wallpaper; the single painting in the room was of the Father sporting a halo. In person, he glowed as though he were made of parquet like the floor and had spent the morning rubbing oil into his skin and buffing himself with a soft cloth.

He dusted his fingertips together, cleared his throat, and in a quiet voice that managed to sound shrill, he said, "You have consorted with a member of the Angelic race." He stared at her as he had that day she'd first heard him speak, withering her with his fierce divinity, and then reached for another pistachio.

It was during this pause, while he raked his fingers through the bowl of nuts, that the girl looked to the seated angel for help. The angel named Miss Love Dove lifted her eyes and smiled back, her soul so chock-full of happiness that it was clear the serene expression on her face would never change, not even if someone poked her with a pin, not even if someone whipped her with a belt, beating her merci-lessly, turning that soft, sweet-smelling skin to pulp.

"Mama!" cried the girl, feeling as though she'd suddenly been turned inside out and given a violent shake. But her mama just looked down at the notepad in her lap and smiled that smile that said *I got everything I'll ever need locked for safekeeping in this old heart of mine.*

"You are limited in your conception of the universal," the great man continued, but the girl interrupted, begging, "Mama, say some-thing!" Mama went on scribbling shorthand, and His Holiness carefully selected another pistachio. "Therefore you cannot see me as I am."

"It's me, Mama! Your own Sheebie!" the girl pleaded, forgetting that her mama had never known her as Queen Sheebie.

"And you have pursued what is forbidden—"

"Mama!"

"Defying me—"

"Acting stone-cold—"

"God Almighty—"

"—like you don't care about nothing—"

"—at the same time that you partake of our bounty—"

"—lessin you crazy—"

"—seeking refuge amongst us—"

"—course you ain't crazy!"

"—and will remain welcome—"

"You just forgetful!"

"—as long as you believe—"

". . . All mixed up . . ."

"—in my omnipotence."

The Father bent his right forefinger in a gesture to signal that the meeting was over. Miss Love Dove marked it with an emphatic period and smiled at her daughter. Miss Pleasing Joy took the girl's hand. The girl felt herself being tugged backward, and though she didn't resist, she remained facing the front of the room, trying one last time to compel recognition.

"Mama, you know Granny's gone." Not a flinch. "Dead, Mama!"

And that was it. Before the girl could say another word, she'd been pulled back into the waiting room and the door to the office had snapped shut, apparently of its own accord. The meeting had lasted for less than one minute. Efficiency, like abstinence, kept the empire functioning smoothly.

And how efficient the girl proved to be, startling herself with her decisiveness as she left the waiting room, walked down the hall, and went out the front door into the street, not stopping until she'd reached Rexall's and then only briefly to orient herself, for during her three months at the kingdom she hadn't ventured outside, there had been no reason to, what with all the activity going on inside and winter souring the streets.

It was snowing, but she hardly noticed. The snow fell in a fine, wet mist, veiling her hair with silver beads and melting on the sidewalk, making the concrete shimmer. At first the echo of her voice drove her on—*your own Sheebie, your own Sheebie*—but after a few minutes she stopped listening, and her mind filled up with the knowledge of her body's discomfort. It was snowing, and the snow felt fiery hot against her face. It was snowing, soaking her thin white blouse, turning the cotton to ice. It had always been snowing. It would never stop snowing. Queen Sheebie was afraid of snow and would do anything to escape it. Just about anything, except go back to the kingdom. Anything else.

She tried moving in a purposeful way, as if she'd stepped out for some ingredient her granny needed for her baking, an egg, some flour, and was only going to the A&P so hadn't bothered to put on her coat. Though she wanted to run, she didn't go faster than a fast walk, which meant she was going along slowly enough for her mama to catch up before she crossed the street. Her own mama, who was suddenly there, grabbing her, hugging her, asking, "What we gonna do now, baby? What we gonna do?" Stuck inside the circle of her mama's squeezing arms, the Queen of Sheba didn't even try to think up an answer.

YIP

ip.
Yip.

Yip.

This is a tape of Harold Linder. Brilliant young Harold. I want Harold to be the star of my show. Listen:

Yip.

Yip.

His brilliance lies in his uninhibited love of his own voice. It doesn't matter to him what he says. To speak aloud is everything. No, not quite everything. To speak aloud in front of an audience is everything. This is my discovery.

Yip. Yadderyipip. Yadderyipiphipippityhiphop.

Yip.

Yip.

Charlie looks forward to a tempting meal. Oh, Charlie. Yip. Oh, Charlie. Yip. Hap. Haphop. Do you like soup, Charlie? Yip. Soup, Charlie? Yip.

Yip.

Yip.

I found him in Bellevue, where I'd gone to see Mr. Jack Dawes, the leading man in my last production. Jack had been hospitalized after he was found wandering along Madison Avenue *in puris naturalibus*. Uncased, as it were, and obviously enjoying the attention. I'd received an anonymous phone call alerting me to the fact that another member of my company required immediate medical attention. As I expected, the reporters were waiting outside the hospital armed with cameras, pens, and their ubiquitous notepads when I arrived. They are always ready to publicize a celebrity's embarrassment. They have built their careers upon such exposure, and those of us in the limelight must accept it as a sort of tax upon our fame. Which is not to say that one must lose all dignity at such moments. As I stepped from the taxicab I raised my hand as though preparing to make a speech, then I strode solidly, full of purpose, toward the entrance and into the lobby.

After signing the necessary papers to commit Jack Dawes for forty-eight hours, I took a stroll along the corridors of the locked ward. That's where I met young Harold, who was leaning against a wall and yipping.

Yip.

Yip.

Yadderyipyip.

The clarity of the sound, even amidst the hubbub of insanity, impressed me, and I stopped to listen. At the time I believed he was unaware of me watching him, but now I understand how important it is for Harold to have an audience. No one can be a spectator to his performance without Harold's tacit permission.

Yadderyip. Yadderyip. Oh, Charlie. Poor Charlie. Do you want something to eat, Charlie?

Yip.

Yip.

Yip.

This boy is not mad, I told the doctors. They disagreed and named his disorder, one of those tangled Latin names that always seems to celebrate exaggeration. I asked to take Harold along home with me, but the doctors said I would need his mother's permission. So I called her, Mrs. Linder, and asked if I might borrow her son. She refused, of course. Then I told her who I was, but as it turned out she was one of the few people in the city who had never heard of me.

"Mrs. Linder, I want Harold in my play," I explained. That interested her.

"What would he do?" she asked.

"I want him in my show," I said.

"But what would he do?"

"I don't know. Whatever he wants to do. Whatever comes naturally to him."

She said she'd think about it and call me back. A few minutes later the pay phone rang, and it was Mrs. Linder, who during the interim must have called some acquaintance of hers, who warned her against me. "No," she said. "Under no circumstances will I permit you to put my son on stage." I tried to convince her to lend me Harold for a two-week trial period, but she refused. I assured her that I was no circus impresario. I was a famous theater director, a modern artist, and I could make her son famous. Rich, too. Still she said no.

Charlie looks forward to a tempting meal. Soup, Charlie. Oh, soup, Charlie. Oh, steak, Charlie. Oh, corn, Charlie. Oh, butteryip, yip. Butteryoyip, oh butteryoh, ow, ohwa, ohwa, ohwa.

I'm certain that a production with Harold at its center would be a wild success. It's the seduction of shame again. The potential for embarrassment is great when lines haven't been memorized and rehearsed. Imagine the twelve-year-old boy standing in the circle of a spotlight on a bare stage—no painted background, none of my extravagant props or music, only Harold and his voice. The show's suspense would be predicated upon his composure. Should he lose it, the spectacle would become the kind of event that takes its place in theater history: "I was there the night that boy . . ." whatever. The possibilities for failure are limitless.

Suspense is essential to all performance, from symphonic music to vaudeville. Without the element of suspense, Harold seems to most people no more than an insane creature capable only of babbling on and on. But put the boy on stage, and mere babbling would turn into artful improvisation. It is not just for my own sake that I want to make Harold a star. I am concerned about the boy and want to save him from a lifetime wasted inside institutions. Besides, Harold enjoys having an audience—I could tell as much right there in the hospital while I watched him. He pretended not to notice me, but I knew he was grateful for the attention.

Yip.

Yadderyipyip. Oh, Charlie. Do you want something to eat, Charlie?

The first time I applauded him I detected the barest ripple of a startle, a slight tremor in his arms, a twitch of his jaw. I stopped clapping and waited for the boy to continue, but he stared past me at the peeling white wall. Imagine a silence so powerful that you can feel it wrapped around your body—and just beyond, the clamor of other patients. If I'd had any doubt about the boy's remarkable ability, I lost it during that nearly endless silence. And then, the burst of sound:

Yip.

Yadderyipyip. Yadderyipyip.

The fact that Harold cannot carry a tune makes him even more unique. Mrs. Linder and the doctors look upon the boy as a malfunctioning machine and keep trying to tinker with the gears and cogs of his mind. But I know that the boy is perfect. In the corridor at Bellevue I recognized in his voice the precise expression of my own artistic ambition. It felt as though he were calling to me out of my past, a voice rising with the night mist from the estuary bordering our estate.

Yip. Yadderyipyip.

A strange seabird calling a warning, splitting the silence into halves, the voice of the bird separating past from present and defining the space of my solitude.

Poor Charlie. Do you want soup, Charlie? Soup, Charlie? Steak, Charlie?

How tempting it is to twist my life into a dramatic tale of suffering in order to explain my dark art. But I might as well come out with it and admit that I've had more than my fair share of privileges. As a boy I was treated, along with my older brother, to all the pomp and rigorous training befitting the sons of a man who had made millions in the insurance business. I grew up in a stone mansion on sixty rolling acres overlooking Long Island Sound. My brother and I had nannies and tutors and chauffeurs protecting us from the world. We attended a small Jesuit day school. Through those early years my happiness was as solid and encompassing as the house, and I believed that the same was true for my brother, though I couldn't be sure. He was an athletic boy, handsome in a puckish way, an apt enough student but a dull companion to my young mind. He and I were strangers to each other not because of any perceptible dislike but simply because we had such different interests. When we weren't studying, he'd go for a swim or gallop his pony, Turl, along the beach; I preferred to occupy myself indoors.

Our home had a library with paneled oak, a splendid living room with a period Adams mantel, three kitchens, and two dining rooms, one of which we used only on holidays. A circular staircase led up from the reception hall to the second floor. The master bedroom was painted a light peach with ivory trim, and the master bath had coralline tile and Tang red fixtures. My own bedroom had buff walls and a bay window with a leather built-in seat. I liked to sit there for hours, reading and watching the color of the sound change from silver to a satiny black as the afternoon wore on.

I have no disclosures to make about unloving parents or sadistic priests who whipped knowledge into their stubborn pupils. My teachers, most of them tending toward the plump, were more inclined to whip cream into peaks for their cranberry cobblers than to whip the tender buttocks of young boys. And my parents were like children themselves, dazed by their ingenuity, for their wealth seemed to them something they'd accumulated while out on a Sunday stroll—a pocketful of pebbles and seashells and feathers and gold. And though my father outlived both his eldest son and his wife, even in his last months he could be seen shaking his head in disbelief at his fortune as he walked around the grounds of his estate, his Stetson sennit at a tilt to shade his eyes against the sun. Life had stunned him from the start—and for this, more than for the privileges, I am grateful.

I inherited from both my parents a sense of wonder and so have devoted myself to sharing that wonder with others. How indifferent we quickly become if we're not careful. Nothing kills interest like routine, day in and day out spent measuring percentages or hauling trash or teaching young girls how to type, and then at night an hour of the Wayne King Orchestra or maybe a boxing match broadcast live from the Bronx Coliseum. The tedium of competition. No, I am not a sportsman. Neither do I take any pleasure in the dance orchestras that lull their listeners to sleep. I prefer long periods of silence punctuated by unexpected sound.

Yip! Yip!

My dear Harold, so strange and wonderful. With the boy as my star, I would be able to shake my audience out of the slumber of routine once and for all. People know that they shouldn't come to my theater if they want to be reassured that all is right with the world—they can go to the movies for that. My shows are never reassuring. They are as jolting as the modern world, as full of surprises. Harold would be my consummate theatrical surprise.

Poor Charlie. Are you hungry, Charlie? Do you want something to eat, Charlie? Strawberry short-Charlie-cake, Charlie, strawberry shortcake, Charlie, if you please, oh please oh please.

Yip.

Such is the force of a vital personality unimpeded by social consciousness.

Yip.

An individual, alone but not lonely.

Yip.

If I had half his ego I would be satisfied. The critics complain that my art is marred by my vanity, that I lack discretion, that I'll put anything and anyone into my productions because I'm too vain to subject myself to aesthetic discipline. My last show, *Garden City*, which featured Jack Dawes, along with two dozen amateur clowns, a marionette troupe, and fifty retired chorus girls, was nicknamed *Garbage Dump*. This wounded me—proof that I'm not vain enough, not compared to young Harold, who exists only as a performer, never stepping outside the role to consider the value of his art. How I envy the boy. He wants an audience, but he cares nothing about the impression he makes—just like a bird that calls out for no other reason than to be heard.

Oh, Charlie. Charlie looks forward to a tempting meal. Wait, Charlie, I've got something for you, Charlie, soup, Charlie, steak, Charlie, strawberry oh . . .

His voice is so completely expressive that any word, any sound, is revealing. He could count from one to one thousand, and the audience would be mesmerized. Yes, I like to imagine this: Harold counting aloud, one, two, three, four, and so on. It would take three hours, and after Harold finished counting, he would remain silent for as long as ten minutes. He would just stand there in the spotlight, his body pressing against the empty space behind him, and then, at last, he would utter a single yip.

Yip.

If you've ever blown a gentle breath into the face of a dog and heard the animal gasp, then you'll know how the audience would react when Harold yipped that final yip. Spot off, and my treasure would once again be hidden in darkness.

Brilliant, yes? I'm sure any skeptic would be quickly converted and would forget the hows and whys and wherewithals of Harold's speech, for all that matters is the boy's acrobatic voice and his admirable self-sufficiency.

Yadderyip. Yap yap yap.

Yip

I knew what I was hearing in the corridor in Bellevue: it was the sound of a solitary creature calling out to the world and expecting no answer, like that strange seabird I heard one night when I was a child. Alone in my buff-colored room with its red-leather-upholstered window seat—

Yip.

Yip.

Poor Charlie. Yip. Do you want soup, Charlie? Yip. Soup, Charlie?

Strange sounds—you'll hear them in the dead of night, on any night, if you listen carefully.

Yip.

Just as I heard the seabird on that summer night when I was ten years old. Not gull, not tern or cormorant. An albatross? No. A great auk? No. A loon or grebe or piping plover? No, no, no. It was a sound I'd never heard before, and when I looked out my window to find the bird I saw nothing but the shrugging forms of boulders and the iron-colored water. I slept, finally, and awoke the next day to the news of my brother's accidental death by drowning.

Yip.

For years I'd thought of that bird I never saw as a messenger announcing the passing of my older brother. Eventually I came to think of it as a coincidence—a strange sound in the middle of the night coinciding with my brother's death.

Yip.

Yadderyip. Yadderyip.

Listen. Listen closely to the silence. There's always something new to hear.

The silence bearing the meaning of the sound.

Yip.

Water sloshing against the pylons of our dock. A body sweeping up and back, up and back, curling around the wood like a hand, then letting go. Clenching, then letting go. I never saw this; I never saw my brother's lifeless body at all. My parents did everything they could to protect me, short of keeping my brother's death a secret.

The vague details surrounding my brother's drowning led me to think of death not as the exquisite sleep described by my parents but as a terrible mystery, and so I made my theater terrible and mysterious, for art must show us what we fear most. In the corridor in Bellevue, young Harold had me remembering the night my brother died, and in the silence that followed our exchange I found myself wondering whether the sound I'd heard in my buff-colored room had really been a bird's cry at all.

Yip.

It might not have been a bird. It might have been a boy yipping as he leaped from the end of the dock into the water. Leaped, not fell— such a sound is not born out of terror.

Yip.

A bird's voice, or a boy's? This much I know: Harold deserves to be heard by others.

Charlie looks forward to a tempting meal. Soup, Charlie. Yip. Steak, Charlie. Yip. Corn, Charlie. Strawberry short-Charlie-cake-Charlie. Poor Charlie.

My marvelous boy.

Do you want something to eat, Charlie? Charlie, are you there? Charlie? Charlie?

HAROLD HAS LEFT THE HOSPITAL and gone to live with his mother. I call her daily, I plead and reason and praise. Yesterday I went to meet her in person. They live in a tidy six-room brick Tudor out in Queens, just the two of them for the time being, until Mrs. Linder can place her son in an adequate "facility," as she says. She is a thin woman, fiftyish, a widow, I presume, with hair bleached an unnatural yellow, and she was obviously none too pleased by my visit, though she did invite me in and offer me a cup of tea. I saw no sign of Harold, no evidence that the boy lived there at all. The house was as oppressively still as a museum after hours, with every piece of furniture looking as though it had been glued to the lime green carpet and the air devoid of any fragrance other than the light tannic scent of tea.

Mrs. Linder was out in the kitchen preparing the tea when I became aware of Harold's presence in the house—the very walls seemed to wait tensely for something to happen, for me to leave, I supposed at first, and then I realized that the tension had nothing to do with me. The house was waiting for Harold to continue yipping. I had arrived during one of his lengthy intervals, and the stillness was of the boy's making, defined by his voice and as integral to his performance as any sound he might utter.

His mother clearly does not understand him. She refers to Harold as her "poor little imbecile" and scolds me for wanting to exploit him. She did, however, give me this tape of Harold, apparently in hopes that it would satisfy me and I would leave them alone. But Harold does not want to be left alone—I knew as much while I sat in Mrs. Linder's house listening to the silence, and I knew it again when I was leaving and glanced up from the front walk at the curtained windows on the second floor.

I called Mrs. Linder this morning, and I will visit her again tomorrow. Sooner or later she will have to give in, and I will finally be able to offer my public a theatrical experience unlike anything they've ever known. Imagine: the lights go down, the audience settles into an expectant hush, spot on, and after a long, clenched silence my magnificent little seabird comes back to life:

Yip.

Yip.

Yip.

EVERYBODY LOVES SOMEBODY

Simple words have simple meanings. He can sing, "Everybody loves somebody," and he knows what he means. When he exclaims to no one, "Life is good!" he knows what he's feeling. The word *good,* though, spoken aloud, has a leaden sound. *Happy* is more fun to say, especially with the roof down and the speedometer's needle hovering at sixty miles per hour. "I am happy." The emotion doesn't need explanation. But since his voice is sucked into the vacuum of the wind, he has to say it again: "I am happy!"

Bob is driving in his red MG south to Larchmont along a road that tumbles through the valley like one of the region's sparkling brooks and then climbs up to a flat-topped mountain, up and up and then down again in a precipitous drop. On an icy winter day this would be a perilous journey. But today is a clear, breezy fall day, the Catskill slopes a patchwork of yellows and reds, the mountains capped with the greens of spruce and balsam at the higher altitudes, the air warmed by a week of Indian summer. Today is the kind of day when a man can open the soft-top of his convertible and finally begin to relax.

Bob is heading home from a client's country house near Oneonta, where he'd been sent because of his notable powers of persuasion. Most of the negotiations had been conducted at a table in the deserted dining room. Strangely, though, the only food offered all day long was a single platter of cream cheese canapés. But the client generously kept refilling Bob's glass with mimosas, and together they'd gone through four cigars. By the end of the meeting, the client was ready to sign on the dotted line of a contract worth a quarter of a million dollars.

Bob, the son of a school janitor, finds it difficult to understand why everyone isn't rich. In his experience over the last decade, desired results have been eighty percent obtainable. Considering the stakes, one hundred percent effort equaling eighty percent return is a reliable formula for growth. The advertising firm where he is an employee has grown considerably in recent years, thanks in large part to Bob's influence. For months there have been rumors in the office that he will be rewarded with a significant promotion.

He enjoys the challenges of his work. In a fundamental way, he thrives on the suspense of a client's resistance. Skepticism is the puzzle he sets out to solve. If he's really as effective as his colleagues say, it's only because he has honed his interpretive skills and can slowly tease out the interests hidden behind apparently impenetrable facades. Slowly, one cigar after another, he coaxes a client to tell him what the client wants to hear so he can say it back in his proposal.

When work is over, though, Bob likes to forget the complexities of business. Having applied himself to an assigned task with focused concentration, he rewards himself with a tremendous calm. On his own time, he prefers to see things as they are—all surface, integral and irreversible. Simple things to go with simple words.

Bob is happy to be on his way home, happy to be driving through the Catskill Mountains on a perfect autumn afternoon. Today his baby daughter is six months old, and his wife, Trudy, is baking a cake. He promised to be home by five thirty. If he doesn't run into traffic near Larchmont, he could be home by five.

But when he passes a sign advertising an upcoming turkey roast at the local VFW post, he realizes how hungry he is. He'd eaten only a bowl of oatmeal for an early breakfast, he hadn't been given a proper lunch back at his client's house, and he has two hours of the journey ahead of him.

He drives for another twenty minutes before he passes a sign advertising a house specialty of chicken wings at a roadside tavern up ahead. He pulls into the parking lot, and as the front of the MG tilts over potholes and a thick dust rises around the wheels, Bob has the sensation that he's falling, sinking through a cloud. He pushes his foot against the brake with unintentional force, jerking to a halt.

The stillness of the area suggests abandonment. He idles in neutral for a moment, wondering if the tavern is open. The windows are dark, and Bob's MG is the only car in the lot other than a pickup truck parked at the back corner of the building, its dented rear bumper secured with rope.

He turns off the engine. Dry leaves tumble in the wind across the surface of the lot, crackling like ice under a stream of water. He waits for a long minute, vaguely hoping that someone will come out and greet him. Finally he decides to test the door of the tavern and is surprised at the ease with which it opens on creaky hinges into a paneled space cramped by the presence of an oversize, dusty bubblegum machine. After this decrepit foyer, the second door opens with a jingle of bells into a room that is unexpectedly elegant, with a long mahogany bar and tables draped in white linen.

He stops in the men's room first, and when he emerges there is a woman standing behind the bar, wiping off the keys of the cash register with a rag. Bob remarks, "What a fine day!" as he takes a seat on a bar stool. The woman greets him with a shrug. The mound of her gray hair, fixed in a tall bun, wobbles with the motion of her shoulders. "It's gonna rain tomorrow," she says as she hands him the menu. "It's gonna rain, and then it's gonna sleet, and then it's gonna snow. Now tell me what you want."

Her odd way of soliciting an order unnerves Bob. "I don't know," he says. The woman replies, "Then you want wings and beer." Amazingly, she's right. Wings and beer—that's exactly what he wants. "With a side of hot sauce," he adds.

Her eyes flash with impatience. "We don't have sauce," she says.

"You don't have sauce?"

"Didn't I just say that?"

"You did, yes. Then how about ketchup?"

"We're out of ketchup."

"You're out of ketchup?"

"You got a hearing problem?"

"I just, I can't believe it!"

"Then maybe you're not of the believing disposition."

Bob decides to pity her. He knows from experience that pity is a fortifying emotion, especially when it's directed at a stranger.

She sets his beer in front of him. He feels the weight of her stare as he sips the foam, but when he looks up she has already disappeared into the kitchen. He studies the bottles on the shelf behind the bar. After a few minutes, the woman reappears with the chicken wings.

He eats noisily, greedily. While he eats the woman tells him about what happens to disbelieving individuals. "First you stop believing what you hear. Then you stop believing what you see. When you stop believing what you feel, it's over, you walk straight into the sizzling hot fires of hell." He drops his napkin, and before he can reach down to retrieve it she slaps a stack of napkins on the counter beside his plate. "You burn in hell," she says in emphasis. When he finishes his beer, she brings him another. "You burn, and you keep burning. You never stop burning."

Bob gulps his second beer. "That so?" he says mildly.

"Course, I could be wrong," she adds in a conciliatory tone as she hands him the check.

When he puts down his cash, she seems to forgive him all his sins. "That your car?" she asks.

"Sure is."

"Nice car," she says softly.

"Thanks."

And that's that. After paying his check and leaving a generous tip, Bob is back in his MG, gently pumping the gas pedal to encourage the reluctant engine, pressing it on through its usual opening sputters, picking up speed suddenly, tires spewing dust as he leaves the parking lot.

The stretch of road in front of him lies in a shadow cast by the mountain to the west, and though the sky above is still a bright blue there's an evening chill in the air, filling Bob with a sweet, melancholy awareness of endings. Not only is the day ending, but the warmth of a late Indian summer is coming to an end as well. A glance at the road in the rearview mirror makes him wonder about the unknown that will fill the same space he'll leave vacant. Someone else will take his place at the tavern. Someone else will hear about the costs of sin.

For no good reason, he pushes in the lighter to heat it. And though he tries to be prepared, the *pop* of the chrome knob startles him, prompting him to give a little jerk of surprise, a reaction that briefly distracts him from the road. Refocusing his attention, he sees about twenty yards ahead a doe emerging from the woods, high-stepping cautiously, as though along paving stones. At the sound of the approaching car the animal pauses, bending her tawny neck to look back behind her. Even the squawk of the horn doesn't faze her. She just stands there, evidently counting on Bob to steer around her, so that's what he starts to do, slowing, curving to the right to make an ample arc.

He's late to see the speckled fawn bouncing out of a tangle of briars. He veers onto the shoulder to avoid hitting the fawn and then has to stop short over crunching gravel to let a second fawn pass in frightened leaps, the two babies racing across the road while their mother waits with a majestic stillness, her eyes locked with Bob's, holding him in place. Only when the fawns have disappeared safely into the woods on the other side of the road does the doe rock forward and clatter after them.

With the road empty again, Bob puts the car in gear and drives at a more cautious speed, savoring the memory of the encounter. The regal aspect of the doe had seemed tinged with a knowingness, as though she had the ability to communicate with words but was too proud to speak. Why did she need words if she could stop time with a glance? Unlike the waitress in the tavern, the doe seemed to think speech an unnecessary effort, a waste of breath in a world where nothing should be wasted. Bob marvels at how wild animals have no difficulty matching effort with intention. To live only with natural light—maybe this is the source of their commanding manner. They can blend magically with dawn and dusk, rippling along the surface of half-light, always unfailingly accurate with their distrust.

Bob is deep in thought, preparing the story he will tell his wife about the deer, and at first he feels the uneven motion of the car as an inevitable thing. Instead of moving smoothly, the MG is bouncing like it had bounced over the potholes back in the parking lot. But Bob doesn't have to be told that he isn't driving across the parking lot. He's traveling along a smooth road, a road without potholes, yet still the seat is shaking on its tired old springs, and Bob has to grip the steering wheel to keep himself from bouncing out of the car.

He's reluctant to stop along the side of the road here, in the middle of nowhere, so he keeps bouncing, trying to convince himself that he's not ruining the rim of the tire that must already be flat. The fact is, the spare mounted in the trunk is flat, too. It's been flat for months. He's been meaning to have it repaired or replaced, but he hasn't had the time.

The MG limps along in second gear. A black hardtop Mustang tailgates for a while, and as it speeds up and passes, the driver signals at Bob with a thrust of his fist. Bob ignores him and continues urging his car forward, the flat tire slapping the road with a steady rattling.

Miraculously, he reaches a gas station before the MG's steel disc wheel falls off entirely. The garage doors are open, and when Bob turns off his car he hears the whir of a drill. After examining the flat front tire, he enters the garage with a loud greeting. The whirring ceases, and from behind the front end of a Buick a man emerges, his white face striped with wide smears of grease.

"Hiya," he says, extending a hand almost too oily for Bob to grip.

"Can you fix a flat for me?" Bob asks, motioning to his car.

"You got a flat?"

"I have a tire flatter than . . ." He pauses, momentarily at a loss for words. "Flatter than a crepe," he says emphatically.

The man echoes in bafflement, "A crap?"

"A French pancake, I mean."

"You French?"

"I'm talking about a flat tire."

"You got a flat tire?"

Bob, who isn't the bristling type, feels like bristling. Instead, he admits that the spare is flat as well, and he finishes with a sigh to express humility, which seems to please the mechanic, who wipes his hands on the dirty rag he's holding and says, "Let me take a look."

"You, T-Rex!" a man yells from the office next to the garage.

"You, Cyril!" T-Rex yells back.

"Willa's on the phone."

"Tell Willa I'm busy."

"You tell her."

T-Rex gives his round belly a pat. "My Willa's on the phone," he explains. Bob signals him to answer the call and follows T-Rex into the office.

"Cyril, we got a foreigner here," T-Rex says, picking up the phone and repeating, "Willa, I got a foreigner here. What? French. What?" He covers the mouthpiece of the phone for a moment and asks Bob, "Willa wants to know, are you real French or Canadian French. She just wants to know."

"I'm not French."

"You're not French?"

"I'm from Larchmont."

"Willa, he's from Larchmont. What? England, I guess. No, I made a mistake. What? Now? Right now? Can't it wait? What? Why?"

While T-Rex is talking to Willa, the second man, a younger man with an ample blond beard, leans across his desk to offer his hand to Bob. "Name's Cyril," he says.

"Bob."

"Hiya, Bob."

"I've got a flat."

"We'll help you out."

"Yeah?"

"Sure thing."

"I got to go bring Willa some eggs," T-Rex says, handing the phone back to Cyril. "She's baking a cake."

"My wife's baking a cake, too," Bob announces abruptly.

"That so?" Cyril says with interest that is obviously feigned.

"I'll be back," T-Rex promises.

"Sure thing, go on," Cyril urges. When T-Rex has gone, Cyril explains, "He had to go buy eggs for Willa."

"Oh," Bob says, as though he only now understands.

"You got time to wait?"

"Well—"

" 'Cause you're gonna be waiting."

"Fine."

"Have a seat."

"Thanks."

They sit in the office in silence for a few minutes while Cyril pages through a magazine. Bob eyes the phone, wondering if he should call Trudy and tell her he'll be late.

"Ever eat muskrat?" Cyril suddenly asks.

"No."

"It's not bad."

"Really?"

Cyril reaches into the deep drawer on the lower side of his desk and pulls out a bottle and two plastic cups. He fills one with two shots' worth and gives it to Bob, then fills a cup for himself. "Bottoms up," he offers. Bob takes his first gulp out of courtesy and his second because he's pleasantly surprised at the quality of the triple malt.

"Thank you, sir," he says, feeling less in a hurry.

Cyril waves away the gratitude. "Ever eat moths?" he asks, refilling the cups.

"Moths?"

"Moths. Mayflies. Grubs. The fact is, you can't starve if there are bugs around. Though I have to admit, I'm not partial to ants. Bottoms up."

"Cheers."

"Did I hear you say you're French?"

"I'm from Larchmont."

"Mmm." Cyril flips the pages of the magazine, then looks up at Bob with renewed interest. "I hear in France they pay more for frog meat than for prime beef. That true?"

Bob pushes his empty cup toward Cyril, who generously refills it. "I don't really know."

While Cyril browses through his magazine, Bob sips the whiskey and gazes contentedly at the tear streaks of dirt on the window.

"You ever find yourself lost and hungry in the woods, you can try salamanders," Cyril says.

"Good idea," Bob replies.

By the time T-Rex returns from bringing eggs to his Willa, Bob is feeling warm inside and happier than ever. While Cyril pages backward and forward through his magazine, Bob wanders out to watch T-Rex work on his car.

"You musta run over a bottle full of nails," T-Rex says without looking up.

"I guess."

"Don't know why you never patched the spare. I can patch the spare for you. Too bad you didn't stop sooner. You did a job on it, mister. But don't you worry. I can patch the spare."

"Well, thanks, thanks a lot."

"Won't take me no time at all."

Bob watches in a pleasant daze as T-Rex unbolts the spare. After a few minutes he wanders back into the office. Cyril is nowhere in sight, so Bob sits at his desk, fills a cup with another swallow of whiskey, and picks up the phone, meaning to dial home. But when he sees Cyril plugging the gas nozzle into a car, he decides he'd better ask for permission to use the phone.

"Hey, Cyril," he calls.

"Hey, Bob, you doing okay?"

"I'm doing fine."

Bob decides to put off calling Trudy and wanders outside again to watch T-Rex, who, with unexpected alacrity, has already started to patch the spare. Bob considers the remarkable skills divvied up among the population: *Everyone's an expert in something,* as his own dad used to say.

"You mechanics," Bob says. "You're amazing. I'm very grateful."

T-Rex declares matter-of-factly, "Wait till you get the bill." He slaps the tire and lifts it off the mount. Bob follows him back to his MG, making feeble gestures to help as T-Rex loosens the bolts of the damaged tire. "That's all right," T-Rex says, waving him away. As he watches T-Rex work, Bob feels deeply, but without embarrassment, the irrelevance of his own skills.

"Willa is baking a cake," T-Rex announces, grunting each word as he jerks loose a bolt.

"I know."

"You know?"

"You told me."

"That's all right. I bet you're wondering why my Willa is baking a cake. I'll tell you why. She's baking a cake to celebrate her ex's birthday."

"That so?"

"The thing is, her ex is dead. Been dead for twelve years."

"I'm sorry."

"I'm not."

Bob watches in thoughtful silence as T-Rex lifts off the flat. Soon the patched spare is in place, the jack has been disassembled, and Bob is in the office, writing Cyril a check.

"I mean it, you guys are great. I don't know what I would have done without you."

"Take care, fella." Cyril's expression suggests that he's eager for Bob to leave. The ringing phone helps to hurry things along. Cyril picks up the receiver before the end of the first ring. "Hey, T-Rex, Willa's on the phone. Yeah, he's coming. What? Sure, if you want me there. When? That's impossible!" He waves impatiently to Bob, and Bob backs out of the office, bumping into T-Rex on the way.

"Hey, thanks, thanks again."

"That's all right."

Though the MG goes through its usual opening sputters, Bob isn't worried. If the car stalls and refuses to start again, then there's a good man named T-Rex who will take the time to fix it. Bob's sense of relief swells as he thinks about the luck of finding this garage, where whatever might go wrong can be fixed.

Soon enough the laboring motor settles into a steady purr, and Bob is speeding along the road again, enjoying the power of the modern B-series engine as though it were his personal accomplishment. He's proud to be the owner of a snappy red car that handles curves so efficiently. Yet as the minutes pass he becomes aware of his growing discomfort. His throat stings with dryness, and the warmth from Cyril's whiskey has already cooled inside him. The miles ahead are beginning to seem as endless as time seems short, with the dusk darkening rapidly into night. He wants to be home. He misses his family and feels a foggy awareness of regret for not calling Trudy to warn her that he'll be late.

He's wearing glasses, but still his eyes are tearing from the wind, and the double line in the middle of the road blurs into a single cord of yellow. Everything is beginning to blur, including the recent past. How much whiskey did he drink back at the gas station? Intoxication is a hypothesis that he can disprove with careful calculations. But how can he be careful when he's seeing one line where there are supposed to be two?

It helps, he discovers, to picture sobriety as a bright white seashell visible through a few feet of murky water while he's swimming— it's right there in the sand, but for some reason he can't find it when he dives. Isn't this always the case? Then he will try again, or at least he will enjoy imagining the sensation of swimming underwater. That's all right, as T-Rex would say. He's heading home. Hit the road, Jack. He sings the few lyrics he remembers from a song, then fiddles with the knob of the radio. Unable to find music, he settles on what he thinks at first is a sportscaster's appraisal of a game, the voice almost shouting, as though competing with the wind.

". . . Result is bound to be apocalyptic terror attended by plagues, conflagrations, seven-headed beasts, and the flaming horsemen of hell. It's the same hysterical old Pollyannas and their liver-lillied calamity howlers who called Eisenhower a baboon and Wilson a Casanova and will tell the average American to hold even our Holy Savior in contempt. But you all out there making up the majority of our great country know how to think. You, my fellow average Americans, know how to use your brains. You are the equals of Jefferson and Hamilton and can be certain of the virtue of . . ."

The radio is replaced by static as the road dips between two steep slopes, the crackling sound reminding Bob of the leaves blowing across the parking lot back at the tavern. How many beers did he drink at the tavern? He can't remember. For the moment he can't remember much of anything.

". . . The wide popular supp . . ." The voice fades in and out of static. ". . . Including the United Na . . . as idiotic an assump . . . I believe . . . that justifies America . . . government being an instru . . . what you can to pro . . . the apparition of . . . arouses no—" As the MG reaches the summit of the hill, the voice emerges from the static with a new clarity: "The gutters awash in blood."

An interlude of harp music follows the final pronouncement. Perplexed by the broadcast, Bob turns off the radio. It's a strange world, he muses, where you can drive along a blurry country road and listen to a stranger spout opinions that make no sense. He is surprised to find himself imagining a face to go with the voice—a pasty, wide face of a man who has made all the wrong choices and has nothing better to do than whine into a microphone about anything and everything.

In an attempt to sharpen his focus, Bob lets his thoughts travel ahead of him along the winding country route. He considers how darkness is like seawater—murky and vast, penetrated rather than illuminated by artificial lights. Fear belongs to the night; violence belongs to the day. And then, at the end of the meeting, Bob will hand you the pen. Please sign on the dotted line. A quarter of a million dollars later, he can sit back and relax. But he can't relax, not until he has figured out how to get from here to home without any more delay.

Is he imagining it, or is the patched spare out of alignment, causing the right front wing to veer to the side? Or else the road is tilting. He's in a bowl made of mountains, the dark ridges spinning counterclockwise beneath the sky. Everything seems to be moving in the wrong direction—except Bob. He's driving from Oneonta to Larchmont. He'd be home by now, but he had to stop to have a flat repaired. Trudy will understand. All he has to do is tell Trudy the truth.

Usually, the truth is what he says is the truth. Not this time. He's not sure what to believe. That he will burn for all eternity in hell? Nonsense. Oh, Willa, bake me a cake. A song beginning with the dream of a song. Everything makes sense, except in songs.

He tries to remember the joke his client told him earlier—something about the Russians and their missiles. If, then. Which will end first, the world or human consciousness? So what. If, in fact, Bob drank too much over the course of the day, with every passing mile the alcohol's effect is diffusing. Soon Bob will be home, and home is where he will be sober.

It strikes him as a fortunate coincidence that Route 28 merges eventually onto the familiar highway. He doesn't even have to wonder if he's lost. Another car politely yields as he enters the right lane, and the whole world seems to click back into place. Bob is beginning to feel like Bob again. After humming at least one verse of all the songs that come to mind, he reaches his exit.

He can't wait to be home. But as he drives through the center of town, he begins to wonder if Trudy will guess that he's been drinking. He's more than two hours late. He should have called. Of course he'll apologize for being late, but once he explains about the deer, the flat tire, and Cyril's garage, she'll realize that it couldn't have been helped. Will she let him take her in his arms? Oh, Trudy, give your husband a kiss, show him that you love him. But she won't love him, not if she assumes he's intoxicated. Her attitude will need no more expression than what her body will convey as she pushes him away.

Although he's only a couple of miles from home, he decides to stop for a cup of hot black coffee at HoJo's. The hostess greets him by name and leads him to a booth by the window. He moves with slow, deliberate steps to keep himself steady. While he's waiting for his coffee, he uses the restaurant's pay phone to call home.

"Trudy," he says, half covering the mouthpiece with his hand.

"Bob, is that you? I've been so worried!"

"Some . . . ting, thing, something unexpected . . ."

"What's happened?"

It takes an effort to speak precisely. "I had a blowout on the road. I'm here . . . where am I? They're fixing the tire, here at the garage."

"I can hardly hear you."

"A bad connection. Listen, I be—will be home in an hour. They're fixing the flat."

"What?"

"I love you."

"I love you too, Bob."

Back at his booth, sipping his coffee, he imagines the scene he has managed to avoid. If he'd gone home too soon, his wife would have smelled the whiskey on his breath and responded with the cold resistance that he has envisioned countless times, though never actually witnessed. In the six years of their marriage he hasn't given her any reason to doubt him. But if she did doubt him, if she thought him less than worthy simply because he'd had more than a few drinks, wouldn't he have tried to turn to his child for affection, his darling little baby, perfect in every way? What young father doesn't live to hear the sound of his child's laughter when he tosses her into the air and catches her, tosses her again and again like a beanbag? Up the stairs he would have pounded, every stride heavy with the vivid awareness that he was a man who others assumed had *made it*. Heading directly into the baby's room, he would have fumbled with the wall switch, and when the light flicked on, he would have found that Trudy had managed to arrive before him and already planted herself in front of the crib, as placid and powerful as the doe who'd made sure that her fawns crossed safely from one side to the other of Route 28.

Women always think men are blind to their own faults. The truth is, Bob knows the dangers of liquor and is able to remain in control. But it's not easy when business and related situations demand the courteous acceptance of whatever's offered—mimosas and beer and whiskey. Because he's a courteous man, Bob is at HoJo's drinking coffee instead of trying to prove to Trudy that he can put one foot in front of the other.

It occurs to him that *flabbergasted* is a good word, a word that can fill the mind like helium in a balloon. Though the scene will never be enacted, he still can't believe that if he were home by now, his wife wouldn't let him hold the baby. But he has to believe it. Confronted with what she'd interpret as the evidence of his intemperance, his wife would refuse to let him reassure her. He can predict the outcome of their argument, if they'd gone ahead and argued. But isn't it always better to avoid a conflict than to persist in stubborn self-righteousness? He won't make the same mistakes other men make. It's really very simple: he'll stay at HoJo's drinking black coffee, then he'll go home.

OR ELSE

PART I

In the Automat

Nora Owen had never arrived alone in the city before, and now she found herself swept toward the exit by the pack of morning commuters, most of them businessmen who proceeded in a vaguely furtive manner, as though they were secretly and independently trailing someone who was trailing someone else, the crowds separating into currents up the escalators and across the main concourse beneath the vaulted ceiling and its pinpoint constellations, carrying Nora this way and that and finally to the end of a taxi line. But she didn't want a taxi, and once she realized what the others were waiting for she headed in the opposite direction, downtown on Vanderbilt, no, uptown and over to Fifth, yes, this was correct. Firmly en route, she swung her arms, fingers balled into loose fists. The ridges below her cheeks swelled when she tightened her jaw. Every few steps her lower lip disappeared beneath her upper teeth and then reappeared as she exhaled in a long, determined sigh.

She paused to study a window display. A fan blew sparkling ribbons around a mannequin draped from head to toe in mink. Inside the store, a clerk moved slowly, like a fish along the bottom of a clear lake. Nora watched the clerk adjust a blouse on a hanger. She watched the mannequin. She watched the shadowy reflection of herself watching and with a start noticed the image of a man looming behind her— a ghost, or a trick of perception, and when she turned he shouldn't really have been there. But he was there—a black man in a speckled wool coat holding in his outstretched hand a worn red leather wallet identical to the one she'd been carrying in her back pocket.

"Does this belong to you?"

He had stolen her wallet. Next he'd hit her, knock her to the ground, and race away, taking with him the seventy-eight dollars she'd managed to save over the past year. She knew that such things happened routinely in the city. Except . . . what did he say?

"Um . . ."

"Yes?"

"Me?"

"You dropped this."

"I did?"

She wanted to thank him, but first she had to check to make sure her money was still in the wallet. When she looked up again the man was walking away with a decisiveness that from behind conveyed a fierce disgust, though the tilt of his head suggested that he might have been laughing. So Nora laughed, too, along with the rich old matron who'd been laboriously entering the store with tottering, high-heeled steps and had paused to witness the conversation.

"It's your lucky day, miss!" cried the old woman in delight. Nora made a motion as though tipping a hat, and she continued on her way, heading uptown on Fifth Avenue. She rested the fingertips of one hand on the wallet in her pocket. She intended to be more careful with her belongings, though not careful enough to guard against the sudden blinding of the winter sun as she crossed the street, the glare dissolving the oncoming taxi into a watery nothing. The taxi honked, Nora jumped, and that was that—the taxi had already entered the jam on Fifth Avenue and Nora was safely up on the curb.

She stopped to examine a store's display of robes and slippers. She stopped again to admire the diamonds in Tiffany's window. She crossed Fifth Avenue beside a man walking a poodle, both of whom, man and dog, were haloed by white puffed curls.

Up the carpeted steps of the hotel past a doorman who was helping a woman into a limousine. Through the revolving door and into the hushed lobby. Red-capped wooden soldiers dangled on gold threads from the branches of a ten-foot Christmas tree. Piles of gift boxes sparkled in the light cast by the immense chandelier. Everyone seemed to be floating a few inches in the air, except for Nora. What was she doing there? Blink. Um. The pale, freckled face of a girl inept at deception. She felt like she would collapse in a faint if someone asked her what she wanted. But staff and guests alike seemed absorbed in some important communal task, and Nora could move among them along the main corridor without any objections. She could muse over a breakfast menu posted on a pedestal. Even better, she could retreat into the shadows of stairway number 5 and sit on the bottom stair, settle herself, relax. She could listen to the pleasant music coming from the Palm Court. She could savor the mingling scents of perfume and cinnamon and cigarettes.

Eyes narrowed into a squint, shoulders hunched, back stooped, knees indecorously apart. She held steady, but the longer she sat and watched, the more her attitude expressed uncertainty. She stared at the ladies in their furs, watched one and then another as they made their way along the corridor. Not many people noticed her. A bellman wheeling his cart nodded with a hint of complicity, and one elderly man circled back after passing her once, tapped his cane near her feet, and hissed something, though whether it was an admonition, an insult, or advice, she wasn't sure.

She sat there for a long time, long enough to think hard about her strategy. The plan she'd devised at home did not include a detailed vision of action. And so she sat and thought and thought some more. And then all at once she sprang up, seized by an idea, fumbled for her wallet, slipped a bill from it, and discreetly crumpled it in her hand.

"Ma'am, excuse me, ma'am, I think, um, you dropped this." Nora held up the dollar bill. The woman, a wispy, fragile thing enshrouded in a lavender silk pantsuit, looked at her with disbelief that within seconds had transformed into disdain.

"Pardon?"

"You dropped this?" She could only cast the possibility as a question. This, um, here—a whole dollar. Actually, it was Nora's dollar, but Nora was pretending otherwise, earning no more than the woman's cough of scorn and retaining the dollar for herself.

Although shaken, she wasn't yet defeated, and after a few minutes she tried again, catching a woman on her way to the powder room down the hall. But the woman, who had dark eyes furrowed with thick, extravagantly arched brows, spoke little English. She shrugged and took the dollar from Nora, then searched in her own purse for change. Confused, she thrust the handful of coins toward Nora, and Nora was obliged to accept it—a total of one dollar and thirty cents, unintended profit that had a heartening effect.

She decided that one dollar wasn't enough. Next time, she tried a five-dollar bill.

"Excuse me, ma'am?"

The woman glared at her. Her dyed blond elegance looked coarse at close range. Nora smiled weakly. Without a word, the woman accepted the five dollars and clacked away on sequined shoes before Nora could explain.

She would have no other opportunity to try again, for a concierge came striding toward her, obviously preparing to ask if she was indeed staying at the hotel or if she was what she appeared: an abominable vagrant off the streets.

No need to bother asking. Nora brushed past him, ducking to hide her face and keep him from enjoying the pleasure of her humiliation. He stood with folded arms, watching to make sure she reached the doors without an escort.

On the morning of the day that I first met Nora Owen, I was at the main branch of the public library, though not in my usual place, which had already been claimed by a woman who was bent over the desk, studying her documents with a magnifying glass. I was impressed by her absorption in her work. Taking a seat at a table across the aisle, I set out to mimic her concentration.

I'd intended to spend the whole day working on an extensive footnote, but as the hours passed, I became convinced that I'd been wasting my time. I'd wasted the morning on a footnote, and I'd wasted many months on a project that would come to nothing. The more I considered it, the more defeated I felt: the subject of my research was arcane, and my information came from questionable sources. I might as well have been transcribing the documents word for word. I'd been working intently, with the effort that as a child I devoted to color-by-number kits. I'd been too pleased with the precision of my study to wonder about my purpose, and I'd forgotten to ask myself whether the fantastic claims I'd been recounting were true.

Shortly after eleven o'clock I left the library. Instead of going directly back to my apartment, I set out walking. I stopped in a shop on Madison and bought a pair of leather gloves—a Christmas present for my fiancé—and a scarf for my sister. At noon I decided to have some lunch. Back then, in the winter of 1972, there was still an Automat on the southeast corner of Third Avenue and Forty-second Street, and this is where, after I finished my sandwich, I spent a lazy hour sipping coffee cranked from the mouth of a brass dolphin and reading the newspaper. This is where I first laid eyes on Nora Owen.

A COUPLE OF LONG BLOCKS west of the hotel, Nora decided to try again, acting this time with a jittery boldness that made itself visible in the ten-dollar bill she pretended to scoop from the sidewalk.

"Excuse me—"

"Mmm?"

The woman's age was hard to gauge beneath the mask of rouge and eye shadow. She could have been forty-five or twenty-five. A tall white woman with a wide-brimmed black hat, a white lamb's wool coat, and black boots, she inhaled smoke through her long cigarette holder and studied the money Nora offered.

"I think you dropped this?" Nora leaned her weight forward on the ball of her left foot. For a few awkward seconds the woman didn't say anything. Then she did something remarkable enough to draw stares from passersby: she withdrew her cigarette holder from the corner of her mouth, pursed her glossy lips, turned her face aside, and spit onto the curb.

"You are a dear," the woman growled, her English tinged with a slight accent that Nora couldn't identify. "You are truly the sweetest thing I have seen in months, and for your kindness you must come home with me and enjoy a cup of hot cocoa, yes?"

"Um . . ."

"Yes!"

Later, Nora would tell this story more than once to me. In one version, the woman took her by the hand and forcefully led her into a nearby building. In another version, the woman delivered a lengthy monologue right there on the street—a speech about the rarity of a girl as innocent and sweet as Nora in a world rife with criminals.

Whatever the exact sequence of events, Nora eventually found herself crossing a Beaux Arts threshold whose door was held open by a man in tails and white gloves. She rode with the woman up the spacious elevator to the sixth floor, filed down a plush hallway, and entered a dank, unpleasant box of a studio overlooking an airshaft, a single room furnished only with a mattress on the floor, a card table, a small refrigerator, and an electric burner. The coil, left on, had heated into a pulsing red.

"Trust no one, *chérie*," the woman said, bolting the door and turning with the flare of an experienced dancer to place her hat on a brass wall hook shaped like a beckoning hand. "Except yourself. Trust your instinct." This last word she pronounced with emphasis on the second syllable. "Instinct will serve you well. Instinct will give you access to the true self behind the mask." Behind what mask? What did she mean? And why did she tuck a new cigarette into her holder and light it, only to leave it burning in the ashtray?

Nora indicated her puzzlement with a shrug, at which the woman seemed to take offense. Rapidly unbuttoning her coat, she said, "You have already concluded I am raving mad!"

"No, really! I was, you know, just wondering where you're from?"

"From?"

"From wh-where are you?" Nora stuttered through the jumbled syntax.

"I am third-generation American, if you please! But I have invited you here not to answer your questions but so you may confirm a hunch for me."

"A hunch?"

"You want cocoa, yes? And what stupid ass left the burner on! Mother of God. It couldn't have been you, pussy-puss-puss. Somewhere in this room there is my little pusswillow."

Whether this woman was as raving mad as she dared Nora to consider her or whether she was amusing herself with the performance, Nora would never know for sure. She was calling for her cat; obviously, there was no cat. It wasn't hiding under the one table or in a cabinet. "Here, sweetbit." It wasn't anywhere to be found. "Ah, mea culpa, little dandelion puff." The cat clearly didn't exist, even if the woman thought otherwise.

"Love-pie!"

This was the moment when Nora should have excused herself and headed toward the door—except that the cat suddenly was there, a blue-veined hairless feline lump, uncovered when the woman peeled back the bedspread. Pussy-puss-puss, with squinting eyes and tuftless ears flattened in annoyance at the woman who had roused it from sleep. And suddenly what seemed mad was not the woman herself but the Chinese box of a world which she inhabited, a cell inside a cell, which happened to be the same world where Nora was trapped, a world designed to make no sense.

With the hairless cat on her lap, the woman positioned herself amid the pillows on the mattress while Nora took it upon herself to heat milk and measure out the cocoa. They conversed about the weather—yesterday a storm, today clear, tomorrow predicted to be overcast, perhaps with morning flurries. They talked about the carriage horses and the dangers of Central Park at night. Then, out of the blue, the woman said, her gaze resting heavily on Nora's back, "By the way, the money you purported to have found belonged to you, I know. I never carry a bill so grand. Nothing more than three dollars, in case of purse-snatching. I think, therefore, you have a secret."

Nora flinched, startled by the woman's insight, and her right heel slipped out of the suede nest of her desert boot. She struggled to reset it while she stirred the cocoa and sugar into the milk.

"I don't have any secret," she murmured.

"Everyone has a secret. And your own has to do with money, I believe. A girl your age who returns her own money to a stranger is looking for a gift she cannot bring herself to request directly. You have a need for charity, yes? You are looking for a mother, yes? Perhaps it is that you are an orphan, yes? This is my hunch. Wrong or right?"

Nora had to bend over and untie her boot in order to fit her foot back into it. The action gave her a chance to formulate a reply.

"Wrong."

"Oh!" The woman voiced her surprise with this delicate exclamation and picked up her cigarette to indicate that she would forget the subject altogether. Between puffs she sipped her hot cocoa. She told Nora about her dream of someday moving from the back of the building to the front, into a luxury apartment with a view of the park. She said she had many boyfriends who were contributing to her cause. They were none of them hippies, she said. This was her choice. She did not like hippies. Peace signs pasted on their jeans. Hair down to their knees. Stay away from hippies, she warned Nora in a fading voice. Hippies and dogs. There was no reason for dogs to exist, as far as the woman could see. And she could see very far. Hippies, dogs, and purse-snatchers. Begin with instinct, she said, drifting off into a dream. And from there . . .

The sleeping, hairless cat floated like a strange seabird on the waves of the sleeping woman's chest. Nora watched them for a few minutes, then she turned off the burner, unlocked the door, and let herself out.

I'm NOT SURE EXACTLY HOW Nora occupied herself during the next couple of hours. She didn't go into any stores or hotels, and I don't know if she approached any more women. But the day wore relentlessly on, and finally Nora Owen was standing beside me in the Automat, looking famished and exhausted, her nose red from the wintry air.

"I think you dropped this."

She held a crumpled bill, which I started to accept with gratitude. But when I saw it was a twenty, I withdrew my hand, convinced that the money wasn't mine and suspecting the kindness to be followed by some quick, clever swindle, likely with an accomplice appearing on the scene any moment.

"Please—" She thrust it back at me.

"You're mistaken."

"I found it . . ."

"It's not mine."

"It is—"

"Not."

"It must be."

"No!"

My raised voice hushed the voices of diners around me, but only for a moment. After the pause, the murmur in the Automat resumed, and I tried to continue reading. But the girl kept herself planted stubbornly beside my table, so I began gathering the sections of the newspaper, preparing to leave. Then I looked up and saw that her face was damp and puckered from crying.

I figured that I was more than twice her age. I wasn't ready to trust her completely, but I wanted to help. My work, I decided, could wait while I bought this poor girl some lunch and listened to the story she had to tell.

With the money, Nora's money, I bought her what she requested: a tuna sandwich and a cup of coffee. I pocketed the change, intending to give it back to her as soon as she was ready to accept it. I was surprised to hear she wanted coffee but was less surprised as I watched her dilute it with cream and three packets of sugar. She appeared relieved to have food in front of her, behavior I initially misinterpreted as evidence that she didn't usually know where her next meal was coming from. But after we'd introduced ourselves I soon learned that she had a home in the suburbs and, I could guess, a mother who kept the refrigerator well-stocked. She was in Manhattan because, well, um, to tell the truth, she was playing hooky, she confessed with a grin.

I was starting to feel some impatience with her and suggested that she go ahead and eat her lunch. She took a sip of her coffee to oblige me, then she clapped a hand over her mouth. Before I could ask her what was wrong, she'd gotten up from her seat and rushed out the nearest exit. Through the window I watched her lean against the side of the building. She stood there with her eyes closed, her hand tight over her lips, while people made a wide arc around her.

I stood up, meaning to offer assistance, but sat down again after deciding that my presence would only add to her discomfort and embarrassment. Watching her, my suspicions began to clarify into a new formulation. The girl was no swindler. She was not using money to make an illegal profit. She had no accomplices.

After a few minutes she recovered from the nausea, dabbed at her face with a paper napkin, and stretched her arms before she returned to join me at the table in the Automat. I tried to lock her gaze with mine, but she shook her head, shaking away unpleasant thoughts.

"You feel better now?"

"Sort of."

"Good."

"Mmm."

"It's really not my business . . ." I began.

"What?"

"I hope you don't mind my asking . . ."

"What?"

"Are you in trouble, dear?"

She watched a customer poke change into the slot for the sandwich case. "I hate tuna," she said idly, as though to herself.

"Then why'd you order it?"

"I didn't order it. You just bought it for me."

I bristled, hearing the ring of contempt in her voice. There would be no shaking her belief that the mistake was mine.

"Does coffee often make you ill?"

"No."

"Do you think you're coming down with the flu?"

"No."

"Then there's the other possibility to consider. The possibility of trouble. Now do you know what I mean?"

At the time, I judged her to be seventeen or eighteen. If I had known that she was only fourteen I don't think I would have confronted her so bluntly. Her sudden intake of breath suggested more the shock of guilt than of surprise. She started to rise, then sat back down and rested her hands on the edge of the table. I expected her to begin to sob. Instead she leaned forward, looked me straight in the eye, and, with a prepossession that made it my turn to cringe, said simply, "Yeah."

"Yeah?"

"Yeah."

This, I thought, was just how the girl, so sensible when faced with the world's insanity, would have said it to her mother, if her mother had known to ask. Yeah. That's right. Big deal.

SITTING ACROSS FROM NORA OWEN in the Automat, it occurred to me that she was *made much of,* to borrow a description from one of the historical documents I'd been reading recently, but the details were eluding me. The turning point came when I decided I would not badger the defiant girl with more questions. After waiting for the explanation that didn't come, I stood up, preparing once more to leave her on her own. Truthfully, I wanted Nora to experience the force of my impatience. She'd singled me out for a reason, but if she wasn't going to say what, exactly, she needed from me, I wasn't going to linger.

I'd gotten halfway across the room before she rushed over to stop me. Wouldn't I listen to what she had to say, she asked me, the challenge colored with an accusatory emphasis. I'd only meant to encourage her to be forthright with me, but instead she was acting as though she'd been abandoned. I felt an urge to do just that—to get on with my life and leave her to ensnare some other willing stranger.

I motioned to the stools at the counter by the window and said I'd be right there. I filled my cup with more coffee and bought a ginger ale for Nora and joined her a minute later.

I pushed the soda in front of her. She took little sips through the straw while she stared out the window. Maybe she needed a prompt from me, but I preferred to wait. She waited with me. Through the smudged plate glass we watched the crowd swell at the intersection and with a surge move forward with the light. We watched a man who'd been pulling a reluctant child by the wrist scoop up the boy and carry him across the street. We watched a woman hail a taxi.

"You wouldn't believe the day I've had," Nora said at last—not what I'd been expecting from her. "This crazy lady I met on the street, she invited me up to her apartment, and when we got there—"

"You shouldn't be so trusting."

"That's just what she said. But I could tell right away that she was harmless." She went on to recount the adventure from the moment she'd met the woman to her culminating hunch.

"Her hunch?"

"She thought I wanted her to be my mother!" We both laughed at this, but our laughter soon evaporated into an awkward silence. Keep going, I thought. Tell me the truth.

"The truth is," Nora said, startling me with the echo of my thought, "she was sort of right. I mean, I am looking for a mother. Are you my mother? Ha, just kidding. Anyway. The truth is, I am looking for a mother. But not for myself, not, I mean, it's just . . ."

She sipped her ginger ale between lips pressed into a tight, flirtatious smile. I felt suddenly as though I were being teased with a strange kind of courtship, though I was stupidly slow to guess the content of her insinuations.

"What I'm saying is . . . it's all about . . . it's about how I'm looking for a mother. I mean a mother for my baby."

"You're having a baby?"

"That trouble we were talking about earlier. Get it?"

She'd thrown me off guard. I was supposed to offer help in the form of guidance, but now I couldn't match her obvious implications with their meaning. The trouble, her trouble. Get it? She was just a child herself. She didn't know what she was saying. What was she saying? "This guy, you know, he just." The motor of her voice shut off again, but only for a few seconds. "Forget it. Don't ask me to talk about it!"

"That's fine." I was conscious of the stares of other diners and made a gesture with my hands to calm her. I had no sense how to articulate my sympathy, partly because I still hadn't quite let myself understand what she was telling me.

"So anyway." She touched her belly. "Here we are." She closed her eyes and settled back into her chair as if she were preparing to sunbathe.

I wanted to suggest that surely there was someone else in her life more deserving of her confidence. But her tone of voice conveyed fragility. I watched her, trying to imagine her thoughts.

"It's so hard to explain," she finally resumed, leaning forward. She'd slipped her straw from the glass and was drawing designs on the counter with dribbles of soda. "Everything was fine, and then this happened. This shit. I could, you know, get rid of it. But I'm going to do it." She was drawing loops and crosses. Or was she signing her name? "I mean, go ahead and have it." She sucked air through the empty straw, then held it like a cigarette between her fingers.

"Nora . . ." It was the first time I'd spoken her name aloud.

"I'm just looking for someone to take care of it. Not just anyone. Someone who can buy it stuff and take it on vacations." She spoke as if she were recounting a dream. "And give it the kind of bed with a canopy or maybe bunk beds, depending, you know, and a pool in the backyard, and on visits to the city you can eat those little tea cakes and take carriage rides and see a show. This is why . . . why . . ." She inhaled, drew back her head, squeezed her eyes shut. I thought she was going to vomit all over the counter. Instead she sneezed violently. Once she recovered, she said in a quavering voice, "This is why I'm here."

ALTOGETHER, Nora and I spent about an hour in the Automat. Only an hour—the brevity still amazes me. I'd gone in to have lunch, and I'd come out with the prospect of adopting the child of a child. How could I accept? How could I refuse? I wanted to help, and at the same time I felt the need to protect myself. Although I wouldn't have been willing to admit it at the time, an awful part of me still distrusted Nora Owen and wanted nothing more to do with her.

But I was twice her age, I reminded myself, and I could show her the proper concern. Yet she didn't seem to want my concern and made it clear when she'd finished her appeal that she preferred not to return to the subject, at least not right then. We exchanged phone numbers and addresses and parted with the ease of strangers who had become acquainted under more typical conditions. At no time did I actually agree to Nora's proposal, but neither did I directly refuse. We would continue to talk, we promised each other. I gently suggested to Nora that she see a doctor. I didn't offer to give her money or even to return the change from her twenty, and she didn't ask.

I told no one—not even Paul, my fiancé—about meeting Nora Owen. In the weeks that followed, weeks I spent privately struggling to come to terms with my responsibility to the girl I'd met at the Automat, she called me three times: once to say that she was doing well, though she hadn't made an appointment with the doctor yet, and once to say that she'd had an episode of bleeding. It was then, during this second phone conversation, that I asked her whether she'd ever had a test to confirm the pregnancy. She said she didn't need any test. The third time she called she asked to see me in New York. We made plans to meet at the Automat again, and there she told me that she was no longer pregnant. Or perhaps—a suspicion I kept to myself—she'd never really been pregnant.

Nora refused to speak about what had happened to her and brushed off my suggestions that she talk with a doctor. She insisted that she was fine. Better than fine, she assured me. She readily accepted when I offered to buy her lunch—though not tuna, I promised. Roast beef, I offered. Cheese, she said, and with that she began to laugh.

We stayed in touch through the next couple of years, meeting once in a while for lunch or a walk in the park. It was during these subsequent conversations that she offered, in bits and pieces, a more extensive explanation of what had happened.

Her story turned out to be a familiar one. She'd been drinking rum and Cokes at a party and ended up in bed with a boy she'd been infatuated with for months from afar, a high school senior. Nora was so disoriented from the liquor that afterward she hardly remembered the experience. Word, though, traveled quickly around school—what she'd done came back to her in the gossip of her friends, whose disapproval made it impossible for Nora to confide in them or anyone when she began to suspect that she was pregnant.

She didn't know what to do. The days passed, she said, like pages she was turning without actually reading. She forgot to wash her hair or do her homework. Afternoons she hung out in the cemetery adjacent to her school, smoking cigarettes, watching the squirrels and birds, sometimes alone and sometimes in the company of a neighbor, an older boy she'd known for years, a boy of sixteen with the mind of a seven-year-old who, she felt a need to add, had a talent for catching frogs in the cemetery pond. He was a gentle kid nicknamed Little John, though according to Nora he was more than six feet tall. Believing him to be her only true friend, she finally confessed that she was going to have a baby. He explained that the best baby stores were only a train ride away, in the city. He offered to help her choose a good baby.

She left the cemetery when a younger boy named Larry came along to catch frogs with Little John. Nora went on her own to New York. Somehow her path led her to the Automat on Forty-second Street. I regret that I was initially so resistant to her, though she never seemed to hold this against me. I tried to find ways to repay her for the twenty-dollar advance she'd paid for my confidence.

In the time we spent together after our initial meeting, she interrogated me about my own life. I showed her a photograph of Paul, and she declared that she approved. In an atlas we found in a bookstore near the Automat, I pointed to the general location of the town in Ohio where I'd grown up, a town so small it didn't even merit a dot on the map. I told her that I'd married my first husband at the age of twenty-two, and we'd divorced three years later. I explained how I'd supported myself in graduate school with waitressing jobs, and since earning my degree I'd been bouncing from one temporary teaching post to another.

At one point she asked me about the papers in my briefcase. I briefly described my current research. I didn't admit that I'd given up on the project and would never finish it, though I did complain that in the documents I'd been dealing with—old diaries and letters and odd scribblings in the margins of books—I couldn't tell the difference between legend and history and wasn't even sure if the events I'd set out to describe had ever actually taken place. Nora replied, "So what?"

PART II

What Will Happen

O r else Nora *doesn't* get hopelessly drunk at a party and lose her virginity to a boy she hardly knows. In this version, the year passes uneventfully, and in tenth grade she joins the junior varsity basketball team and becomes known in her school as a rising star.

I picture her on the first day of her future, doing what she always does after basketball practice: she puffs rings into the damp air with the smoke from her cigarette as she walks home along the top of the low stone wall bordering the cemetery. The Baggley boy is at the pond today, as usual, scouring the mud for frogs. Though he's known to be a major creep, Nora has always tried to be friendly with him. But today for some reason she prefers to ignore him; she doesn't wave back when he waves at her.

She jumps off the wall into the meadow separating the cemetery from the woods backing up to Willowbend Lane, which leads to Flanders Street and Nora's house. She is deep in thought, planning the order of phone calls she will make to friends, when twelve-year-old Larry

Groton lunges from behind the thick cover of a hemlock bush with a roar, shaking what she thinks is a baseball bat. She's slow to figure out the joke and staggers back a few steps, causing Larry to double over with laughter. He thumps his bat against the ground, the hollow sound revealing that it is just a plastic Wiffle ball bat. "Don't pretend you weren't scared, Nora!" he shrieks, delighted with himself. But she's not scared anymore. She's only appalled at having to deal with a stupid little brat like Larry Groton. "Now get out of my way," she demands, whipping her book bag through the air and knocking the bat from Larry's hands. When he bends over to pick up the bat, she hip-chucks him, pushing him to the ground.

She stomps toward Willowbend Lane while Larry, after scrambling up, takes off in the opposite direction, plunging through the wet grass and heaving himself onto the wall. Hearing the loose stones clattering, Nora looks behind her to watch Larry stumbling along the top of the wall, heading in the same direction from which she has just come. "Who's scared now!" she shouts after him. In response, he raises the bat and brings it down with a pathetic popping sound, the effort causing him to lose his balance, and he falls backward into the cemetery, disappearing from sight.

Nora hesitates, suspecting another one of Larry's tricks, and in the time it takes her to consider that he might be hurt, she notices that the Baggley boy is loping along the paved path from the pond, heading toward the place where Larry has just fallen.

Even at a distance, the Baggley boy looks like a creep. His hands are weirdly small for his long arms. His face is a mulish oval, crowned with brown, stringy curls. Nora even thinks she hears gulps of hee-haws coming from deep in his throat.

Why would the Baggley boy be laughing? There is only one reason Nora can think of, and it has to do with Larry Groton, who probably

isn't hurt at all but instead is lying behind the cover of the wall waiting for Nora to come help him so he can scare her again. Whether
they are creeps or stupid little brats, boys will go out of their way to
torment girls. Larry is probably preparing to pounce on Nora—that's
why he hasn't yet clambered to his feet. And if the Baggley boy can't
stop laughing as he runs along the path, it means he's in on the joke.

Nora turns and heads away from the cemetery, leaving Larry and
the Baggley boy to their idiotic games. At home she takes a long
shower, toasts a couple of frozen waffles, and eats in front of the television. She wants to call someone and tell what happened, but she's
embarrassed by her own foolishness.

She's asleep on the couch by the time her mother returns home,
though it's only 7:15. Her mother, who is lucky to have income from
a family trust fund to compensate for her meager alimony, has spent
the day shopping in New York. She wakes Nora to show her the new
navy cardigan she bought at Saks.

THE NEXT DAY, Nora is invited by two friends to skip lunch and
join them in the cemetery to smoke cigarettes. On the way they talk
about how to cheat on the state driving test. They talk about diets.
They are listing the foods that make them fart when a girl named
Lizzie Marshall comes running across the field to warn them not to
go to the cemetery because some kid had been murdered there yesterday and now the place is crawling with police.

They find out from the group gathered around the tennis courts
what Nora has already guessed—that the dead boy is Larry Groton.
Little Larry Groton. He was a good sport, someone says, and someone

else agrees: Larry Groton was the kind of kid who just went along with everything.

For the next two days rumors swirl around the school. Larry Groton had been stabbed in the heart. Larry Groton had been shot. Larry Groton had been chopped into pieces by one of the cemetery's walking dead and the police still hadn't found his hands and feet. That Nora is more visibly shaken than her friends only confirms her reputation as an acutely sensitive girl. She keeps her thoughts to herself, reliving the memory in secret. Not even when Lizzie Marshall tells her that the elder Baggley boy had confessed to killing Larry Groton does Nora speak up.

The teachers explain to the students that after Larry Groton had taunted him and hit him with a Wiffle ball bat, the Baggley boy fought back. A heavy rock he'd thrown had struck Larry in the head. The local newspaper describes it as an accident. There is no trial. The elder child in the Baggley family simply disappears from his house. Some say he is hiding in the cemetery, feeding on corpses. Others say he's been sent to a maximum-security prison. Lizzie Marshall says he's in Fairfield Hills, in the psychiatric hospital.

Though Nora doesn't admit it to anyone, she is convinced that she, not the Baggley boy, is responsible for Larry Groton's death. Little Larry Groton. She can't stop thinking about him. She no longer trusts herself. She has lived for fifteen foolish years and doesn't deserve to live any longer.

Larry Groton Larry Groton Larry Groton. Home after basketball practice, Nora looks into the bathroom mirror that has steamed up from the shower and imagines Larry Groton's ghost staring back through the fog.

•   •   •

LET'S SAY NORA DOESN'T GO to college, though not because of Larry Groton. She doesn't go to college because her father gives her his car and his three-bedroom house in Providence. He says she can have the house all to herself while he's in Indonesia, on the condition that she pays the utilities. The Buick, he tells her, is hers for keeps.

Let's say she moves to Providence in the summer when she turns eighteen, against her mother's halfhearted protests. Her mother has been thinking about putting their Connecticut house up for sale so she can move into an apartment in Manhattan with her boyfriend, Gus, who has a great proud mane of white hair and only ever wears sandals, even in winter. He tells Nora that she is always welcome at his apartment—she can consider the sofa bed hers.

She makes new friends quickly—friends who still live with their families and go to high school and who treat Nora as an exotic creature welcome in their group because she lets them use her house for parties. Nora gives duplicate keys to whoever asks and encourages them to walk right in whenever they please.

She finds a waitressing job that pays well enough. Her tips, though, don't come close to covering the utilities bills. She has lost track of her father's route in Indonesia, and he is too involved in his work to write. Her mother is devoted to Gus, and Nora doesn't want to give the two of them any indication that she is less than self-sufficient. She has no grandparents living. She has only her ancient great-aunt in New Jersey, who is wealthy enough to give money away.

Great-Aunt Lucy, who was a concert pianist and once performed in New York's Town Hall, generously sends Nora one thousand dollars and advises her to go see the world. The recklessness of the idea makes it irresistible. Nora pays the overdue bills, finds some college students to stay in the house, sells her father's Buick to a dealer for an ample eight hundred dollars, and buys a one-way plane ticket to Paris, along with a rail pass and a backpack. The challenge she sets herself is to stretch the cash in her pocket into a lifetime of adventure.

IN EUROPE, Nora is surprised to feel at home almost everywhere. She is adept at edging her way into groups of students and will travel with them on the trains from city to city, hostel to hostel, sharing their meals and parties and gossip. After a few weeks, she still has plenty of money to spend on whatever catches her eye. She believes she can return to America as soon as she is ready to go.

With a Danish girl she meets in Paris—an eighteen-year-old girl graced with snow white teeth and a stout bosom, the daughter of a dentist—Nora travels through Germany and Austria into Hungary. The border is sealed with barbed wire, the station platform full of soldiers and their guard dogs waiting to board the train. Nora and the Dane pretend to be asleep when two guards enter their compartment, but the guards wake them with rude nudges and proceed to rummage through their backpacks. Nora is afraid they'll confiscate her dollars as contraband, so when they find her cigarettes she motions them to take the whole box. This is enough to persuade the guards to leave them alone.

Nora stays in Budapest for less than twenty-four hours—long enough for the Danish girl to fall in love with a Hungarian waiter she meets in a park. Nora is disappointed to lose the company, but she'd rather sleep on a train than on a floor in the waiter's apartment listening to the noises of lovers in the dark.

She heads back to Austria on the night train. She is alone when an American enters the compartment. He is a student from Dartmouth, an eager, blond rugby player named Trevor. They are both relieved to share a language, and after a short hour of easy conversation Nora is already suggesting that they travel together for a while.

In Vienna they share a hotel room with twin beds. The first night they sleep separately. The second night they move tentatively into each other's arms only after they've turned out the light. They linger in the mornings over a breakfast of bread and sliced meats and coffee topped with mounds of sweet cream. After three days they head south.

They are in Switzerland when Nora learns that her great-aunt died two days earlier from a massive stroke. Nora's mother gives her the news over the crackling connection of the call Nora makes from a phone center in Lugano.

"But I just bought her a present," Nora protests, as though this would be reason enough to undo reality. "I bought it five minutes ago," she lies. She'd bought it yesterday in Bern. "A music box. A little chalet thing with pebbles glued to the roof and window boxes with tiny velvet flowers. You open the roof to start the music."

"I'll keep the ashes," her mother says. "We'll have the service when you're back." Even with the poor connection Nora can tell that her stoical mother is already used to the idea that her aunt is dead. Nora is silent, unable to come up with words of sympathy because what she wants is to ask permission to come home. But her mother urges her to go on with her travels because that's what Aunt Lucy would have wanted.

Nora says that she has to hurry to catch a train. She promises to call again soon. After she hangs up she lets herself sag into Trevor's arms. Trevor's kisses on her forehead are more comforting than he could ever know. She dries her eyes with her shirtsleeve and hooks her arm around his, hoping he can sense her gratitude.

Trevor suggests lunch. Trevor loves to eat. Trevor has a little pot of a belly now, the kind that foretells a big pot spilling over a tight-cinched belt in middle age. Trevor loves to sample regional special-ties, which in Lugano is a first course of wide flat noodles in cream followed by a horse-meat stew.

Nora watches him eat. After their meal they rent a paddleboat and paddle far from shore and make out, nibbling at each other's tongues as they bob over the crisscrossing wakes, their kisses gentled by their understanding that they won't speak about the future.

The next day Trevor and Nora take the train back to Paris, where it is raining. They split the cost of two-star accommodations in the Marais. That evening, Nora counts her money and is aston-ished to find that she has just short of one hundred and fifty dollars left. She stiffens with suspicion and glares at Trevor, who is lying in bed reading a comic book, but when he looks up at her under the pressure of her stare, his innocence is plain. Trevor doesn't need Nora's money. Nora needs Nora's money, and she's been spending it carelessly over the past weeks, leaving herself less than the cost of a plane ticket home.

Trevor's offer to cover all expenses arouses scant protest from Nora, since Trevor is the one with his father's credit card. Thanks to Trevor's father, they can keep moving. The next day they go to Bil-bao, the day after to Madrid. "Where are we?" Trevor asks when they are eating a lunch of sausage and wine on a park bench. "I mean, what city?"

In March, in Barcelona, Trevor confesses that the last time he called home his father objected to the girlfriend and her expenses. Nora, who by then has less than fifty dollars left, is furious, for as she sees it she let Trevor pay for her only because he insisted. But she keeps her voice low, and as they finish their paella, they work through their argument toward the quiet agreement to go in separate directions.

Nora adds easygoing-Trevor-from-Dartmouth to her list of regrets. She is sorry she ever befriended him, sorrier to lose him. She takes the train back to France, while he heads toward Portugal.

In a compartment by herself, Nora props her backpack in the seat next to her and fiddles with her music box, opening and closing the lid, starting and stopping the whir of its tinkling melody while she imagines her great-aunt's cold fingers reaching through the darkness, tapping Nora's arm to hush her.

LET'S SAY THAT ON A WARM SPRING AFTERNOON in April, six months after she left home, Nora is alone, stranded in Rome during a national strike. The rail workers are on strike. The tram and bus drivers are on strike. The postal workers, the museum guards, the street cleaners, even Nora in her own way—everyone is on strike.

She figures she can sleep on the floor of the train station if she can't find anything better. She's done it before—once in Nice, once in Brussels. She's been spending next to nothing these past weeks and still has thirty-four dollars in her backpack, along with a mix of foreign currency in change. She is surprised by how little she needs day to day. She wants to test herself to see if she can live on even less.

She is sitting on the steps of the fountain in front of the Pantheon when the piazza fills with a parade of bicyclists. There are young people, old people, children, babies in baskets, unicyclists, and even a blind man pedaling on the backseat of a tandem. Though the scene should have been boisterous the mood is somber, the wheels creaking slowly over the paving stones, the cyclists singing in subdued voices. They are all singing—pedaling forward through their song and circling round to a simple chorus of *Ciao, bella, ciao, bella, ciao ciao ciao!* . . . circling like some of the cyclists circle around the fountain, drawing the people idling there, Nora included, to their feet.

The two young women beside Nora start singing with the cyclists. A waiter clearing a table stops and sings. A mother clutches her two children by their hands and sings. The stooped beggar woman lifts herself up, floats her cane above the stones, and moves her lips to mouth the words: *Ciao, bella, ciao, bella, ciao ciao ciao!*

The parade straightens, and the cyclists ride on toward Piazza Navona, their voices lingering in the air behind them. Nora feels cheered by the song, though she doesn't understand its meaning. She is used to not understanding what she hears around her. She doesn't even know whether the cyclists are celebrating or protesting, or whether the song is about saying hello or good-bye.

The singing fades back into the clamor of the piazza. Nora watches the beggar resume her stooped, plaintive appeal. She watches children chasing each other. After a few minutes she decides it's time to move on, thinking that she might try to catch up with the bicycle parade. But when she reaches for her backpack it isn't there on the steps where she'd left it. It isn't on the other side of the fountain or even in the arms of a boy running from the scene. It is nowhere. Or it is somewhere and Nora is nowhere—without her money, her address book, fresh underwear, an extra sweater and jeans, a sleeping bag, a music box, a rail pass.

What can she do now? She'd be wasting her time if she went to the police to file a report. And she doesn't want to ask for help at the Embassy. She hasn't had a proper shower in days. How would she explain letting herself sink to this state of carelessness?

She does the thing that comes easiest: she wanders—around the center of Rome, through the ghetto, up the lush, quiet streets of the Aventino, heading uphill by instinct.

The park beside Santa Sabina is empty except for a few mangy, watchful cats and an old man who is playing simple scales on the flute—trilling up the scale, trilling down. Nora sits on the grass with her back against an orange tree. Soon the sun will set. Already the sky is crisscrossed by pinkish wisps. It is pleasant here with the music of the flute and the perfume of oranges in the air. Although she's lost everything but the few coins in her pocket, the parade she'd watched has revived her sense that she is living through an adventure that can only turn out all right in the end. Isn't it much better to be alone on an adventure than alone in a lonely house? She will be all right. She is living bravely, taking in the world. She is free.

But she's too skittish, or reality is too dangerous, and when some rough-looking boys enter the park and light up a joint, Nora decides that it would be best to leave the park. She heads down the hill into the darkening twilight, the smoky blue of the sky visible above the knobby limbs of the sycamores. She follows the rim of the grassy bowl of the Circus Maximus and heads toward Piazza Venezia. She lingers at the bottom of the dirty white stone of the Campidoglio stairs. She watches a girl tip with her Vespa as she buzzes around a corner.

Nora could just as easily turn left; she turns right. She could go around the piazza; instead she follows the maze of crosswalks. She could go anywhere, do anything, and for this reason can only wander deeper into the night.

She passes a drowsy little girl sitting on the sidewalk with a kitten on a leash and an accordion on her lap. She passes a German tour group gathered around a juggler, who is setting up his stage. On the wall, an allegory of what? A portrait of whom? The Sabines are being raped, manna is falling from the clouds, the wind is picking up, and there is a smell of rain in the air. *Ciao, bella, ciao, bella, ciao ciao ciao.*

She stops at the first hotel she sees, a hovel not far from the train station. The man behind the desk looks her over, from the filthy frizz of her braids to her muddy boots, and answers her inquiry with a single word: *Completo.* The same is true at the next hotel. She heads down the Corso. When she passes a small but elegant hotel, the Hotel Ricci, on the corner of Via Piemonte, she hesitates, and then keeps walking down the block. But when she feels the first raindrops she turns around, heads back to the Hotel Ricci, and pushes open the heavy glass door while a uniformed doorman helps a woman into a taxi.

What could she possibly want from the concierge? He stands behind a high wooden counter and lowers his glasses, propping them on the tip of his nose, to stare at her. He has grown what remains of his brown hair long enough to tie it back in a ponytail. He looks to Nora like he has stepped from the eighteenth century.

He is half Dutch, it turns out. She explains her situation in English and asks if she can sleep on the floor somewhere, in the basement, on the roof. He smiles at her—or is he leering? He says he will help her; he directs her to come back at midnight.

Okay. Midnight. She'll walk into this lobby at midnight and offer herself to this man in return for a bed to sleep in. Sure. Other girls do it all the time.

She whirls around, offended, and marches through the door that this time is held open for her by the grinning doorman.

It is raining, though not hard. Nora considers her predicament. How can she stretch what she has left until the end of time? She would call her father in Indonesia if she had a number for him, but she won't call her mother at Gus's. She doesn't want to admit to her mother that she needs help, and she certainly doesn't want Gus to know that she needs anything. Though he's never breathed a word of criticism, she can just tell that he's the kind of person who would treat her forever after with the condescension of someone who knew long ago that she'd never amount to anything.

She takes shelter under an awning of a closed store on the Via Ludovisi and watches the traffic. Every other car is a taxi transporting stranded tourists. Water sprays from the windshields, splashes up from the gutter.

She spends seven hundred lire on a tepid *caffè*. She stands at the bar's window with her empty cup for an hour or more watching couples huddled under umbrellas walk past. Inevitably, the women stumble on their high heels, one foot twists under, but they are able to steady themselves with the help of their escorts and go clacking on.

The barista watches a soccer game on television. Other customers come in, down a drink, and rush out. Nora is the only one in the world with nothing to do. She glances at her watch. With an unconvincing gasp of surprise at the late time, she hurries out the door.

The rain has stopped, though the wind is sharp and damp. She enters an all-night pharmacy and bides her time browsing until the glare of the pharmacist becomes unbearable.

She is an innocent American girl on a European tour, she's cold and exhausted, and she's not to be blamed if at midnight she makes her way back to the Hotel Ricci and goes in to find the man she'd spoken with earlier sitting on a chair in the lobby like a king on a ziggurat, waiting for her.

There's a cot in the hotel dining room, the cot this man who introduces himself as Frederic usually sleeps on during his shift. Nora can have the cot. Frederic will sleep in a chair.

He's leering again, obviously plotting how he'll use his strength and twenty years' superiority to do whatever he wants to do to her tonight. His fingernails are long for a man's, filed into smooth arcs, the whites tinged with yellow. He walks around the lobby in his brown socks. But he is eager to help Nora, and she's too tired to go through the dance of polite refusal. He has offered her a place to sleep. She has accepted. She doesn't have the stamina to be afraid. After he leaves the room she collapses on the cot, drawing the starched sheets and heavy wool blanket over her.

She wakes often during the night—every time the hotel's front bell is rung by a guest wanting entry. As she drifts back to sleep she wonders when Frederic will come for her, when he'll ask for payment. At one point she is vaguely aware of him standing in the doorway watching her.

The Baggley boy passes through her dreams, along with Larry Groton, Gus, Trevor, her mother, her great-aunt, her father, all of them ringing the bell to bring Frederic to the door.

And then, miraculously, it is morning, and Frederic is urging her to wake, bending over her with a smile that in daylight has lost its quality of greedy insinuation and is simply expressive of his curiosity and kindness. He must set the tables for breakfast; Nora offers to help. They fold napkins, arrange bread and pastry in baskets, and when they have finished they sit down together to big milky cups of coffee and a plate of *cornetti*. When his shift is over at nine, he will take Nora to the American Embassy a few blocks away. She doesn't bother to point out that they'll take one look at her and decide to ship her home.

What is she doing in Italy? he wants to know. How long will she stay? Where has she been? She tells him that she has come to work on a photography project for school, but her camera and film were stolen along with her backpack. She spins the lie easily, for no other reason than to try to prove to him that she hasn't been lazy.

When two waiters arrive, Nora retreats into the bathroom and leaves Frederic to his work. She washes her hair in the sink with the foam of hand soap, shakes a cracked tooth from her comb after pulling it through a tangle. She pauses to study herself in the mirror, her reflection familiar and foreign and inadequate, like an old photograph of herself—the narrow nose, chapped lips, brown eyes, and heavy brows all sharing the label of her name.

Back in the lobby she sits in a chair and waits for Frederic to return so she can tell him that she doesn't want to go to the Embassy. She tries to concoct a new lie in order to get away, though what she'd really like is to stay here for a week at least and sleep on Frederic's cot, eat a hotel breakfast, wash up at the sink in the ladies' room.

The desk phone rings. Frederic doesn't arrive to answer it, and there is no doorman at this hour. The ringing stops for a few seconds and then begins again. Nora feels herself drawn to her feet by the responsibility. She wants to answer the phone herself and almost does, but it stops again. She waits for Frederic. He has left a newspaper open on the counter and his jacket hanging on a hook. He has left a pack of cigarettes in one pocket, his eyeglass case in another pocket, his wallet in the inside pocket.

She lifts a few cigarettes for herself and then reaches for his wallet, struggling against the impulse to hesitate. She pries open the billfold, takes out a lira note, another note, another. She has no idea how much she is stealing. She just takes the paper money from the wallet, tucks the jacket closed again, and bolts. The glass door eases back on its hinges behind her, closing with an accusing groan as she hurries up the sidewalk.

·   ·   ·

THE THIEF KNOWS that the thief's remorse is worthless, as long as the thief takes no reparative action. The thief knows that it is better to be free than in prison. The thief is three hundred thousand lire richer, and that's plenty to keep her going for weeks.

The strike is over, and the thief takes a train north toward Milan. She stops off in Florence because she has never been to Florence. She visits the Duomo, dodges taxis, explores the San Lorenzo market. She discovers that stolen money isn't easy to spend. She can't find anything to buy that is worth the value of her guilt.

After a few hours the rain begins again. The thief is wet. The thief is weary. The thief walks past a Gypsy huddled on the steps of a church and takes refuge inside. She rests there, revives, and because it is still raining she wanders around inside the church trying to see the paintings through the thick darkness. She fiddles with the light switch of a nearby lamp and fails to make it work. The best she can do is drop a five-hundred lira coin into a slot, lighting one electric candle in a row of twelve.

It's a cheap, pathetic light, but still it's something—enough to cast a glow on the back of her hand. It's true, isn't it, that this is the same hand that stole a good man's money? If someone had told her a year ago that this hand belonged to her, she wouldn't have believed it. But the truth is the truth, and based on what she has learned about herself, she can only imagine a future that is a continuation of the present. It will always be raining. She will always be a thief. One electric candle in a row of twelve will always be lit. The present will always be the present, and it will always be raining in the center of Florence.

She is tired. She is hungry and alone and foolish. But where do you go if you are condemned to be a good-for-nothing thief for the rest of your life? You proceed in an arbitrary direction, not just away from where you've been but toward whatever destination you happen to choose.

As she leaves the church her right hand brushes against cold marble. Her left hand is thrust in her jacket pocket. On her way down the steps she bends beside the Gypsy and with a clumsy motion she drops all the money she has left in her shallow plastic bowl. She hurries on through the rain. Though she doesn't turn around, she imagines the old woman behind her nodding in a routine fashion, as if she'd received exactly what she expected to receive—no more and no less.

PART III

Rain on Concrete

Or else Nora Owen never encounters little Larry Groton in White Oak Cemetery—then she doesn't have to decide whether or not to help him after he falls from the stone wall, she won't just turn and head home, she won't move to Providence and then leave Providence for Europe. Instead of going to Europe, she'll do what's expected of her and go to college.

Her hair, a dense brown with a surface film of frizz, hangs to the middle of her back. Her unplucked eyebrows rise in fluffy peaks. She wears jeans and T-shirts year-round, desert boots in cool weather, flip-flops in summer. By her sophomore year she has a strong, if not spectacular, academic record and plans to declare her major in psychology. But first she wants to stop pretending to be what she's not.

Her boyfriend, Max, and her roommate, Sophie, think they know what she wants. They've been conferring privately, and Nora is supposed to be too naive to guess the plan they've concocted. As she approaches their table in the cafeteria, she sees them stop talking. She sets down her tray with a bump that sloshes Mountain Dew from her glass. Max's expression is tranquil as he watches her mop up the mess with a napkin. Max has a reputation for tranquillity. Born and raised in the Maryland suburbs of Washington, D.C., the son of two State Department bureaucrats, he openly aspires to a career as a high school swim coach.

"Hey, Nora."

"Hiya."

Sophie has a reputation for spunk. The eldest in a family of eight children, she is putting herself through school, supplementing financial aid with tips she earns as a waitress. With her cap of glossy dark hair and her mocha skin she is by far the most attractive of the three and is inevitably the one who draws unwanted attention to their group. But Nora and Sophie and Max have learned to negotiate their relationships with what they consider sophisticated ease. Max has been Nora's boyfriend since they met at a party three months ago. Sophie, who has her own boyfriend in New London, is Max's confidante. And at some point Max confirmed to Sophie that Nora really does have some hang-up about chastity.

Nineteen years old and still innocent—though only by reputation, and not for long, if Max and Sophie are successful. Combining encouragement with convenience, they will help Nora Owen lose her virginity. Or, more exactly, though they can't know it, they will help her lose her virginity again.

Night after night these past few weeks, Sophie has been peppering Nora with information. For instance, the average length of an erect penis. The chemical composition of semen. The mechanics of orgasm, male and female. Working from the assumption that Nora's prudishness began as childish disgust and evolved into stubborn ignorance, Sophie has sat propped against pillows on her bed across the room from Nora and tried to explain everything, talking at Nora, talking and talking, until eventually Sophie talked them both to sleep.

And off Nora has marched each morning across the quad, an unremarkable female student who still refuses the full experience of love. The emotion of love supposedly connected to the action of love. But the logic is flawed. She wishes she could explain this to someone. How would she begin?

As she watched her chemistry professor diagram conversions on the blackboard during the day's first class, she imagined her cool, precise testimony in a court of law. Given her decision to keep her secret to herself, she can't turn around at this late point and confess. The idea of confession, though, intrigues her. Isn't Saint Augustine more forthright than Rousseau? she wanted to argue later in her political science class. But she kept her mouth shut. It's always best to keep your mouth shut unless you can predict at least in some general way where a conversation will go.

The conversation with Max and Sophie at lunchtime in the cafeteria, for instance: this, she's sure, will lead to a good end. Here's Sophie demanding that Nora go back to the counter and add a pile of bologna to her sandwich. Two pieces of white bread, mayonnaise, and relish do not make a sandwich, Nora! Her loud reprimand draws glares from other students. The disapproval of their peers rebinds the three of them into an impermeable triangle. And now it's time, as good a time as any, Sophie coaxes Max with a nudge, to ask Nora to dinner at Chanterelle's on Saturday night.

Chanterelle's! Nora knows that Sophie will be in New London celebrating her boyfriend's birthday this coming weekend—which means Nora and Max can have the dorm room to themselves. But though she's been expecting this invitation, she feigns surprise at the extravagance. Not just pizza this time, eh, Max? Not just sausage and beer?

"Okay?" Sophie prompts. "Okay, Nora?"

Nora examines her fingernails. She sighs. She peels the top crust off a slice of the sandwich bread. She thinks of the previous evening, sitting with Max on the secluded stairs leading to the basement laundry room, their lips wet from kisses, her T-shirt pulled up in a crumpled necklace. She considers how serene Max is in manner and speech, how he accepts whatever limits she imposes. He loves her too much to take advantage of her. She'll never have to defend herself against him. But neither can she go on perpetuating this notion that she is what she isn't.

Okay, Nora?

As if she could persuade herself that the past has no verifiable reality. As if, without cause, there were no lasting consequences. Is she willing? A nice dinner, and then she and Max can spend the night together?

"Okay," she finally says, raising her eyes, locking startled stares with Max. For a few seconds they are silent while Max and Nora regard each other and Sophie looks on. Then Sophie swallows a burp with a hiccup, and they dissolve into hilarity.

BUT BY THE NEXT MORNING Nora has changed her mind. Through lunch, which she eats alone because Max is swimming and Sophie is in class, and on through the afternoon, she searches for an excuse to renege on the commitment. She thought she could convince herself to be willing. But she doesn't feel willing. Why not? She, who is usually admirably in command—why can't she just get it over with and move on with her adult life? Why won't they just leave her alone? Why can't she be lighthearted on such a fine spring afternoon, apple blossoms browning on the sidewalk, cottonwood seeds floating in the light breeze? Even the rattling of a bus engine at the intersection is soothing. Even the smell of old, percolated coffee in the 7-Eleven when she goes in to buy some groceries. The fluorescent lights. The rapid exchange in Arabic between a customer and clerk. The quiet voice of a man turning to ask, "You're Nora Owen, right?"

Nora Owen. You're Nora Owen. And that's your political science instructor in line ahead of you, the one who assigned the whole of *City of God* for next Thursday—this after a week spent on the *Confessions*. Dr. Eric Harrison, associate professor, office number 316, Packard Hall.

"Yes." She is impressed that he remembers her name.

"Taking a break from Augustine?"

She forces a polite chuckle in response. He waits for her to put her change in her wallet. They leave the store together, and as they cross the parking lot Nora becomes abruptly conscious of the intense resin scent of his aftershave. Four thirty in the afternoon, and Professor Eric Harrison appears to have alighted on this dingy city street fresh from a bath, with his salt-and-pepper hair brushed neatly in two stripes on either side of the bald ridge of his scalp. His even teeth, Nora notices, stealing a glance as they walk along the sidewalk, are an unnatural white. His eyes have a copper tint. He's a short man whose bulk makes him look taller, with imperfections enhanced by age. Thick black nose hairs, expansive pores, oversize ears, and beneath his chin a little fold of skin that trembles as he guffaws. But the smell of pine is delicious, and he walks with a boyish bounce, springing forward off the soles of his shining loafers.

He's amused by her comment that her favorite passage in the *Confessions* is where Saint Augustine of Hippo admits he'd been doing nothing more for a decade than telling stories to himself. Indeed. The joys of self-deception. Professor Harrison hopes Nora is liking his class. She babbles something about the pleasures of studying a subject unrelated to one's field of expertise. Not that she's an expert in anything, she adds with a short laugh. He points out that fundamental connections can be perceived between the most disparate subjects. "In the Taoist scheme . . ." he begins to explain as they turn the corner together—but look, here's his house, a modest, well-kept lemon Colonial on a side street shaded with new maple leaves. Won't Nora come in for a cup of tea?

How easy it would have been to thank Professor Harrison for the invitation and excuse herself. Too easy. Instead, knowing full well the implications of acceptance—

"Okay." With a shrug meant to convince both of them that there's nothing at stake.

"Good. Come on in!"

The room is lit with afternoon sun. A bamboo screen painted with spirals of blue and white and gold casts its shadow across the wood floor. Two wicker chairs flank a low, cream-colored sofa. Nora, uncertain where to go, drifts toward the bookcase. She doesn't recognize a single title, and her dismay over this extends into surprise as his fingers brush against the back of her hand.

"May I?"

Nora has bunched the top of the 7-Eleven bag, and her fingernails have left little tears in the paper. She realizes that he merely wants to relieve her of the bag of groceries. Not really groceries. Just some cans of soda, Triscuits, Tootsie Rolls.

"May I?"

"Oh. Sure." Another shrug.

Already the air has become charged with the prospect of dangerous intimacy, though before they walked out of the 7-Eleven together it hadn't ever occurred to Nora to think of the professor in these terms. She's one of twenty-seven students in his class. She received an A- on her midterm exam. Sometimes she'll work on a chemistry assignment while he's lecturing. Even when she has an opinion relating to the discussion, she'll keep quiet.

She's quiet now while he bangs about in the kitchen, clattering pots, dragging warped drawers open and shoving them closed. Does she have a preference? he asks from the kitchen. The question strikes her as both significant and silly. She has to stifle a laugh. He appears in the doorway with a tea canister in hand.

"Lapsang souchong?"

Fine. She flashes him an inappropriate grin. He grins back, and Nora suddenly imagines herself watching him from the back of the class. Why does she think this now? Why does she think anything? Because of who she is. The stamp of personality. He. We. A professor who invites his students in for tea. A saint who spends a decade telling stories to himself. A young woman who is supposed to show up for work at the library's reference desk at six o'clock.

Coincidentally, she forgot to wear her watch. She interprets this as a sign that she shouldn't worry about the hour. She shouldn't worry about anything. For a long while—long enough to switch from tea to wine—they talk about Saint Augustine. They discuss his theory that some parts must disappear in order to make room for new parts before a whole entity can be created. The crackling music of an old record establishes the ambience. "It ain't necessarily so." The inch of tea left in Nora's mug is a translucent caramel. Her wineglass is empty. "It ain't necessarily so." Remember, Nora, how Saint Augustine offers the example of a sentence to demonstrate that disparate parts cannot be perceived simultaneously? And his conclusion: we should not attach ourselves to objects cursed with a temporal existence. The professor quotes the relevant passage as he refills Nora's glass: "If the soul loves them and wishes to be with them and finds its rest in them, it is torn by desires that can destroy it."

Nora doesn't even know if she is already late for work. She's not used to this. She's used to knowing exactly where she should be at any given point. Now, as if to persuade herself that she belongs where she is, she hides a forced yawn behind her cupped hand and sinks deeper into the sofa.

Perhaps responding to her cue, the professor reaches across the small coffee table and lays a hand on her knee. He begins humming a few bars and then adds words, singing along with the final chorus. "The things that you're liable"—he is an unexpectedly strong baritone—"to read in the Bible . . ." She laughs softly, nervously, idiotically. He sings with gusto. "It ain't necessarily so."

When the professor saw her in the 7-Eleven, he apparently decided that Nora Owen could be seduced. His expectations, she believes, are her fault. She'd given him some subtle signal, invited him to pursue her so she could lead him on in a direction that would be familiar to both of them. He knows what he's doing. He is obviously a man used to success, someone who sleeps with his students whenever the opportunity arises and then rewards them with casual appreciation. And she is a young woman used to reneging on commitments. Together, Nora and the professor are a volatile match—

surely he understands this as well as she does and has already guessed that she intends to extract herself from this tense situation before it is too late. Which is why he's resting his hand on her knee. And singing. And trying to capture her with his gaze. He doesn't just want her to look at him. She is supposed to look through him into his soul and to consider the possibility of union.

The song ends, and the room fills with the scratching noise of the needle sliding along the empty groove at the end of the record. Then the series of clicks as the bar rises automatically.

His goal, the professor explains after a moment, is to be able to reflect back on his life from old age and feel no regret. What he says seems to be related to the music they've just heard, yet it's as though he's speaking English in translation, using words drawn from the mysterious context of a language Nora doesn't know. His intensifying solemnity has the effect of thunder rolling in the distance. Nora wonders where Max is, whether he's gone to the library to find her. And Sophie? She imagines ahead to the carefree future when she and Max and Sophie will laugh together about how Nora was delayed on her way home from the 7-Eleven.

"Um . . . do you know what time it is?"

"Does it matter?"

Somehow she musters the poise to thank her host for the wine and tea and conversation. It's been interesting, but it's time for her to go.

She can't go, not yet. The water for the pasta is boiling. Won't she stay for dinner?

"Sorry, Professor Harrison."

He wants her to call him Eric.

"I really have to leave."

When the phone in the kitchen begins ringing, Nora flinches. The professor gives a sympathetic nod, indicating that he understands why she is scared. The ringing seems to grow progressively louder. Why won't he answer his goddamn phone! Nora rises from her chair. The professor mutters something—a *w* sound, *wait* or *won't*. His expression suggests that he is about to reveal some terrible secret. Instead, with a nimble motion, he grips her wrist.

A man expecting more; a woman expecting less. She'd meant to stay in control of the situation and make her limits clear, but she was not prepared for such an abrupt escalation. Her awareness is clouded by confusion. She can't figure out why she is unable to summon the strength required to resist, why suddenly she feels dizzy, drained, as in the aftermath of a high fever. She can hardly stay on her feet. What is happening? She can't tell whether she is following his lead, or he is following hers. When did the phone stop ringing?

She tries to regain her balance, buying time with nervous laughter. Really, it can't be as serious as it seems. Surely he's joking when he tells her that he knows what she wants and wraps his arms around her. He's relaxed into laughter again, and now she's laughing, both of them admitting the inanity of this embrace. How can he know what she wants when she doesn't know what she wants? Then and now. The present offering no more than a repetition of the past.

He combs his fingers through her hair until they're snagged by a tangle. He brushes his lips against her cheek. His touch is surprisingly gentle, and this gives her the momentary impression that she can trust him. She wants to trust him. She wants to be able to anticipate what will happen next. And the possibility that what happens will injure her reputation stirs in her a vague, odd sense of relief. Whatever happens, she won't be able to go on pretending to be innocent.

Tentatively, she parts her lips. He slips his hand inside her T-shirt, caresses the curve of her waist and climbs upward. Slowly, cautiously. See how easy it is? Show him what you want. Okay. The soft exhalations as they settle into each other. Okay. Here you are. She isn't wearing a bra—a simple discovery that has an animating effect, and suddenly he is all over her, his tongue is inside her mouth and he is fumbling with the zipper of her jeans.

Feet bare, jeans down. He pushes her backward, back farther, back through a doorway and across a hall, back into a room until she tumbles onto a bed. He falls over her but catches himself with his hands and peers down as though from a great height.

If he is using her, then she is using him. Looking up at the professor, she could almost convince herself that there's nothing wrong with this, as long as the satisfaction is mutual. Yet now that it is too late to refuse him, she wants to refuse him. All her strength goes into the effort of escape. She tries to lunge out of his reach, but he's got his hands inside her shirt again, and he manages to hold her in place while, with a single swift motion, he turns the shirt inside out and pulls it over her head. At the same time he nudges her legs apart with his knees, and after an awkward series of jabs he's tearing into her.

His face is hidden over her right shoulder, which he presses down with a hand that is too soft to be so strong. His other hand is rubbing her left breast. One of his knees is on her thigh, pinning her to the bed. When he bears down, his weight squeezes the breath from her lungs. She can't breathe. If she can't breathe she can't think. That's good. Without thinking, there can be no memory. Only the thudding of the headboard against the wall.

"It follows," Saint Augustine explained, "that the very thing which by its presence causes us to forget must be present if we are to remember it."

What is the professor trying to say?

He's telling you, in case you hadn't realized, that you're something special. My love, he calls you.

The only word Nora hears is *my*. The assumption of possession. A word that should repel her, she knows. But her response is like this effort—raising her pelvis to push him away only makes the grinding fiercer, the sensation more intense. Wanting to belong to no one only makes her more dependent. She belongs to him. That's good.

But you see, Nora, he's far more experienced than you, with precise ambitions and self-control. How artfully he thrusts, once more, a strong, groaning thrust, and then withdraws, spilling onto the sheet, an accomplishment that instantly becomes in Nora's mind the distinguishing factor. Because of this, the professor is nothing like the boy who attacked her when she was fifteen. That boy was under the delusion that he had to hurt Nora Owen. The professor would never set out to hurt anyone. He'd found a willing partner for a mild spring afternoon. She belonged to him only for the minutes he remained inside her. Now she is free to go.

He doesn't actually send her away. Lying beside her on the bed, spent and pleased with himself, naked from the waist down only, he makes an effort to demonstrate affection. As he reaches across her to turn on the lamp, he tells her she's beyond wonderful. He tells her she'll get an A on her final essay, though she has yet to write it. He chuckles to indicate that he's only kidding. He remembers he left the pot of water to boil and jumps up in a panic, pulling on his boxers as he stumbles toward the kitchen.

Nora looks down at herself, trying to see what the professor saw. Her body, slick and veined with blue in the lamplight. The curls of pubic hair. She notices that the thigh of the leg turned outward is broader than the other. She waits for the professor to return. She hears water running, a toilet flush. After a few minutes she goes into the living room and pulls on her jeans and shirt. Deliberately, she leaves her underwear on the floor.

When he appears again he is dressed in gray sweatpants and a red muscle shirt that must be new, for it still has the creases from the package. He settles into a chair and rubs his arms as though to warm himself. He asks, "Now where were we?" He says it in jest, but there is also something different in his voice, an inkling of annoyance, which Nora interprets as impatience. He says nothing about dinner. As far as she can tell, he's just waiting for her to leave.

He reminds her how the turn of the afternoon's events came without warning. The day was supposed to be ordinary. He'd gone out for a quart of milk and had been planning on staying up late to grade papers. He has forty papers to mark for another class. He'd promised his students he'd have them done by tomorrow.

This is his most obvious hint——he has work to do, and it's time for Nora to leave. Okay. So long. She doesn't know what to call him. He'd wanted her to call him Eric, but that was before.

He accompanies her to the door and kisses her softly, with a lingering wisp of passion meant, she knows, to signal an end. They'll not meet again, except in class. He won't be caught carrying on a romantic relationship with a student. He doesn't want to be in any relationship. He is a puckish, independent sort, fun-loving but ultimately solitary.

"Good-bye, my love."

This time it's the last word that she hears. *Love* used in mockery of love. The sound of the word, emptied of meaning, fills her mind as she walks through the evening darkness back to campus. Love. Love. Love. She doesn't even look when she crosses the street and doesn't jump when a blue Ford Escort swishes toward her. Go ahead, smash her. It would be a perfect ending. But the Escort veers around her with an angry honk and disappears down the block, leaving Nora to continue on her way.

The dorm room is empty. Nora takes her time showering—a long, hot shower to wash off the wintry smell of pine—and then she sits at her desk and picks up a pencil. Catching sight of her reflection in the mirror, she's struck by how composed she appears, poised and focused, as though she's completed one necessary task and is ready to start on another.

WHAT DON'T YOU WANT to forget? What don't you want to re-member? What exists in your mind without consequence, like empty suitcases taking up space in an attic? A dusty old volume in your father's house: *The Natural History of Selborne.* What else don't you need to know? Do you really need to know who George Borrow was? Do you care what happened to Hajji Baba of Ispahan?

Gusts rattling the leaves. The soil is dry for this time of year, but the prediction is that a steady rain will begin to fall the next day. Two crows in a tree, waiting for the rest of their flock. What matters? Company. One stone on top of another.

"Why didn't you show up at work? I went to look for you. Nora, what's wrong?"

"I had that lab report to finish."

"You sure you're okay?"

"Yeah."

"You're really sure?"

"Really."

"Night, then."

"Night."

You, Sophie, can't know how much I appreciate your concern. Our hours of schnapps and pot and conversation. And you, Max. And Mom and Dad. Mom? Yes, dear? Nothing.

Dad is off in Indonesia exhuming pottery shards and bones. Mom is living with Gus in New York. But even if they were all here in the room with her, Nora wouldn't know what to say.

When, therefore, the memory loses something—and this is what happens whenever we forget something and try to remember it—where are we to look for it except in the memory itself?

Remember?

She remembers that Edward I. Koch is mayor of New York. She remembers that Leonid Brezhnev is president of the USSR. She remembers Saint Augustine's theory of parts. The first half of the sentence disappearing into the meaning of the second half. Experience disappearing into dream. And then, in the morning, the whole page is blank, everything is new, and you can start all over again, from scratch.

SHE HOLDS A TORN PIECE OF FABRIC that she'd found between her dorm and the quad. Lengthwise, she estimates, it is about three inches. Two inches across. The pattern consists of colorful oblongs, jelly beans in yellow, orange, lime green, pink, purple, and teal. As she waits, she folds it in half, then in half again and again until she has a cushion of fabric the size of a pea, and then she unfolds it, flattens it against her leg, and begins all over again, keeping her eyes on her hands' activity while students skip up the stairs into Packard Hall. The cloud cover sinks toward the ground under its own weight. Fat, scattered drops leave stains on the concrete squares of the walk. The music of a violin can be heard through an open window of an upper-floor rehearsal room. Grackles poke around in the newly seeded grass beside the steps. A flag furls and flattens with a snap in the wind. Behind the building, a truck beeps a warning as it backs up. A girl heading toward the door drops an unwrapped straw on the step and scoops it up before Nora can retrieve it for her. Nora pulls a few stray threads free from the piece of fabric. Red threads tipped with black. She folds and refolds, unfolds, smooths the fabric against her jeans.

She recognizes his shoes first—brown loafers, polished and comfortable—and then his voice. She can tell from the forceful emphasis in tone that he is talking to a colleague rather than a student, though she can't make out the content of the conversation. When she hears the pause in his speech, she knows without doubt that he has seen her sitting there on the step. For this brief moment he is trapped between what he wants to say and what he will say. He is not used to feeling awkward. This in itself gives Nora some satisfaction. She has made him feel something he is not used to feeling. The space between intention and action. The blank space between one word and the next when we can't be sure what will happen, when the chaos of memory threatens the coherence of understanding. When it's possible that we might be held accountable. When anything is possible.

The pause lasts long enough for his colleague, a woman, to notice the break within the phrase and to coax him on with a *Hmm?* It doesn't last long enough for him to fill the silence with Nora's name.

As he was saying.

She folds and unfolds her piece of fabric. She watches a fat raindrop melt into the pavement. She watches the grackles bob for grubs. She hears the whirring sound as the electric chimes in the tower prepare to ring the hour.

AND NOW, at last, it's Saturday night, and Nora lies in her bed beside Max, who sleeps soundly, stretched prone, his head framed by the arc of his arms, his skin dimpled around the junctures where the ribs meet his spine. His breath moves through pursed lips in gentle whistles. He is exhausted by sex. She is exhausted by confession. She hadn't meant to tell Max about what happened at Professor Harrison's on Tuesday, but somehow he'd drawn it from her, motivated by the suspicion that she'd generated with her reticence over the past four days. He'd sensed something was wrong and had even guessed the nature of her secret, if not the details. He couldn't make love to her freely and completely if he was tense with suspicion. So she'd told him everything she could allow herself to tell.

"He must have forced you," Max said quietly.

"It was my fault."

"It was his fault."

"Blame me."

He refused to blame her. He knew her too well to blame her. He'd never blame her—a promise he wouldn't be able to keep. It might take months, even years, but at some point he would think about what happened, and he'd blame her.

But for now he loves her and can speak the word straight—*love*—unshaded by doubt. He would never suspect that she's a fraud. Twining his fingers with hers. Let's be together forever.

Her sweet, forgiving lover. If only she could have included in her confession the relevant facts. Watching him sleep, she imagines what she wished she could have told him: not the story of last Tuesday, but, rather, the story beginning that afternoon four years ago when she was walking home from school through the cemetery and the Baggley boy ran up to her from behind, smacked her on the head with a hollow plastic bat, and then jumped on her and raped her.

She would say it boldly, confidently. Rape. Noun and verb. She imagines Max's astonishment, and even more, the dismay he would express when it dawned on him that Nora had waited so long to tell him about this. She'd have to explain why she'd kept the truth a secret, why secrecy was her first, spontaneous response and why, after a week had passed, secrecy became absolutely necessary.

You let a guy like that go free, he'll do the same again. He'll do it again and again until someone comes along who has the guts to make an accusation.

Nora imagines Max's anger—really just frustration, knowing that his girlfriend had been harmed. She couldn't fault him for wanting to protect her. She could only try to make him understand.

Listen, Max.

Why didn't you tell me?

I am telling you now.

You lied to me. You said you were, you hadn't . . .

I never said that. Sophie said it, not me. I'm trying to explain. If you'll listen. Are you listening?

She was raped by a sixteen-year-old boy—a sick, gross kid who didn't know what he was doing. The smell of him. The sounds he made. Her face in the grass. Afterward he'd scrambled over the stone wall bordering the cemetery and run like a little boy who'd broken a window with a baseball. She had continued to lie there until it started to rain, and then she, too, went home, though she walked slowly, limping slightly, for she'd turned an ankle trying to escape him.

At home she stood in the shower until the hot water ran out, then she planted herself in front of the television. The puzzles of *Jeopardy!* had a soothing effect. By the time her mother returned home, Nora was calm enough to pretend that nothing had happened. Coward that she was. Don't ask her to explain.

He lived near her—across the street, a few houses down. For years she'd seen him wandering the neighborhood at night, shining his flashlight into mailboxes. Sometimes he'd use a sharp rock to make long scratches along the side of a parked car. He was the kind of boy whose usefulness the other children were taught to appreciate, the way they were taught to appreciate their nightmares, his example demonstrating the scope of human variation, preparing them for the unexpected.

Creep was the name the children used when they were calling to him. *The Baggley boy* was the phrase they used to identify him in their conversations. But their cruelty toward him was restrained simply because he had a younger brother who, though reserved, was an all-around good kid, smart and cute and promising on the lacrosse field. As long as the younger brother had potential, the older brother would be tolerated.

No one would ever know what the older Baggley boy did to Nora Owen. She missed only a single day of school and then resumed her life. A social studies unit on South America; algebra; French; filched cigarettes; intramural basketball, though she had to sit out two games because of her sprained ankle. Six days passed. Her period began on schedule, with cramping that was blessedly normal. Everything was normal. The arguments with her mother about money. The gossip with her friends. The crisp fall weather.

And then little Larry Groton had to go walking alone through the cemetery. And instead of minding his own business, he stopped when he saw the Baggley boy hunting for frogs in the reeds around the pond. Is that what happened? He had to strike up a conversation. Is that what happened?

Watcha doing?

Mmm.

Huh?

What?

You know me. I'm Larry.

Yeah.

So watcha doing?

Dunno.

Looking for frogs?

Mmm.

Did you catch one yet?

Mmm.

Where is it?

Mmm.

Can I see?

Naw.

Why not?

Ummm.

Why not? Maybe you didn't catch a frog. I bet you didn't catch any frogs, not even one.

Two boys, one twice the weight of the other, seven years older, with a mind that didn't understand the concept of morality, though no doctor had been willing to treat him, since no exact diagnosis had yet been determined. A boy who couldn't have been uglier. Fat, grayish lips. Fat fingers and toes. Fat arms. Fat butt.

Fatso!

Larry, don't. You should know better.

Creep!

What happened next? Larry would have experienced it either as unreality slowly unfolding, as in a dream, or as a real sequence in real time. Whatever the quality of impression aroused by experience, Larry would have understood that he was in danger. He was a small child for his age, and though he knew himself to be a fast runner, he wasn't fast enough.

And what about the Baggley boy? How much did he understand? Nora could guess what was going on inside that fat brain of his. The way memory exists within forgetfulness. Remembering that he couldn't remember what he'd done wrong. You dummy. Fatso. Creep. Anything he ever did was wrong. He understood that in order to be himself, he had to keep doing wrong. Last week he'd done something wrong. He'd done it because he was who he was. Creep. It was wrong to jump on a girl. It was wrong to grab this little boy by the neck. Of course it was wrong. That's why he did it. If wrong is what you always are, then wrong must always be what happens next. He couldn't remember what, exactly, he'd done wrong to the girl, but his action had left behind an impression, like the stain of a raindrop on concrete. He remembered the forgetting. Before he forgot the remembering, he'd have to do it again.

He did what he did to little Larry Groton because he'd done what he'd done to Nora Owen. It was as simple as that. He was someone who could only ever do wrong. He was a creep. He was ugly and fat. Fatso. That's who he was. That's what he'd done. A boy lying with his face in the grass. He'd done that. The smell of wet leaves and pine needles, mud, pond water. The hissing of the wind. A half-grown boy who would never move again. He'd done that. He'd done it because he remembered the forgetting. Make no mistake—he'd meant to do it. And later when the police came to talk to him, he would remember that he'd meant to do something, but he wouldn't remember what the something was until they told him.

Is that what happened?

Creep.

Run, Larry. Or even better, stick to the road. Walk around the cemetery instead of through it. Start from the beginning and change the sequence. Save your life.

PART IV

That Place

O r else Larry Groton didn't even exist—then the Baggley boy couldn't murder him, and Nora wouldn't bear some responsibility for his death. Maybe the Baggley boy never attacked anybody in White Oak Cemetery. Let's say Nora grew up without ever being assaulted. After completing her graduate degree, she found work in public school administration. She fell in love, married, and moved to Philadelphia. And eventually she came home to take care of her mother, who was battling cancer.

When Nora's mother developed a low-grade fever, the doctor prescribed erythromycin. By the next day her lips had swelled and turned the pale, pinkish hue of the underside of her tongue. The doctor changed the antibiotic and prescribed a course of antihistamines to relieve the symptoms of the allergic reaction as well as reduce the stiffness in her neck. The next morning, she sat propped up in bed, a coffee mug tucked in the crumpled sheet between her thighs. She felt improved enough to request a breakfast of scrambled eggs.

Returning to Bev's bedside with the plate of eggs in hand, Nora thought that her mother had fallen asleep and the mug had overturned. But the way her mother's head, tilted back against the pillow, moved in a rhythmic twitch indicated that either her sleep was troubled or she was having difficulty breathing. Nora tried nudging her awake. Bev kept twitching. The cracks between her eyelids showed only white.

The seizure lasted less than five minutes, but by then the ambulance was already en route, and Nora agreed to let the medics transport her groggy mother to the hospital. After a wait that extended into the early afternoon, the emergency department physician diagnosed a brain abscess.

An anticonvulsant was given to prevent repeated seizures—this, a nurse explained, would act as a sedative, so Nora shouldn't be surprised if her mother remained difficult to rouse for another day or two. By ten p.m., Bev was resting comfortably, and Nora's husband, Adam, who had driven up to Connecticut from Philadelphia, took Nora to her mother's house.

A call from the neurologist early the next morning brought Nora and Adam back to the hospital. A corticosteroid, administered intravenously to control the swelling in the brain, had failed to have the desired effect. The neurologist needed consent to drain the pus, which involved drilling a small hole through Bev's skull. This, or Nora's mother could suffer permanent brain damage.

The procedure took less than half an hour, though Nora imagined that she would have to wait for time to move in reverse before she saw her mother again. While she sat with Adam in the lobby outside of surgery, she heard a buzzing sound—the sound, she was convinced, of a drill grinding through bone. She touched her husband's arm to draw his eyes away from the soccer game on television and told him she was going to be sick. He grabbed a plastic wastebasket and held it in front of her. It was empty except for a piece of white gum stuck to the black disk at the bottom.

Nothing more than old peppermint gum. Shimmer of a fluorescent light overhead. Colors flickering on the TV. On again, off again. Who's winning? Everything conspiring to remind her of the contest between life and death.

"Do you still feel sick?"

"I'm fine. Thanks."

She leaned back into the curve of his arm and took in the action on the screen, the players' leaping jubilation, a World Cup game, United States leading Spain, 1–0. And then the long exhalation in the aftermath. Bev Knox, formerly Bev Owen, born Beverly Diamond, topped with a turbaned bandage, scrubbed and ruddy and looking younger than she had in years, was wheeled into a private room in the critical care unit.

"Bev? Bev, it's me, Nora." The stupid human need to be oneself. And even stupider—"How are you doing?" As if she expected her mother to lift up on her elbows and say through the artificial airway, I'm fine, dear. And you?

"She looks good, doesn't she?"

"She looks peaceful."

"She looks like photographs of herself when she was in her thirties. Bev? I wonder if she can hear us. Bev? Can you wiggle your finger for me? This finger here, on your right hand. This one. Can you lift it?"

Between the *shush-shush*ing of the ventilator, the heartbeat graph on the monitor, and the flat gray sky outside the window, the room had a contagious serenity. Adam and Nora stayed with Bev through much of the afternoon, passing sections of the newspaper between them. They spoke in whispers. Adam stared out the window for a long while. When he turned back he seemed to be trying to hide his confusion, as though he didn't want to admit that he didn't understand how he'd come to be here.

"We're not doing much good," he finally said, stretching out his arms. "Why don't we go back to the house?"

"You go on. I'm going to stick around for a while."

But she needed to eat, Adam pointed out. She said she wasn't hungry. She needed rest, he insisted. She said she'd stretch out on the cushioned alcove bench. She'd stay as long as hospital rules allowed, and then she'd take a taxi and join Adam at Bev's.

"Look," she murmured with her eyes closed, "I'm already asleep." He kissed her on the forehead beneath the peppered arc of her bangs.

SHE MUST HAVE SOME IDEA that she's not lying in her own bed in her own home. Not working in her garden. Not dancing with Gus. Bev can't have forgotten that Gus is dead. His final whisper of a groan. Who could forget? The man who had been described to her as a shrink with a passion for tofu. His shroud of gray curls. Straw sandals. Remember the evening of his first visit to the Ridgefield house, Gus chasing a bat around the kitchen with a broom? He finally managed to trap it beneath an overturned pot, and they all relaxed with tall glasses of lemonade and then watched in amazement as the bat flattened itself into a puddle and seeped from under the rim of the pot, unfolded its wings, and flew across the room and out the open door.

Or the time she was pregnant with Nora, and she and Lou stayed in a cheap motel in the Berkshires. Animals crackled through the dry ground cover outside their open window all night. And then when Lou was getting dressed the next morning he discovered a chipmunk asleep inside his boot. Bev, come see!

Lou's ambition to follow the example of the Raytheon executive who at the age of fifty quit his job and took his family to live among the Bushmen in the Kalahari. Bev, out of necessity, adept at pretending that anything is possible.

Making puppets out of rose hips. Making whistles out of acorn shells.

Benny Goodman's thin lips and rimless glasses. Good night, my love.

Thinking about all this while she listened to a bird in the garden and waited for Nora to bring her breakfast. *Chickadee-dee-dee-dee-dee.*

IT FELT GOOD to give in to fatigue. But when Nora found herself awake later in the evening, she wasn't certain she'd actually been asleep. How much time had passed since Adam had left the hospital? Since her mother had gone into surgery? Since her mother had been diagnosed with ovarian cancer? Since Nora's birth?

The strange fact of passing time. Acceptance had felt like defeat when she was a young girl and her mother finally convinced her that the Earth was turning beneath her feet. Even now, what she knew to be the truth seemed the opposite of such dependable impressions as these: the day's filmy residue on her teeth, the steady breathing of the ventilator, the bulge of her mother's eyeballs under the thin skin of her lids, the figure of a man in the doorway, backlit by the recessed ceiling lights.

"Nora, honey . . ."

It was her father's voice, all right, and her father's bald, freckled head and full beard. Nora half rose, then settled back onto the bench.

"Lou! You startled me."

"Didn't Adam tell you I was coming?"

"What are you doing here?"

"I'm here to see your mother."

Why? she wanted to ask—a purely spiteful question that would have put him on the defensive. Instead, she remained silent while he stepped into the room. He stepped forward again with a jerk, as though moving through an invisible barrier, and stood beside Bev's bed.

Watching him graze his ex-wife's hand with his forefinger and then lift it, tubes and all, to his lips, Nora didn't know whether to feel embarrassed, offended, or impressed. She couldn't muster pity; she couldn't tell whether the gesture was purely for show—an old gentleman's debonair display of affection. A display for whose benefit? Nora suspected that Lou would have done the same whether or not he'd had his daughter for an audience. He even seemed mildly surprised by either his own impulsive action or by the taste of Bev's skin. Beverly Knox, formerly Owen. This wife Lou had left thirty years ago for another woman and who wouldn't take him back when he came begging.

Lou gently lay Bev's hand back on the mattress and bowed his head with a solemnity that Nora thought both tender and portentous.

"Were you planning to stay with us at Bev's house?" she asked.

"Is that all right?"

"I guess so."

"I appreciate it."

Nora was used to Lou's habit of visiting without invitation. He moved around so frequently he used a post office box for his home address. But she was surprised by how old he looked. She'd seen him last . . . when? Summer a year ago, and he'd been fit enough to dive naked from the dock of the lake house. Shedding his jeans right there in front of his daughter and son-in-law, he'd squeezed together those skinny buttocks of his, pushed off his toes, and with a yelp dove into the water that by then, mid-August, was topped with a thick scum of algae. Right through the green bloom went Lou, and he didn't surface again for so long that Nora had risen to her feet in panic and was about to dive in after him when he finally did bob up ten yards away, on the other side of the dock.

Rising again from the murky depths in Bev's hospital room after an absence of eleven months.

"How is Brunswick?" she asked him.

"I moved down to Harpswell for the summer. How is your mother?"

"For a woman with a hole in her head, she's managing."

"What in heaven's name have you let them do to her?"

Nora explained to her father the reasons for the surgery. Lou wanted to know if she'd gotten a second opinion. Yes, she lied. She'd gotten a second and a third opinion, and all the doctors had said the same: surgery or brain damage. Which would you choose, Lou?

"What about surgery *and* brain damage? What's the point of that?"

Nora wasn't sure how best to respond. It always took some time to size him up after a long absence. *Youthful* was the word others used to describe him even into his seventies. The better word, Nora thought, was *incomplete*. Whoever her father had been the last time she'd seen him, he'd be more stubborn, more resigned in his misgivings about his past actions, and more blatantly contradictory when she saw him again.

More Lou than Lou. A man who couldn't see the point of putting a hole in an old woman's head.

Nora might have folded her arms and scowled. Or she might have given Lou a detailed description of traumatized brain tissue. Instead, she decided to challenge him: "What would Bev have wanted?" she asked.

"Bev?" he echoed, unexpectedly deflated. The Bev who had been his wife, or the Bev who had become a stranger? How about both? Nora had heard him talk on many occasions about his regret over the split. She knew what he would say—he'd never gotten over Bev and had spent the last three decades longing for reconciliation. What unnerved Nora now was that he would say it in Bev's presence.

He sat on the lower corner of Bev's bed near where the catheter emerged from under the sheet, and he lifted a cigarette out of the pack in his shirt pocket. Nora reminded him that smoking was prohibited in the hospital. He left the cigarette dangling unlit from the corner of his mouth and looked at his daughter with a raised-eyebrow expression clearly intended to challenge her to pay attention.

OR THE TIME Bev called Nora into the kitchen to examine a germinating bean. Forget the television show, for God's sake, and come see this. The seed coat disintegrating. The withered cotyledon. Trying to explain the paradox of loss and gain, all that we have to give up in order to move forward, arriving in this place. What place? And who asked Lou to come along?

Deep in thought, running her fingers over the velvety purple sepal of a larkspur. Doesn't that feel nice? Clouds gathering for a late afternoon thunderstorm. Her garden. Her house, 7 Fairport Lane. Built in 1890, the floorboards warped, the chimney crumbling where the vines had grown into the mortar. The place Gus and Bev went to live out their last years together. Sweet Gus. Plucking dead blossoms off a rhododendron. The perfume of lily of the valley hanging in the humid air. The wind picking up. Silver shine of the poplar leaves.

ON THAT TERRIBLE NIGHT ending with Bev's assurance that she would never again speak his name aloud, Louis Owen drove north. It was summer, between semesters, and he would miss nothing more than a couple of conferences with inconsequential panels about theoretical rubrics and anthropology's hidden bias. Talk, talk, talk. Lou had always been too eccentric, as he liked to think of himself, or too lazy, as others thought, to have anything productive to say about theory, and he'd lost interest in the social element of the conferences. He'd met the woman for whom he'd left his wife at one of those conferences; he wasn't in the mood to meet another woman right then.

He'd intended to keep driving up through Canada into the wilderness of the Northwest Territories, but his car broke down in Niagara just before he'd cleared the border. So he booked the cheapest room he could find in a motel across from a Nabisco factory. How many times had he told Nora about this motel? Seventy dollars a week, morning coffee included, the smell of burned sugar clinging to the sheets and towels.

Finishing this first part of the account, he paused, and, through his unlit cigarette, drew in a long breath that was synchronized with Bev's ventilator. Lou breathing on his own; Bev being breathed for.

"So you hung out in Niagara Falls for a while."

"Feeling sorry for myself, I admit. Having lost the love of a good woman, I'd lost my future."

You and your sentimental clichés, she wanted to say. Instead— "What's that supposed to mean?"

"You know how many people throw themselves over the falls each year? You don't want to know. Every morning I'd walk from my motel room to the park and spend the day there. What a wreck I was, destined for the junkyard. And yet somehow I found ways to make myself useful—snapping photographs for tourists, pointing them in the right direction. I got friendly with the grounds staff and when one of the guys quit I was offered his job. Did you know that your dad had a job picking up trash?"

"You've always kept yourself busy."

"Collecting soda cans and hot dog wraps, newspaper, old socks, and lost hats. I wish you could have seen me."

"I can imagine."

"I was missing you like crazy, Nora. Believe me, I never wanted to stop being your father. You know, I wrote to you. More than once." *How come you never answered me?* he would say next. "How come you never— forget it." He gave a dull shrug. "Your mother forwarded the bills. Of course she did. I'm not complaining. And wouldn't you know, she sent along the certificate confirming our plots at White Oak Cemetery."

"Where?"

"Crazy business, eh? We bought our little patch of land on sale. And she'd sent a copy of the certificate to remind me of our commitment."

"Where did you say?"

At first he'd thought it was a nasty joke designed to remind him that his life would add up to no more than dates carved in stone. But the more he'd thought about it, the more he'd studied the paper and traced his fingers across the numbers, the more he'd been comforted by the idea. He and Bev would be together in the end.

Where?

She'd heard correctly. *Cemetery,* he'd said. And *White Oak.* It had to be White Oak. He'd never mentioned this before, and neither had Bev.

"I can't believe it."

"A pact made long ago," he said, his irony tinged with pride, though he admitted it must be disturbing for Nora to imagine her parents, given their years of estrangement, together in the end, planted side by side.

Or the time Nora stepped on the spiny husk of a chestnut, and to stop her from crying Bev split open the nut and showed her the shadow of the seed leaf inside. Then they went inside and Nora dressed up in Bev's old belted blue dress with padded shoulders. Bev painted Nora's eyelids blue and dusted her cheeks with cyclamen rouge, and Nora went clacking around the house in her mother's high heels. Hey, gorgeous!

Or the time, the last time, Lou came to dinner. Asking for Bev's forgiveness. Begging for Bev's forgiveness. Demanding Bev's forgiveness. Don't you dare threaten me, Lou! Get out! No. Yes. And snap, she's an old woman pulling out a maple sapling by its roots and trying to recall a song she once knew about mandrakes. Her back aching, her head throbbing, only wisps of hair left after the chemo, her ears ringing, and Nora's at the kitchen door calling—

Bev! Bev! Telephone.

Did someone say something, or is that sound the dry leaves moving in the breeze? Sky darkening. All the work she wants to finish before the rain.

IT DIDN'T HAVE TO BE THAT WAY, he reminded Nora. She thought he meant it didn't have to be White Oak Cemetery—he and Bev could have chosen a different place. But he meant that Bev didn't have to refuse him. She could have forgiven him and taken him back. That they were never a family again was her decision.

He spent that whole summer hanging out in Niagara, having decided that he could never love anyone else but the woman he'd betrayed. What a mess he'd made of his life. Had he ever told Nora about the bar in Niagara? That dingy saloon, where he could drink away his sorrows. A white man adrift. The linoleum floor was sticky with beer. Cigarette smoke hung so thick that he could hold it in fistfuls. Two men were singing with the jukebox. A drunk old woman laughed in delight, her wrinkles like a fine net pressed against her face. Her joy was infectious.

"Did I ever tell you about that woman in the bar?"

"No," Nora said, though she was thinking *yes*.

OR THIS SAME DREAM that returns to her when she's ill: she is in a waiting room. There are strangers sitting in seats against the opposite wall. They are reading books they had the foresight to bring with them. Bev brought nothing with her, so she sits there bored with her thoughts. Idly, she scratches her shoulder and feels an odd patch like hardened syrup stuck to her skin. She touches her elbow and feels the same. She is spotted with this hard, transparent substance—tiny crystals, she sees upon examination. They are on her arms, her legs, and at the base of her throat.

Beverly Diamond Owen Knox is becoming the woman she'd been named to be. At first she's not sure whether to resist or give in. There are patches on the back of her hands. Brilliant crystals picking up the buttery tint from the surface of her skin. The ache in her joints is worse than arthritis. The discomforting bristle of crystals between her toes and behind her ears. The sensation of being buried alive inside precious stone. Help me, Nora. I'm not ready yet. Her lips tearing at the corners. Help me. The taste of blood. Help me.

"Bev!"

"She said something. What did she say?"

"Bev, it's me, Nora. Lou's here as well. Can you open your eyes? Do you think she can hear us? Bev? Maybe we should call the nurse. Bev, are you okay?"

The nurse, summoned by Lou, listened with a stethoscope to Bev's chest and checked fluid levels in the IV bag. Any sounds she made, the nurse explained, were the body's normal effort to clear the lungs of mucus. Bev wasn't in any pain, and she wouldn't wake up from sedation any time soon. But it would be best not to disturb her.

After the nurse left the room, Lou needed to be reminded: "Where were we?"

•   •   •

HE'D FINISHED ONE BOURBON. Two. Three. And then he'd realized he didn't have enough money to pay for his drinks. A new crisis to follow the last. What could he do? Stiff the bartender? Admit that he had only spare change in his pocket? His gaze had settled on the drunk old lady with the fishnet face. She represented life and hope, and she would surely have compassion on a man who had no family anymore.

"What did I know? I was an idiot."

There was so much he didn't know. For instance, Nora considered telling him right then and there about what happened in White Oak Cemetery when she was a girl. But now the thought of all the necessary explanation she'd have to offer Lou exhausted her, like the work that would go into renovating an old house that had been shut up for years.

Lou was talking about the old lady in the bar in Niagara Falls: her head tipped back in laughter, skin a toffee brown, darker in the creases, with lips painted a fiery red, and dark, leathery pouches beneath the rims of her eyeglasses. She wore a red saucer hat to match her red shoes, and her summery dress was a loose black-and-white polka-dot wrap. She looked like a charitable person who would lend a few dollars to a man in need.

"I called to her—Ma'am!—but she couldn't hear me above the music. I called louder. Excuse me, ma'am, pardon—but she still didn't hear me. So I went ahead and tapped her on the shoulder. She tipped her head to look at me over the top of her spectacles. She switched off her smile. And at the same time, the music stopped. I don't know whether someone pulled the jukebox plug or by coincidence the song had ended."

This was the scene in the story that Lou liked to label *a situation*. An old woman who happened to be the mother of one of the singing men. And it sure looked like the bartender was her grandson, while Louis Owen was a white nobody who stupidly decided to call attention to himself.

He spoke in the direction of the window facing the hospital parking lot, as though his intended audience were the ghost of his reflection. He didn't seem to care anymore whether Nora was paying attention. And he might as well have forgotten about Bev. He was talking to himself, refining the patterns of experience that had made him who he was. His tendency, as he would say, to put his foot in it. His many attempts to run. His regrets.

"Next thing I knew, one man was holding me by the collar, and another had a knife at my neck."

Nearly had his throat sliced because he'd been bold enough to tap an old woman on the shoulder. And yet he was alive because of that same old woman's dispensation. All she had to do was give a slight, severe nod in the direction of the door, and the two men threw Lou out on the sidewalk.

That was Nora's father: savvy only in the aftermath of his mistakes.

His conclusion, always the same, invited dramatic comment. Nora imagined Bev sitting up and uttering a good, verifying insult. She thought of the fight they'd had in the kitchen when she was thirteen years old, the night Lou returned to apologize. She remembered lying in her bed pretending to sleep and listening for the shrill explosions in Lou's voice when his pleading turned into threats. She thought about how wrong it was that Bev and Lou should be buried side by side in White Oak Cemetery, though she didn't say this. The truth was, though she sometimes needled him, she never meant to say anything that would cause her father pain.

"Sometimes," she said to Lou, who sat waiting for her response, "it's better just to keep your mouth shut."

•   •   •

OR JUST THE OTHER DAY, wasn't it, when a storm blew in. The smell of fresh-cut grass. Screeching of red-winged blackbirds in the marsh. The first syrupy drops of rain. Growl of thunder. Flicker of lightning. On again, off again. *Crash, bang,* run for cover in the shed!

Dripping beneath the cloth hat she uses to hide her thinning hair. The chill of damp clothes. It's not the same kind of chill as the chill in her bones. This despite the doctor's optimism. But she can still notice things. In the corner, for instance, a nest made of dry grass and shredded paper from a fertilizer bag, crowded with four baby mice. And there's the mama retreating with the fifth baby in her mouth to the safe shelter behind an old wheelbarrow that had been overturned and left to rust by the previous owner. Back again, to fetch the rest of her offspring, carrying them one by one while Bev watches.

Nora, come see!

Bev, you're soaked.

Or the time Gus and Bev threw a party for themselves one year after they'd gone off to City Hall to get married. The two of them dancing to "This Year's Kisses" in the center of the crowd of guests while Nora watched from the ballroom's balcony.

Or the day after Lou left for good and Bev hired a locksmith to change the locks. She sipped her coffee and chatted with the man while he worked on the kitchen door. Nora came into the kitchen to pour herself some milk and overfilled the glass.

Nora!

Or watching Nora watching *Jeopardy!,* leg thrown over the back of the couch. Bev gave her big toe a tug.

You okay?

Yeah.

Want to talk?

Nope.

The one thing they needed to talk about kept Nora from wanting to talk at all. She couldn't be budged. Bev had better luck guessing the questions for the answers on *Jeopardy!*: Dale Carnegie's number-one best seller. What is *How to Win Friends and Influence People?*

X-shaped stigma, reflexed yellow sepals. What is an evening primrose? What are ragged robins and corn cockles? Did you know that a fly must beat its wings two hundred times a second to stay airborne? Look: you can tell from the white dots and the red-barred forewings that it's a red admiral butterfly. Nora, take out the garbage, please! Nora, did you hear me? Listen.

"THROWN OUT ON MY ASS," Lou was saying. "First by your mother. And then by two toughs in a bar." His tone was wryer than earlier, his eyes narrowed in a slightly mischievous squint.

"It's true I learned from you," Nora said, "how to get into trouble. But also how to get out of it."

"And remember that there's rest at the end." He leaned forward and patted Bev's hand, the same hand he'd kissed. "The peace of our eternal sleep together on some shady slope in White Oak Cemetery."

"You did say White Oak Cemetery."

Their own private property in White Oak Cemetery. Two names, two stones. They didn't even have to let on that they'd once been married. Just as long as they were together in the end.

"Lou—"

"The only home I'll never lose to foreclosure."

"Lou—"

"Thirty years I've been waiting to hold her in my arms again."

"Lou!"

"What? You think I'm not sincere?"

"If you'd be quiet and listen, for once."

"You have something you want to tell me?"

He looked at her with a smile she interpreted as smug, as if he were satisfied that the setup had worked and he'd trapped her, making it impossible for her not to match his disclosures with some of her own—and yet because of this expression of expectation he made it necessary for her to resist. This was an unfamiliar predicament. Usually she was adept at closing the conversation with a decisive comment. But she thought she'd had something else she'd wanted to say. What? She wasn't sure.

There was no way she'd tell Lou about what happened thirty years ago in White Oak Cemetery. That place where she and her girlfriends would go to smoke in secret. The same place where strange Johnny Baggley—a boy they understood to be *disturbed*—found refuge from the taunting of his schoolmates. He'd hunt for frogs and birds' eggs, and one day he either fell or jumped from a high perch in a tree. It was Nora who discovered the body. Climbing the hill after she'd said good-bye to her friends, she had seen a boy's sneaker turned at an odd angle. Then she noticed that the fingers of his left hand, curled against his knee, were caked with mud.

Lou had been out of the country at the time, and as far as Nora knew, Bev never told him about Nora finding Johnny. It was important to Nora not to tell him. She hadn't wanted to tell anyone, except her mother—she'd told her mother right away, as soon as she'd raced home from the cemetery. When Bev called the police, Nora couldn't help but feel betrayed. She felt tainted and newly vulnerable in a way her mother didn't understand. She had cooperated with the police and led them up the cemetery hill, but only out of necessity. And afterward, she'd shut up. Even when her friends gathered around her and demanded to know what she'd seen, she'd kept her mouth closed.

But thirty years had passed, and she was ready to talk to Bev about it now. She needed to know why Bev hadn't chosen somewhere else to spend eternity. Why White Oak, the place where lonely children died horrible deaths and were left to rot? Why did Bev want to be buried there—and next to Lou, no less? Why hadn't she ever mentioned this to Nora?

They'd talk as soon as Bev's condition improved. They'd talk about ugly, rotten, horrible death. What, exactly, would her mother have to say? They'd begin with the story of finding Johnny's body in White Oak Cemetery, and from there, wherever. The past or the present. It would depend upon Bev. Nora could only guess what her mother would tell her. But she didn't want to guess. She wanted to know what Bev would say, if she could say anything. That and more. Her mother being far less predictable than her father, complete, though partially hidden from view. Lou, much as he liked to talk, would never adequately answer the one question Nora wanted to ask:

"Why White Oak, of all places?"

"What?"

"Why did you choose White Oak Cemetery?"

"Why?"

"Yes."

"Why White Oak? Why that place? I don't know. Why anyplace? We just wanted to be together, if you can believe it. Doesn't seem possible, does it? Hey, Bev? Can you hear me, Bev? I wonder if she's been listening. Why there? Why us? Why did we spend thirty years

apart if we planned to be together in the end? Why did we do anything?"

Both Lou and Nora watched Bev for some indication that she had
an opinion she wanted to share. She just lay there, unblinking, un-
smiling, her chest swelling and flattening with the action of the ventilator. Lou and Nora would have gone on watching her forever if the
nurse hadn't come in to tell them that visiting hours were over,
which seemed strange to Nora, whose fatigue had led her to believe
that it was the middle of the night. She'd call a taxi, she said. Lou
reminded her that he had his car. They could stop at a diner for a bite
to eat, she suggested, and they could talk some more. They'd have a
good night's rest and come back to visit Bev the next morning. She
would probably be awake by then. Lou said he'd bet she had heard
everything and would give them an earful!

THE VOICE OF HER OWN FATHER. The red circles on his cheeks.
He was telling her about Joe Louis KO'ing Natie Brown in the fourth
round. One cigar after another.

Bev, phone's for you!

What?

The whir of a fan. The roll of a carousel horse. The swoop of a
swallow.

Or the time she found her husband's lover's name and number
written on a slip of paper in his wallet. See how it is, Nora, when we
have to make do with suspicion? Sometimes it's best to tell.

Two cups of flour. Cream the butter with the sugar. Crack an egg
against the rim of a bowl. The satisfaction of catching the yolk whole.

The time Gus came out to the garden, where Bev was trying to screw the nozzle of the hose on a spigot, and she could see from the look on his face that something terrible had happened. More precisely, somehow she knew that his son was gone. She didn't yet know the details—that he'd been killed in a bus accident while traveling in Mexico. But in that flash of a glance, she felt as though she knew everything.

Or the days following the day Nora ran home to tell her mother she'd found something in the cemetery. Nora wore her softball cap around the house to hide her eyes in shadow.

Or the time Bev was about to remind her again how much she loved Adam and was grateful for Nora's happiness, and the next thing she knew . . .

What?

She's not sure she weeded the garden before she left. Those stubborn little maple saplings, as tough as mandrakes. The songs she used to sing. Gus, according to his wishes, reduced to ashes and scattered over the north Atlantic. Lou, come closer so I can look at your face. The wiry white curls of your beard. The wide pores of your tanned skin. And you, Nora. Sitting in the garden cradling cups of coffee. We must do something about the potato vine tangled in the pachysandra. Is that what she wanted to say? Also, the thicket of loosestrife at the top of the front walk.

THE LUCITE CANE

Blue sky. Summer day. One car after another. A woman talking back to the radio, the thread of her voice trailing through the open window of her Chevette. Another woman sucking into her mouth the deflated bubble of her bubblegum. Two boys riding in the bed of a pickup truck, one expertly flicking away his cigarette butt. Yellow ribbon in support of our troops. Ticking of a blinker. An attorney who last year was defeated in his bid for the city school board calling, "Maria!" into the mouthpiece of his cell phone. Another man telling the woman beside him about the television show he'd watched last night. The woman in her Chevette snapping, "Go to hell!" A baby wailing, straining against the belt of his car seat. A brother pinching his sister. A sister slapping her brother. A retired social studies teacher fuming as he heads back to the hardware store to return a garden hose with a cracked nozzle. A retired salesclerk crying silently because today is the twenty-second anniversary of her son's death. An anesthesiologist pretending not to listen to her daughter and two friends in the backseat trading gossip. "It was like, you know, and when she like said she did she really meant she did . . ." Red light remaining red while the green light changes to orange. Cars idling. Cars speeding up. A man with a cane appearing out of nowhere. A fly bumping against a rear window. A squirrel on a branch. The woman chewing bubblegum watching the man with the cane as he steps off the curb. The same woman moving her foot to the brake. A paper flag tied to an antenna. A squirrel leaping. A brass plaque on a stone near the intersection marking what was once a spur of the Ohio Trail. The young mother yelling at her children. The attorney calling, "Maria, Maria, hello, are you there!" Two boys laughing. Three girls laughing. "Because she didn't like have to, you know." A squirrel catching the tip of a branch to save itself from falling. Orange light changing to red, red changing to green. The outrage of money spent on faulty merchandise. The fact of dirt. The annoyance of dry skin. The man with the cane stepping off the curb. A child complaining. A squirrel swinging on a branch above the sidewalk. Boys watching the squirrel. Girls watching the boys. The retired salesclerk noticing the man with the Lucite cane and failing to remember the word she wants to shout in warning. The woman with her foot on the brake wondering if the old man has Alzheimer's. A fly buzzing. The driver of the pickup truck banging his hand on the horn to warn the man with the cane. A woman singing, "If I could see . . ." A cloud slipping like a cutout in front of the edge of the sun. A plastic gallon of two-percent milk lying on its side in the trunk. A flock of sparrows rising all at once, like smoke. "Like yeah, like I was saying." The imprint of last night's strange dream on the waking mind. Imagining the time when she didn't exist. Heading east. Heading south. Twelve minutes after four. Damn. The anesthesiologist furtively slipping her finger under her shirt to finger the lump in her breast. The jolt of one sneeze followed by another. The retired salesclerk staring at the empty place where she'd seen, or thought she'd seen, a man with a cane. The woman with her foot on the brake recognizing that time is moving as slowly and as rapidly as the sun sank into the sea that evening last month when she and her friend walked down the beach to have dinner at the restaurant in a little fishing village on the island of Corsica. The driver of the pickup truck blinking away the hallucination. Boys swearing. Rumble of a jet passing overhead. "Like how typical!" Aware and not aware all at once. The pickup truck driver telling himself that he must have had one too many beers last night. A single feather nestled between a wiper and the windshield. A burp. A yawn. Boys waving at girls. Girls laughing at boys. *Stop,* that's the word the retired salesclerk had been trying to remember, but the light has already changed to green, and she realizes that she'd been mistaken about the man with a cane. There is no man with a cane. At the moment, there are only the people in passing vehicles, girls and boys, men and women—among them three individuals who have realized simultaneously that they didn't really see what they thought they'd seen and now can secretly savor the good feeling of knowing that only they know how ridiculous they are for getting all worked up over nothing.

ONE SUNDAY MORNING in June, in the year 2000, Lawrence Duroy walked with his two old greyhounds across the park that separates the reservoir from Culver Street. Fading lilacs perfumed the air. Yellow heads of dandelions dotted the grass. Thrown off balance by the tug of the two leashes, Lawrence slipped into a rut left behind by bicycle wheels but managed to keep himself from falling by planting the heel of his left sneaker in the mud. His yell halted the dogs, and they both gazed over their bony shoulders with mild impatience.

Lawrence glared back at the dogs. The smaller one returned to him and rubbed its long nose into the creased khaki behind his knee while the other squatted nearby and squeezed out its morning turds. Lawrence tugged on the leashes and tried to head toward the path leading up to the reservoir. But these two dogs, both of them used to losing on the racetrack, were habitually stubborn. They began rooting in the grass beside the tennis courts, pulling the leashes taut. Lawrence threw sticks to draw their attention, but they ignored him. He threatened punishment. He pleaded with them. Finally he indicated with a clucking sound that in his empty hand he held delicious treats—an old trick that never failed, and the dogs lurched stupidly after him up the hill.

The next person to cross the area was a jogger, a middle-aged man who was pleased with himself, for he'd made it up the slope and three times around the reservoir without stopping and had just descended at a spirited pace. Nearing the end of his run, he was thinking about how he couldn't even imagine the feeling of getting old. A strict exercise regimen for twenty years had kept him youthful. He'd survived a prolonged separation and divorce, and now he was newly in love with a woman half his age. He pictured her waiting for him back at the apartment with a pot of coffee and fresh-baked muffins.

More than two hours later, a group of children raced at full speed toward the tennis courts. Their game had been organized by an eleven-year-old boy, who'd announced that tag would soon be an Olympic sport and it was never too early to begin training. A seven-year-old girl had bolted from the pack before her cousin finished counting. Whether or not she'd be disqualified remained to be seen. But she was fast, faster than anyone in her second-grade class, and one day she'd be the fastest runner in the world.

Her ten-year-old stepbrother trailed her, calling taunts at the pair of slower boys behind him, twelve-year-old twins who considered the game juvenile but at the last minute had decided to participate and with their example were demonstrating how to be way cool and agile at the same time. Next came a six-year-old boy, who was missing four of his upper front teeth. He grinned as he ran just to feel the air whistling into his mouth through the gap. The youngest of the group, a five-year-old girl, was at the tail of the fleeing pack, with the eleven-year-old, the organizer of the game and the one chosen to be It, so close behind her that when she stopped squealing she could hear his heavy breathing.

The seven-year-old girl who'd been in the lead, the girl who in the last year had changed her name to Cheeta, flew behind a lilac bush, jumped out, yelled, "Ha-ha!" at her cousin who was It, and ran away. Her cousin ducked behind another bush, made a wide circle, and surprised Cheeta with a roar. She screamed and in a flash was out of reach, so her cousin decided to head after the twins, who had stopped running altogether and were huddling by the tennis courts getting ready to light cigarettes, though they were the ones dubbed by their mothers _in charge,_ the ones who would pay for the inevitable catastrophes that happened when this gang got together.

But what could go wrong in a game of tag? As long as everyone played by the rules, the game could go on forever. Cheeta sprang forward, leaping off the ball of her foot to gain momentum. She would have jumped as high as the radio towers at the top of the hill if the toe of her right sneaker hadn't caught on a root that had suddenly popped out of the grass. She fell onto her knees. And then, just as quickly as she'd fallen, she scrambled upright and was about to bolt. First, though, she had to pause and examine the root.

The root, it turned out, wasn't a root at all. It was a fine plastic walking stick, hooked into a handle at one end, that someone had accidentally dropped or intentionally thrown away, and now, finders keepers, it belonged to Cheeta.

"Got ya!" shouted her cousin, who appeared from nowhere and slapped Cheeta on the back, slapped her hard, harder than was fair in a game of tag. But Cheeta was armed. Cheeta had a cane as long as a gun, which she pointed at her cousin to scare him away. But he wasn't even rattled, and in a quick offensive he leaped to the side, grabbed the cane by its rubber tip, and ran off, waving it above his head, hooting in victory.

In seconds the twins had cast away their cigarettes and set off after him, wanting whatever their cousin had. The ten-year-old joined the pursuit, and Cheeta charged after them, shouting that the stick was hers. She didn't notice that when her six-year-old stepbrother tried to follow, he slipped on the wet grass.

"Yuck!" cried the boy. "Dog poo."

"You gone down in dog poo mess!" announced his delighted little sister.

"Dumb shit," said the boy.

"Don't you call me that!" the girl commanded.

"I didn't call you nothin'."

"You did."

"Did not."

The girl started to cry. The boy started to cry. "Mama," they wailed together, running toward the gravel path leading up the hill, each of them vowing to the wind to tell their mama what had happened. But when they finally made it up to the reservoir path where their mama and aunt were walking off the fat of their behinds, they found themselves caught up answering questions:

"Why you all alone? Where'd your cousins go?"

"They just ran away."

"They ran away and left you?"

"Sure, they just left us all alone."

Forgetting that they were mad at each other, the two children led the women back down to the lilac grove where they'd been abandoned. They found the big kids in a heap by the tennis courts, pounding and pulling in a terrible fight. When their mama found out that a plastic walking stick had caused all the trouble, she grabbed it from the hands of one of the twins and promised to use the stick to whack the butt of any child who wasn't back at the car within ten seconds. "One," she began to count as the children took off, calling, "Twothreefourfive . . ." behind them. With her sister, the mother dissolved in laughter and twirled the plastic cane like a baton before flinging it into the weeds.

THE RAIN STARTED TO FALL at dusk. At first it was a prickling rain—tiny drops like the snipped heads of needles falling from a dull gray sky. Then the cloud bed turned the green of old copper, and the rain stopped for an eerily still period, and the air became thick and damp, sucking the street noises into a vacuum of silence. At about nine the real deluge began, three inches of rain in an hour reported at the airport, the winds breaking branches and whipping apart power lines, the sky pulsing with lightning, bolts cracking trees in two right down the middle, thunder crashing like waves against stone cliffs.

On the reservoir hill rainwater collected in the gully of the path leading down to the field. Soon a full stream was flowing along the track used by joggers and mountain bikers, softening the dirt to a thin mud that bubbled out of the ruts and spread across the grass beside the tennis courts. Bushes crumpled beneath the flattening force of the wind. Twigs and refuse collected in swirling bunches. The rain fell through the night, turning the lilac field into a swamp. Birds clung to broken nests. Worms washed into the sewer. A huge branch snapped from a silver maple and landed on a tennis court, collapsing the net. And in a weedy patch at the base of the hill, not far from the path, the Lucite cane sank bit by bit into the melting earth until, by morning, it was completely buried.

WHEN CORKY'S CRAVING PARLOR at the corner of Monroe and Culver was still Sal's Mini-Mart and Delite's daughter Ta'quilla was three years from being born, two years before Abraham Groslik took his last walk across the park and one year before the city got to work building up the curbs and bricking the crosswalks, the two girls from East High discovered that Sal wasn't easy anymore. "Blame the feds," he said. "No ID, no sale."

Oh, come on, Sal. They would give him ten dollars for a five-dollar six-pack. Fifteen dollars. Okay then, how about twenty dollars? They didn't have twenty dollars between them, but if they did, would he sell them the beer? It's Friday night, they reminded him. They knew what day of the week it was, though they hadn't been to school since April. But Delite knew it was Friday because she'd seen the rabbi covering the temple's bingo sign across the street. And Merry knew it was Friday thanks to the calendar behind Sal. It's Friday, Sal, come on. They weren't planning on getting drunk and running their car into a tree—they didn't even have a car. All they wanted was beer to go with their pizza. But they'd spend the whole night thirsty thanks to Sal, who wouldn't sell them the beer.

"Now get outta here, girls, go on. And hold the door for ol' Abe while you're at it."

But Delite didn't hold the door for no Jew man. Delite was no slave girl.

"Whoa, wait a sec. What did you call Abe?"

"I didn't call him nothing."

"You sure did call him something. You better say sorry for that something."

Abe just stood there blinking against the store's strong lights. He hadn't heard Delite's slur and wasn't quite sure what was happening or why. He'd spent another lazy day in his apartment reading the newspaper. Now all he wanted was orange juice. He was determined to get the carton juice. Sal kept putting the bottled juice on discount, and Abe kept falling for the trick. That's a real entrepreneur who can sell you juice in a bottle when you prefer juice in a carton. Abe intended to ignore all signs advertising sales. But first he had to remedy the situation of the angry girl.

"Hello," he said, blinking.

The girl stared at him. Abe watched as comprehension slowly lit her face.

"You stop condescendin' me!" she said.

What did she mean, condescendin' her? And why for God's sake was she flicking open that sharp little blade? Abe noticed specks of rust on the metal and tried to remember when he'd last had a tetanus shot. He wondered if the girl could be mollified with a dollar. He wondered what her friend was thinking.

One girl was angry. The other was scared. "Girl," the scared friend asked, "what you doin'?"

"Let's talk about this," said Abe, who used to be known for saying inappropriate things to his friends, when he still had friends, before they all died one after the other of heart failure and stroke and pneumonia. He knew that he was awkward and that with each passing year he was getting awkwarder. Or was it more awkward? No matter what he'd heard and read along the way, when old age hit him he wasn't prepared. Old age is a crime against humanity, he thought.

"I done with talkin'," said Delite, clearly borrowing her dialogue from television. That was sad, too—the hours young people spent in front of the television these days.

"Delite, let's go," said her scared friend.

"Sal, we gettin' that beer. Merry, get that beer. We takin' it and walkin' out."

"Let's just go."

"Shut your mouth, pisshead."

The way girls talked to girls. The lives they lived. Their hopelessness. Abe figured the angry girl could tell a lot of sad stories, though she wasn't yet sixteen. Or was she?

"How old are you?" he asked. He knew from the girl's expression that it was a stupid question, unworthy of a reply. She could only roll her eyes at Abe's stupidity. She had beautiful eyes with shapely lids dusted with pollen, yet Abe could guess that she didn't know how beautiful she was.

"I wonder if anyone has ever told you you're beautiful," he said. He meant it only as a compliment. So why did the girl stamp her foot

as though she were flattening a sand castle and say with icy sophisti-
cation, "I declare, I hate this white man—"?

Why did she hate him? Why did the good Lord extend the capac-
ity for hatred to beautiful young girls? Why wasn't tomorrow yesterday? These were a few of the many questions that deserved to be
asked. But Abe knew better than to try to interview a girl who was
holding an open switchblade in her hand. Despite his reluctance to
leave the situation unresolved, he didn't have a choice. "All right,
then. Good day."

But you didn't just up and "good day" Delite when the day wasn't
near good. The day had been flawed by the issue of disrespect. It all
went wrong as soon as Abe walked through the door.

"Dirty ol' man callin' me beautiful without even knowin' me."

Did he have to know her to know the kind of girl she was? Luckily, he didn't ask this question. Instead, he asked the scared friend if
she liked Sal's ice cream. He assumed that the question conveyed his
obvious intention—he would buy an ice cream cup for both the
girls. He thought it a generous offer, and he was surprised by the
girl's expression of bewilderment. "You're looking at me," Abe said
with a gentle smile, "like I'm from another planet." The comment
felt appropriately self-deprecating and helped to put him at ease, despite the confusion and danger. He decided to continue along the
same line. "Like I don't speak English." He knew he could be amusing. If he put his mind to it, he could steal the show. The amateur ac-
tor in him took possession. "I'm a-speaking English, ain't I?" He
tapped his cane against the edge of the door for emphasis. A glance at
his reflection in the glass assured him that he was as funny as he
thought he was. "Ain't I?"

"You," said the angry girl. "You." She couldn't find a predicate
to attach to the pronoun. She couldn't think of anything to say, so

instead she used the knife in her hand to communicate her disgust, thrusting it up until the tip dented the grizzled cushion under ol' Abe's chin.

"Ouch," he said.

"Ouch is just the beginnin'," she said.

"Oh, Delite, we're in trouble now," said her friend.

"I tell you who's in trouble."

"I say we're in trouble."

Even at that moment, when the experience of being in the world was magnified by the possibility of an abrupt end, Abe wanted to smile once more at the girls. And to think that the angry girl was so absorbed in her anger she remained unaware of the scowling man in uniform who had appeared behind her like a shadow when a light comes on.

"Drop the weapon," ordered the officer.

Outside in the summer dusk, a car moved slowly along the avenue toward the intersection ahead. Inside, Abe heard for the first time since he'd entered the store the sportscaster on Sal's radio. He became aware of a rotten smell, the smell of frozen fried fish thawing in the sun. He thought about the castor oil his mother used to serve him in a metal thimble. For a moment he pitied himself, or pitied with cold detachment the individual named Abraham who had survived eighty-two years of indignities. But in the next moment he was remembering the pleasures of lovemaking. He thought about his wife, who'd died in 1989. He thought about how he was prepared to admit that despite the hundreds of times he'd wished himself dead so he could be with her in heaven, he felt lucky to be alive.

Here he was in time—an old man who'd come to Sal's to spend a portion of his Social Security on carton orange juice. What, he asked himself, was meant to happen next? Abe reasoned that he should take the time to think of words that might change the outcome. But the desire to do something immediately was overwhelming, and though he sensed it was a mistake, he couldn't stop himself from knocking the girl's arm away with the handle of his cane in a single brisk motion, which caused the scared girl to scream, the angry girl to stumble, and the officer to pull his finger back against the trigger.

YOU WATCH A MOVIE ON TV, you want the guarantee that by the end it adds up to something. But this worthless movie—Raymond made the mistake of watching the whole thing, wasting the two hours he should have spent finishing his paper on Thomas Jefferson.

It was too bad that Raymond had to think about Thomas Jefferson. All he wanted from the future was to become a rich lawyer and spend his time suing his neighbors for negligence and fraud. He had a plan. It was too bad that his plan involved a little education.

But let me tell you about this movie, Raymond wrote in an e-mail to his girlfriend, Clarisse, who lived in Buffalo.

Theres this teacher accused of downloading child porno stuff
and tho the charges thrown out in court hes fired from his job
and then he cant land another job teaching he cant even get
jack in another state and then he tries to make a living at the
mall but he freaks after lacing up 27 pairs of sneakers for some
idiot who cant decide what to buy he just up and quits and then
he ends up washing dishes somewhere but the manager hears
that this faggot has a thing about kids and thats it the guy is out
of work again and now he cant even bring himself to go

looking for another job anyway it turns out its easier to collect
a check from social services and when its used up he sits on
street corners and begs he does ok by begging but he spends
the money on booze so thats his life he begs all day and gets
drunk all night he doesnt wash he doesnt pick up the phone he
doesn't even have a phone and thats the end.

Raymond didn't add, *It was one of those movies with some sneaky truth
in it.* He didn't admit that the story got him thinking about what mat-
tered. He didn't say that all he wanted in life was Clarisse. He didn't
want to work the graveyard shift at the grocery store on East Henri-
etta plus finish the essay on Thomas Jefferson so he could get his high
school equivalence and apply to college. He didn't even want to go
to college. He wanted to get on the bus and go to Buffalo and spend
the rest of his life with Clarisse. As long as they were together, everything else would work out.

Fingers idling against the keyboard. Desk awash in the white light
from his screen. *Baby,* he wanted to write, *we got to be together.*

Clarisse was everything to him. And yet he'd never been able to
bring himself to tell her exactly this because he was afraid he'd scare
her away. What if he wasn't everything to her? What if she was biding
time, waiting for a better opportunity, and Raymond Johnson was
just a trial run?

Or else she was biding time waiting for Raymond Johnson to
make his move. *What you waiting for, Raymond?* Suppose he wrote,
Clarisse, will you marry me? Suppose she was waiting at the other end
to say yes?

The enigma that is an eighteen-year-old girl. What did Raymond
know for sure? He knew what he felt about Clarisse. He wanted to
believe that she felt the same for him.

Anythings believable, he typed, almost without volition. *One thing leads to another,* he typed, then paused, resting his fingers on the keyboard, and took a deep breath. *One day I met you and the same day I fell in love with you. Clarisse Clarisse Clarisse I love you.*

He didn't hesitate—he sent the message on its way then quickly shut down the computer since he didn't want to stare at the screen waiting for a reply.

He rose from his chair and stretched his arms. His murky potential seemed to come into focus all at once. He'd always known he was capable. Now he felt that he was more than capable. He understood what he had to do to be happy. Don't underestimate me, he wanted to tell someone, even at the risk of sounding like a conceited fool. But he was convinced that he had only to spend his life loving Clarisse and the impression would alter. You'll see. We'll see. Raymond Johnson knew with the certainty of observation that he was right. Loving Clarisse, he would be somebody—not a somebody scrambling to get ahead, but a somebody with vision who could see into the future and know that he and Clarisse belonged together.

He felt a sudden urge to notice whatever he'd overlooked. To see for the first time the variation in the particleboard of his walls, the black casing of his telephone, the shine of his fancy H & K, which his uncle had bought him for bull's-eye shooting and he carried for protection. He was someone who deserved to be protected. He was meant to live a long, long time.

Here I come, world.

After slipping his feet into his oversize sneakers and his H & K into the inside pocket of his jacket, he headed down the steps to the ground floor and out onto the porch behind Sal's. His uncle Sal didn't like it when he entered the store through the back door, but Sal didn't like a lot of things. Sal wouldn't like to hear that Raymond had decided to move in with Clarisse and become a great man. Sal, along with most everyone else, would need proof before he considered Raymond great.

Raymond used his key to let himself into the storage room. As he made his way along the narrow corridor between the stacks of cans, he felt an urge to dance. He'd been lit on fire by a bad television movie and was hot with the good luck of being Raymond who loved Clarisse. The future of the family they would make was directly ahead, clear as the towers of six-packs around him. The future of Clarisse loving him and the good work he would do for her sake. Their happiness together. As he stepped from the storage room into the stale fluorescence of the store, he imagined that it was forty years later, and he, a great man, the happiest man in the world, was returning for a visit.

Two and a half long years before Raymond Johnson was sentenced to twenty years to life for using his pocket pistol to put a bullet in the shoulder of a cop—the cop who Raymond mistakenly thought was trying to kill his uncle—Abe sat on a stool in Jeremiah's sipping the foam off his beer. It was a dreary February afternoon, and the tavern was empty except for Abe, two bikers playing pool, and the bartender, who was watching the TV above the bar.

What was worth saying aloud? Abe wondered as he slid his hands along the tapered glass. He'd already asked the bartender, "How are you today, young fellow?" and the bartender had shrugged, clearly finding the question too dull to answer. Abe would have liked to stir his interest. There were a lot of interesting subjects he would have proposed for discussion—barbecue sauces, gardening, politics, his stamp collection, his nephews, John Wayne. But the bartender was more interested in the two women on TV, a mother and her grown daughter, who were in love with the same man. Apparently the man, a high school principal, was waiting off camera for a turn to tell his side of the story.

Another gray winter day in the gray city that had been his home for more than half a century, and Abe had nothing better to look forward to than the evening's bingo. The truth was, he'd been playing bingo regularly for twenty years and had never won. Everyone agreed that victory for Abe was long overdue. It was terrible to think that time was running out and he might never win.

At least he could still appreciate the simplest of impressions— the smoothness of the glass between his hands, for instance, or the relief of a belch. He always belched politely, muting the sound with his closed fist, an effort he'd perfected at the behest of Edna, his long-ago wife.

Long-ago lovers, you and me, he mused. Young rascals. Edna and Abe, Abe and Edna. Forget about the disappointments. We had each other. Year after year. Remember when. Of course you remember when. You're in heaven now. You remember everything, even the eternity before you were born. Such is the expansive consciousness of angels.

Abe believed that at his age he had a right to believe whatever he pleased. He'd spent most of his life believing in nothing more than possibility, but after he lost Edna he couldn't help it—when he imagined his wife, he imagined her alive, floating comfortably above in a heaven that couldn't be less than heavenly.

Down here, human effort would continue to be riven by bitter disputes. Isn't there always someone ready to take what someone else has? The bartender, for instance, was ready to take Abe's five dollars. Each of the bikers was planning to claim the pack of cigarettes they'd bet on this game of pool. One man's loss was necessarily the other's gain in this world of never-ending competition, where only the fittest are expected to survive.

Gray daylight hung like cardboard against the glass of the front door. Inside, the strongest illumination came from the television, which lit the bottles stacked behind the bar with a faint white glow. Stale smells of beer and cigarettes thickened the air, along with the sharp pine fragrance of Lysol. The bartender wore a plaid fleece vest over a T-shirt. The coaster beneath Abe's glass advertised Budweiser. The mirror hanging on the door to the kitchen had been painted over with red, white, and blue stripes.

Nothing makes complete sense, Abe thought, and yet in theory everything has a logical explanation. Reason assumes a cause for every consequence, birth marking the beginning of the end, the child becoming the widower who is left behind to do the work of remembering.

At least an old man can reward himself with a tepid beer after enduring a long morning alone in his apartment. He can hope that tonight he'll win at bingo. He can think about his wife in heaven.

Hearing a sharp yapping, he looked around for the dog. But it turned out that the dog was a terrier yapping gratefully for his gourmet food on the television. Abe considered how easily he'd been fooled. The trick of false reality. Where does the truth begin? he wanted to ask. He found himself imagining that the interior of Jeremiah's was a stage set and the play was his own life story. The problem was, he hadn't read the script. He could only fumble along, trying to guess the best next line. Actually, he had a knack for improvisation. He remembered how Edna used to watch his antics with her hand clapped over her mouth to keep herself from laughing too loudly. Just the thought of his wife holding back her laughter brightened the gloom. But when he heard the ringing of a telephone on the TV, he was reminded of his loneliness. And when he noticed that the clock on the wall in front of him had no hands, he decided it was time to leave.

"I owe you—" Abe began but stopped short when the bartender held up his open palm in a gesture suggesting refusal. Or was he simply expressing his contempt?

"Excuse me," said Abe, perplexed.

"Merry Christmas," offered the bartender in a defeated voice.

"It's February," Abe pointed out. "Anyway, I don't celebrate Christmas."

"Then happy birthday."

"Is this a joke?"

"The thing is, I've been thinking."

"You were watching the TV."

"I was watching the TV and thinking. And I thought to myself, If I stay in this dump another day I'll die. But I don't wanna die. I wanna quit. So I'm gonna quit."

"What are you saying?" Abe asked.

"It's on the house is what I'm saying. Hey, you idiots," the bartender called to the bikers, "I'm telling you it's on the house."

One of the bikers thrust his cue into the center of the dartboard hanging on the wall and broke the stick in half. "Hallelujah!" he shouted as the bartender reached for the tap to a keg.

This certainly wasn't how old Abe had expected to end the day— celebrating at a party with a man who had decided to quit his job. And what a party it turned out to be! It was a party thrown in honor of spontaneity and renewal and courage, a party as uncontainable as a riot, with the guests multiplying when the waitress arrived for the dinner shift along with two college friends, two girls who'd just finished taking a chemistry exam and were ready to unwind, and then the Chi-Wah Tigers men's softball team and various others off the street who'd heard that the house grog at Jeremiah's was free for the night and came to drink and trade stories about bad dates, flat tires, local bands, body piercing, novelty drugs, probations, rock climbing, and miraculous escapes. It was a deafening, joyous party, and Abraham Groslik sat contentedly on a bar stool in the center of the crowd, understanding almost nothing that was said to him yet having the time of his life.

THE DAY BEFORE Abe's Lucite cane was found in the lilac grove by the tennis courts, more than four years after the party at Jeremiah's, the bartender, whose name was Sam, returned to Rochester and walked right into the bar and ordered a beer. He guessed that the owner still had better things to do than hang around to manage his business. Unfortunately, his guess was wrong. The owner had lost two employees to better jobs the week before, and now he had to wait tables himself. After a few minutes the owner spotted his former bartender in the crowd, and he marched up and demanded the restitution that had been ordered by a judge at the conclusion of a small-claims hearing three years earlier. But Sam had left for Florida without paying the owner a penny. From Florida he'd moved to Chicago with his new girlfriend. In Chicago the girl had left him for another girl, and after a few months of travel out west he'd sold his car and come home.

Sam still believed that he hadn't done anything wrong. "Since when is generosity wrong?" he asked the owner. "Since when is generosity at someone else's expense right?" the owner retorted. They continued to argue, though they kept their voices low to avoid drawing attention to themselves. Finally Sam gave up and pulled two crisp fifty-dollar bills from his wallet—a fraction of the prescribed sum but enough to mollify the owner, who demonstrated forgiveness by offering his popular former bartender his job back.

Sam accepted and promptly took his place behind the counter, sharing the busy night's work with a girl named Clarisse, who had been working at Jeremiah's for nearly two years, ever since she'd moved into her boyfriend's apartment above Sal's Mini-Mart. It took an hour of casual conversation snatched when drink orders drew them together before Sam learned from Clarisse that her boyfriend, Raymond Johnson, was in jail. Sam couldn't believe it. He'd met Raymond Johnson years ago at the Laundromat next to Chen's Noodle House, and though they never became good friends, they'd shared a couple of pitchers. Raymond Johnson was in jail? Yes, Raymond Johnson was in jail for shooting a cop. And Clarisse had moved into Raymond Johnson's apartment in order to devote herself to keeping the memory of their love alive.

Though Clarisse was attached to a man who might never be released from prison, she had a fresh-as-the-morning kind of beauty, with brown curls that still looked damp, her skin scrubbed and shining, her perfume a mix of soapy lavender and cinnamon. Sam just wanted to be near her. They were kept busy through the night, which happened to be a Fish-Fry Friday, but whenever he could he'd shimmy in her direction and lean toward her to whisper in her ear. Did she live alone? he asked. Did she have family in town? Had she ever seen the Amerks play?

Yes was her reply to all his questions. But she looked overfilled with mixed emotions, and Sam thought that if he pushed hard enough she would burst with all the things she'd been wanting to say.

The crowd at Jeremiah's was as raucous as ever, and many of the customers, regulars for years, recognized Sam and remembered his going-away party. They wanted him to throw another going-away party, but he assured them that he wasn't going anywhere. Why not a welcome-home party, then?

Sam was in too ambitious a mood to throw a party. He wanted to drum up tips for Clarisse, and with his swift service encouraged everyone at the bar to drink more than they'd planned. As the night wore on, the crowd grew fuzzier, louder, more harmlessly belligerent while Clarisse seemed to sharpen in focus. At one point Sam slipped behind her and eased his hand into the back pocket of her jeans. For a few delicious seconds she pretended not to notice. And though he couldn't see her face, he was sure that when she gently tugged at his wrist to lift his hand up, she was smiling.

He was confident that at the end of the night they would leave together. And yet when the time came, he didn't know where to go with her. He couldn't take her home to his mother's house, and he guessed that she didn't want to take him home to Raymond Johnson's apartment. Neither of them had a car. He couldn't think of anything else to do but say good-bye to her on the sidewalk as the door to Jeremiah's closed behind them. She said good-bye in return, but as she spoke her hand reached out and hung in the emptiness between them for an uncertain moment, until Sam extended his hand and folded his fingers around hers. He'd already reminded her that they'd see each other back at work on Tuesday night. They were going to shake hands like business colleagues and go their separate ways. But now that he held a part of her, he couldn't let her go.

Hand in hand, they set out walking. Since the reservoir was the destination for much aimless wandering, they headed there. It was a cool spring night, with a half-moon slipping in and out between clouds. Against the backdrop of darkness the faded lilac blossoms looked like straw caps hanging on the racks of bushes. It was too early in the year for the locusts to be buzzing, and the city streets were deserted. The only sound was the occasional whir of a truck traveling on the highway that skirted the opposite end of the park.

Clarisse and Sam walked up the hill in silence. They stood for a moment on the steps of the maintenance building beside the reservoir, and then they pressed together. She started to shake with what Sam would later learn was the pent-up grief from two years of trying to love a man who was too full of rage at the injustice of his fate to keep loving her back. Sam and Clarisse kissed through her crying. They moved up the steps into the small arcade and kissed again. Eventually Clarisse stopped crying, and they settled into each other's arms on the stone bench. Sam brushed his lips against Clarisse's neck and slid his hand inside her blouse. Clarisse rubbed her cheek against the bristle of Sam's three-day beard—a decisive action suggesting that she was ready to love someone new, even if she wasn't ready to give up loving Raymond Johnson. They kissed and stroked and explored each other until the sky was tinged with pre-dawn silver, the rising light bringing with it a sweet, heavy calm. They should head home, they agreed. They didn't say that in this new life they had no home, but neither did they make a move to go. Helpless to fatigue, they fell asleep.

They couldn't have been asleep for long when old Abraham Groslik came tapping up the reservoir road on his early morning walk, huffing at the effort, his huffing worsening incrementally with each step. As he approached the arcade he paused to catch his breath, then he cleared his throat to warn the lovers of his presence. When they didn't stir he inched closer to take a long look, studying, with eyes made keen by a new pair of bifocals, what he understood as the image of pure happiness.

Lovers in love. Sure, Abe knew what that was like. He knew it in the way he knew the warmth of the rising sun. He hoped that these two would be allowed to grow old with each other and to have the luxury of remembering, fifty years from now, the night they fell asleep in each other's arms on a stone bench up at the reservoir.

Their heads were tipped in sleep, their faces hidden from Abe's prying eyes. But he didn't need to see their faces to enjoy a small surge of pride. Just by discovering them on the bench in the arcade, he had earned the right to take credit for their happiness.

Sunlight had replaced the shadows over the flat suburbs to the east by the time Abe decided to get on with his walk and head home. He chose to take the path rather than the paved road down the hill— this was his first mistake. His second mistake was to let gravity speed his descent. For the first few steps he moved at a spirited pace without huffing much at all. But soon he found it difficult to keep up with the momentum as the slope steepened. At the same time, the earth tilted forward, and the sky that had always been above old Abe fell across the space in front of him. He felt himself plunging into it, running straight on, as though toward a closed glass door.

His Lucite cane saved him. He managed to lift the cane in front of him, barely keeping himself upright as he thrust the stick against the air, pushing the sky away. An observer might have thought Abe was lifting his cane in a gesture of freedom or joy, but in reality Abe was using his cane to open the door so he could pass through.

The forceful action caused him to loosen his grip on the handle, and as he stumbled, the cane flew from his hand and disappeared into the bushes. Amazingly, Abe remained on his feet. Monroe Avenue was ahead of him. Across Monroe Avenue was the small apartment complex where he'd lived for thirty years. Next to the apartment complex was the synagogue his wife had attended regularly and where he always lost at bingo.

Somehow Abe made it home that morning on wobbly knees without his Lucite cane. He went straight back to bed. As he drifted off he told himself that after a short rest he'd get up and go find the cane because he really couldn't manage without it.

ABOUT THE AUTHOR

JOANNA SCOTT IS THE AUTHOR OF EIGHT PREVIOUS books, including *The Manikin,* which was a finalist for the Pulitzer Prize; *Various Antidotes* and *Arrogance,* which were both finalists for the PEN/Faulkner Award; and the critically acclaimed *Make Believe, Tourmaline,* and *Liberation,* which won the Ambassador Book Award from the English-Speaking Union of the United States. A recipient of a MacArthur Fellowship, a Lannan Award, and a Guggenheim Fellowship, she lives with her family in upstate New York.